Dréoteth

by
Danielle Bourdon

Dréoteth

Published by Wildbloom Press

Dedicated to my sons, Ayden and Tristan.

My parents: Kathy Sleigh, Tim Sleigh, Jerry Bourdon and Felecia Bourdon for supporting and believing.

A special thanks to Michael Johnson and Kimberly Hoyt for their skill and honesty.

Chapter One

Fall
The Year of the Red Leaf

"*I am called Dréoteth.*"

I enunciated each syllable slowly, unable to abide the pleasure of his death with the wrong name on his lips.

Dray-o-teth.

It was the first time I have uttered it in—I do not know how long. Decades. Centuries. Mister Mathan, a prominent member of society, now knows exactly who and what has been picking off the citizens of Malmsbury.

I worry not for my safety. The dead tell no tales.

If the villagers knew what an atrocity walks among them, as one of them, they would look upon me with horror rather than intrigue and curiosity. But they do not.

The people have no idea that the scribe in their midst is the one responsible for their nightmares, for the dark whispers in the corners of the inns and taverns.

I have been here for six months and have chosen my prey wisely. I have not attacked them in groups even though I have been tempted. Sometimes I want to change right before their eyes and watch them flee en masse, terror thick on the air, their screams layered one over the other.

In this subtle way, taking one victim at a time, I can stretch out the duration of my stay and study them. The townsfolk have concocted many stories about the unexpected disappearances; one rumor insists that one of their own has gone insane. Another is that a curse has been placed upon the village by a troupe of gypsies that passed through not long before I arrived here.

A random stroke of luck, that, since it throws any suspicion off me. As a newer member of their small society, any ill news or bad omens and strange deaths might be blamed upon the man they know the least about.

In an attempt to blend in better, I gave them a false name when I arrived. Here in the village of Malmsbury, they know me as Nehemiah Trimble. I amuse myself with these trivial little details. Centuries past, I never bothered to try and integrate or get to know them. There is danger in doing this, which I suppose is part of the lure. In a fit of brash honesty, I admit that humans have always been nothing more than food in my mind, not worthy of my time or commitment. They are prey, and I am a predator. I found their trials and tribulations tedious. Humans fret and worry over nonsensical things.

However, the longer I spend among them, the more I find myself annoyingly intrigued. There are several men in this town with intellects almost as big as their egos and on more than one occasion we have engaged in interesting conversation. I find myself seeking their company out, shockingly, and could swear that they seek mine out also. I wish that did not fill me with a sense of satisfaction. They are only men, after all, vastly inferior and I know in time they will prove that their true worth is in how well they fill my belly.

In another contradiction, I find myself loathe to target those with artistic skill; painters, architects, musicians. I am secretly fascinated by their abilities, as much as I wish I was not.

A woman who serves here at the inn, Eugenia Bailey, bears watching. It is almost as if she can peel open the layers of a person and take a look inside. I know, because I caught her doing it to me and it was most unsettling.

For a rare moment, I thought she knew my secret.

I have not lived this long to be disabled by a glance, no matter how incisive, and dismissed the notion immediately. I will see her, in fact I will see them all again on the morrow. There is a great festival planned and while they revel, I will do my best not to be incited by their energy.

For now the candle burns low and the hour grows late.

Dréoteth.

The distorted image that stared back at him in the looking glass resembled a gentleman. His coat, black wool with matching trim, fit loose from his shoulders to his thighs. Layered underneath, a black vest and white shirt added contrast but he cast a critical eye on the snug breeches that tapered down into knee high boots.

They were gray, the color of ashes, and he considered changing them to match his coat.

When Dréoteth realized that he was dawdling over his appearance like some *normal* human, he snorted.

Humans and their wardrobes, in his grandiose opinion, were too bright, too frilly, too overdone. If he weren't careful, he would next be shuffling through wigs and ruffles and lace kerchiefs that had absolutely no business anywhere in the vicinity of a man. The thought was laughable if he'd been the type given to fits of amused whimsy.

He was not.

Austere. Over-confident. Aggressive. *Those* were words that better suited him.

Weak fingers of light, the last hurrah of a dying dusk, painted the spartan room more orange than ochre. It turned his olive skin a jaundiced hue and streaked his jet-black hair with bronze.

He stalked to a small desk under the open window and collected his journal from the surface. The covering, brown leather worn soft from so many handlings sported no name, no marking, no initials. He took it to the armoire and crouched down in front of it. Setting the book on the floor, he gave it a shove and watched it disappear into the space beneath. He wasn't *too* concerned with someone stealing it. Any unfortunate soul daring to invade his room would meet with an unpleasant, *permanent* end.

A moment later he stepped into the gloomy hallway, closing the door behind him. Mellow candlelight flickered from sconces on the walls, too far spaced to chase the shadows away. He would not have been hindered had the corridor been totally black.

He encountered no one as he descended three floors to the main room.

The Rose and Lion Inn was said to be the best in Malmsbury, a fact he found ironic considering there were only two. After observing both for several days prior to his official arrival, Dréoteth found that this one served his purposes better than its smaller rival, *Cantley's*. The Rose and Lion backed up to a sweeping forest, giving him some sort of cover if he suddenly needed it. *Cantley's* sat in the middle of the village, providing less protection if he found himself on the wrong end of a hunt.

"Good evening, Mister Trimble."

The intrusion of his name into his thoughts ended them abruptly. He glanced through the empty room to the diminutive woman behind the bar.

He smiled, a slow curve that didn't expose any teeth.

"Mistress Bailey. Are you not attending the festival?" he asked, weaving through the maze of vacant tables with uncanny grace. Arriving at the counter, he rested a hand there, long fingers spare of rings or adornment.

He stared across at the redheaded, gray-eyed woman and drew in her scent: apples, wine, spice, meat and rose soap. It was always some combination of food and flowers.

She lifted her chin and maintained eye contact, drying the goblet in her hands with quick, nervous swipes.

"When Jared relieves me of my shift, yes. You may call me Nia, if it pleases," she said.

He thought Miss Eugenia Bailey must not be overly fond of her given name, because this was the fourth time, at least, that she'd briskly offered an alternative. Intrigued, he watched her present a feisty façade while her fidgety body language suggested unease in his presence.

She set the heavy goblet down, snapped the small

6

towel onto the counter and regarded him with *that* look.

The one that was too sweet to be suspicious and too knowing to be ignored.

In one fell swoop, she set the situation on edge. He stared at her from lidded eyes, nostrils flaring. The predator in him felt challenged by her boldness, real or perceived.

Sixty seconds passed in unrelenting tension until she glanced down at the counter and cleared her throat. The ends of the towel, already fraying, were now shredded into skinny strips. She picked and picked and pried and tugged.

Mollified by her retreat, his aggression eased.

"I will consider it, Mistress Bailey." There was a scratch and rasp to his voice that hadn't been there before.

Her voice cracked with a meek question, eyes downcast. "Will you have a drink before you go?"

He didn't realize he'd leaned a few inches closer until he straightened to step away from the counter for the doors. Fighting for diplomacy he didn't feel, he said, "No, but thank you. Perhaps I will see you at the festival."

The woman tried his patience like no other.

"Have a good time, Mister Trimble!" She sounded stubbornly cheery.

He paused just before he stepped out, looking back, half expecting to see her smiling and waving. She smiled and waved *when* he looked, like they had not just traded several minutes of awkward friction.

Humans were the most confusing creatures on earth. The door whispered closed on his shadow.

Eugenia exhaled a breath she didn't realize she was holding. Positive she hadn't imagined the threat she felt in the air, she willed her heart back into a normal rhythm and released her white knuckled grip on the towel.

Nehemiah Trimble remained an enigma. They had passed like ships in the night for months and she was no closer to knowing him, *really* knowing him, than she had been when he arrived. None of the other women knew him any better than she. Nor did any of the men she'd been brazen enough to ask. They knew the simple things; that he was six months new to the town, that he was living at the Rose and Lion, and that he worked as a scribe for scholars.

Usually, she had no trouble getting to know *anyone*. Exuberant and merry, she asserted her goodwill and compassion onto the citizens and people responded in kind. Except for the shoemaker, grumpy Mister Rou, who scowled and fussed and tried to pretend he wasn't charmed by her smiles.

She wiped down the already clean bar and set a clean stack of trenchers on the back counter. Everyone was at the festival and business would be slow until morning.

Jared, the lumbering, giant man who tended the Inn at night, ambled in the side door a few minutes later. Blocky and bulky, he had the finesse of a bull in a china shop but fists the size of warhammers; it kept any rabble-rousers in check in the off hours. He had sandy blonde hair and gray eyes so light they almost looked white. His clothing consisted of a threadbare muslin shirt and dark suspenders that helped hold up tan colored breeches.

Eugenia perked when she saw him, putting away the last of the goblets she'd washed.

"I am off to the festival, Jared. I do not think you will be too busy tonight." Eugenia didn't expect a verbal answer from Jared, who preferred silence to speaking. Always.

She patted his arm on her way by, whisked out from behind the counter, and hurried to the door.

Eugenia left the Inn for her small cottage nestled at the very edge of the woods, hurrying past the stables where horses nickered when they heard her go by. It wasn't her own, this little house, but she always warmed at the sight of it. Ivy twisted up the outer walls like skinny, seeking fingers. Leaves draped down from broad branches overhead, creating a whispering rustle on the roof that she'd grown used to over time.

Now she found it charming instead of annoying.

Most of the merry flowers lining the cobbled walk were starting to wane as the season inched toward winter. Patches of snapdragons and broad-faced pansies surrounded roses of red, pink and yellow. Morning glory twined around the post of a birdhouse in the yard.

The lock on the door had been broken for some time and she swished inside, closing it soundly behind her.

"I am home, Honey!" She smiled, amused at the ritual of announcing her arrival.

A small living room sat to the right, a kitchen to the left, and a harrowing, rickety staircase between led up to the loft. Straight ahead, two bedrooms split off a short hall.

Bypassing the living room, Eugenia all but ran into her bedroom. A plaintive meow greeted her from the bed. The cat, roused from its sleep, yawned and sat up. Honey had been her companion for six years, twelve days and four hours. They shared a great affection and she paused to pet and coo, earning a lazy lick along the end of her nose.

Moonlight poured through the window in an elegant stream, bathing the dress she'd laid out in anticipation of the festival. It was the best one she owned, bought back in the spring after months of careful saving and planning for just this occasion. Burgundy and cream brocade, it had a fitted bodice, full sleeves and embroidery along the hem. Without any help, it took her fifteen minutes to change. At least it laced up the front instead of the back.

She traded her dusty work slippers for a newer pair and brushed her hair without the benefit of a looking glass, leaving the wavy tresses shining gloriously down her back.

"I will be home late, Honey. Do not wait up for me!" She scratched the purring feline gently under the chin, laughing, and had just straightened when she heard rustling outside the open window. The crack of a twig drew her gaze there immediately. All she could see were deep shadows made by the trees. Eugenia had never feared for her safety until several members of Malmsbury society went missing.

The silence stretched thin, expectant, as if someone was standing just outside the window against the wall, listening to her. Honey's ears flattened and she darted off the bed and under it, disappearing from sight. Eugenia saw it in periphery because she couldn't take her eyes off the window. Any second a dark silhouette was going to blot out the moonlight, sinister and scary, intent on dragging her into the woods.

Eugenia Bailey wasn't having it.

Picking up a heavy stick that she'd set by her bed, she stalked to the window.

"Who goes there?" she shouted.

Leaning out with the stick raised, ready to strike, she glanced left and right.

No one waited on either side. She scoured the shadows and found nothing suspicious.

"A deer then," she surmised, pulling back inside

with an indignant huff. It didn't explain Honey's strange dive off the bed or the eerie feeling of being stalked. Deliberately, she put it from her mind. She'd been listening to far too many rumors flying about town.

She leaned the stick against the wall and briskly left the cottage; the festivities were well under way and time was wasting.

The Fall Festival was the biggest event of the year. Families came out in droves to celebrate the harvest, participate in games, and to see and be seen. Dréoteth, with his hands clasped behind his back, strolled along the heavily decorated main street on the way to the field. Chrysanthemum wreaths hung on the doors of every shop and squat pumpkins sat on the stoops. Haystacks, low candles, awkwardly shaped gourds and scarecrows with potato sack faces all added to the ambiance.

Children ran amuck, absolutely frenzied with excitement. Barefoot, carefree, hair wild, they shrieked and whooped and hollered, running circles around the festivities.

Bales of hay were stacked everywhere in no certain pattern. They provided more than just seating—they became obstacle courses for the children. Up and down, around and around.

Dréoteth took a few steadying breaths. Their darting to and fro threatened his careful control. He waited until there was a break in the madness and entered the clearing.

Long tables were set up on the perimeter, loaded with food. Baskets of apples, pears and peaches flanked platters of roasted pork and fragrant duck. Casks of wine sat at each end with tankards and goblets lined up in rows.

Some of the women wore their better dresses with the necklines scooped low, gossiping about fabric and style and embellishment. There was a hierarchy here, as in most societies, and it was easy to detect the affluent by the cut and expense of their cloth. Men stood in notable groups; the farmers over there, the merchants over here, and the scholars apart from the rest. No matter what group, most doubled as warriors and had swords attached to belts at their hips. The disappearing residents of Malmsbury assured that the men were armed at all times.

Musicians took up a corner and played for dancers that made intricate circles in the center of the haystacks. The crisp evening boasted a clear moon glowing brightly in a black velvet sky. Bonfires spewed serpents of smoke into the air, casting a flickering orange glow across the dark landscape.

He headed for the group of scholars, nodding a greeting to a few couples along the way. It had taken him only a few weeks of intent scrutiny to learn the proper etiquette of polite society.

"Mister Trimble, a pleasure to see you again."

"Mister Trimble."

"Good evening."

Greetings overlapped each other as he reached the circle of distinctive men. William Tuttle sported a cane, a round belly, and had lost all but four strands of silver-gray hair; Ronald Upham stood tall and lean like himself with a hawkish profile that reminded Dréoteth of a bird; Meyer Lyon, younger by a decade than his counterparts, was fit and hale with a full head of dark hair. Tuttle and Upham were attired in expensive surcotes and had an unflappable presence while Meyer wore black chausses and a leather hauberk of sturdy quality.

"Gentlemen. I trust the festivities are getting off to a good start?" Dréoteth asked.

"I'd rather be next to the fire with a good book," Upham said. He had an imperious lift to his chin and he stared at the dancers skeptically.

"There *is* more to life than reading, Upham." Tuttle scolded his hawkish companion, disinterested in the complicated steps that he had long forgotten in favor of other, less strenuous pursuits.

"Says the man who tears through three books a week," Upham said. He scoffed, drawing laughter from Tuttle and Lyon.

Dréoteth examined each man in turn as they spoke, pulling in their distinctive scents with a slow, unobtrusive breath. Experience had taught him how to be subtle about these unusual habits of his. He smiled faintly at the banter, recalling from prior conversations that Tuttle and Upham were both avid and unapologetic readers. He glanced at Meyer Lyon when the man suddenly pinned a direct, jovial question on him.

"What of you, Mister Trimble? Tell us what you think of Malmsbury's annual Fall Festival."

"I hope it will be more exciting than standing here conversing about books with the lot of you." His wry statement earned a rumble of laughter.

Dréoteth had only discovered his own love for the written word mere decades before. There was much to be learned of the ways of men between the covers of a book. One such work, an old diary he'd happened upon, inspired him to keep a journal of his own. Unfortunately, he'd found his entries somewhat lackluster and staid.

He hunted, he killed, he slept.

All the drama he recorded was about *other* people's lives. There were no conspiracies or touching deaths or mystifying puzzles revolving around him. Which was exactly the way he wanted it. The redundant entries ceaselessly reminded him, however, of the limited scope of his life. A restless mind had first led him into the outskirts of humanity. The curious things he found, both annoying and intriguing, held him sway. His loathing for them fluctuated wildly sometimes, tipping between volatile and temperate.

A trio of passing horses led by a farmer shied violently, straining their leads. They drug the man ten feet before he regained control. Tossing their heads, wild and unruly, they seemed to startle in the direction of the scholars.

Tuttle, Meyer and Upham observed the incident with perplexed expressions.

"I say, that's a strange thing," Tuttle said.

"It is a rather large crowd." Upham, barely bothered by the uproar, decided it was the chaos.

Dréoteth subdued the urge to bare his teeth and growl at the horses. He was their natural enemy, as hungry to destroy them as they were to flee. In his time here, he had taken care to avoid them in the presence of others. People would start to suspect something if every animal he came into contact with had such a vehement reaction. It created a tedious and treacherous environment.

He glanced around like the others, frowning, feigning confusion. He spied hound dogs across the field that had also picked up his scent but their baying seemed random from this distance.

"Perhaps the dogs?" Dréoteth suggested.

"Perhaps," Meyer said, glancing away from the horses. "Probably the children, too." Several waved sticks and screamed as they ran.

The scholars were content to let the odd occurrence pass.

"So, Mister Trimble, to pick up where our last conversation left off--" Tuttle was interrupted by a sweet, high-pitched voice closing in from their left.

"Meyer Lyon! You come dance with me this instant!" Miss Merriweather marched their direction with determination. Petite and dark with rosy cheeks, she smiled charmingly. The peach frock skimmed her slim frame, her fingers pinching the skirts to hold them a few inches off the ground.

Meyer laughed and bowed chivalrously. "Or what?"

"Or I will go find Henry Bower and dance with him instead!" She helped herself to Meyer's elbow when she arrived and smiled a greeting to the men.

"Henry Bower has bowed legs and dances like a chicken," Meyer scoffed.

"Chickens do not dance," she laughed.

"And *if* they did," Meyer said, feigning seriousness. "They would dance just like that."

"Did we hear something about dancing?" Tuttle and Upham's wives arrived, smiling, apparently intent to disrupt the men.

"Oh, the wives." Tuttle sighed melodramatically. He rocked back and forth on his shoes and stamped his cane once for emphasis.

"There is more to life than discussing business and books, Tuttle. I have not seen you dance in quite some time." Meyer's dark eyes gleamed with mischief. He was regarded as one of the most eligible bachelors in Malmsbury after his wife of ten years perished tragically two seasons past. He was also known for his good-natured bantering.

"Dancing, pah." Tuttle voiced his discontent and clutched his cane while his wife plucked and picked at the arm of his coat.

She was thin next to his roundness with a pretty face and fair hair touched with silver at the temples. Missus Tuttle wore her age well.

"Oh come now! It's been an age since we danced," she said.

"It will be another age before I do so again!" Tuttle announced, before whispering conspiratorially to Dréoteth. "Don't ever marry."

"I will heed your advice well." Dréoteth replied. The feigned gravity made the men chuckle.

Regarding them all with a neutral smile, hands loosely clasped behind him, he watched as the couples retreated to dance. He was perplexed at the interactions. How the women cajoled the men and although they complained, they pandered to their whims.

Women rarely ever approached him, for any reason, so he was not subject to the ridiculous displays he had just witnessed. Eugenia Bailey was the exception, although even she hadn't gone so far as to touch his arm or ask for escort.

While the men took their places amongst the lines and waited for new music to start, Dréoteth strolled the perimeter of the gathering. He took care to appear casual rather than like he was hunting— which was exactly what he was doing. He took the opportunity to examine the townsfolk while they were unaware of his scrutiny.

Many people were already well into their cups, laughing drunkenly, and several couples slipped away into deeper shadows only to return a short time later with leaves in their hair and their clothes askew. Some of these would have been prime targets, but Dréoteth was not yet ready to kill. Tuttle was also a good choice; too slow to move quickly and the extra mass around his middle made for a tasty meal.

Even as he considered the scholar, he found himself reluctant to end his life. It was a startling revelation. Rarely, if ever, did he second-guess the slaughter of humans. Curious over his own hesitation, he stood at the far end of the clearing, not directly involved but not apart from the festivities.

A small girl, no more than seven or eight, broke away from the other rowdy children. Directly, without pausing to ask permission from her mother and without any trace of fear, she ran past the haystacks for Dréoteth. She halted before him and stretched out her tiny hand, extending a bright yellow dandelion. A pale halo of curly blonde hair framed her face.

"Is this for me?" Dréoteth asked, glancing down. His lips thinned faintly at her intrusion.

She nodded, smiling, dimples appearing in her cherubic cheeks. With her other hand, she reached up to impatiently push a few strands away from her mouth.

He took the weed with care and examined it as if it were the most precious of flowers, as delicate as the girl who gave it to him.

"Then I shall wear it proudly," he said, tucking the dandelion into one of the buttonholes on his coat. As a rule he avoided children at all times, finding them irritating and noisome. This particular one surprised him with her fearless charm.

They made a sweet cameo against the celebratory backdrop. Not one of the townsfolk could have guessed that the small child stood before the very man who had made four of their citizens disappear.

She performed a miniature curtsy, short legs bobbing her down and up in a flawless imitation of women thrice her age. Her dress, a haggard thing three different colors of brown and dirty at the hem, proclaimed her as one of the less privileged.

"What is your name?" she asked.

The abrupt question nearly caught Dréoteth off

guard and he bit his real name back in favor of the fake one. "Nehemiah Trimble. Yours?"

"Miss Thea!" Exuberant, she hid a giggle behind her grubby hands. Dréoteth thought she had the palest pair of green eyes he'd ever seen. In contrast, his own were a vibrant blue.

He spared her a scant smile, head and shoulders bowed just enough to make eye contact less of a strain on her little neck.

"Mistress Thea. I shall not forget it, or your thoughtful gift." In retrospect, he thought he sounded almost gallant. On the heels of that, he realized that he was standing there chatting with a mere child. A *human* child. He should be choosing a victim from the herd and instead here he was, coddling one.

"Charming the ladies, Mister Trimble?" Eugenia asked, approaching the two with a smile.

Dréoteth straightened his posture and glanced aside. Eugenia Bailey, with her lively eyes and freckled complexion, annoyed him. She didn't have a reedy voice or an ugly face and yet he discovered that she put him on edge.

Perhaps his victim had inadvertently come to him. Thea darted away with another giggle, leaving the pair alone.

"My attempts are poor, since they keep running away. If you will excuse me, Mistress Bailey, I was just about to find dinner." Without waiting for her to forestall him, he inclined his head and stepped around her.

Eugenia opened her mouth to speak and closed it when she found herself summarily dismissed. Staring after him, she balled her small hands into fists at her sides. She had intended to apologize and try to open what she hoped would be enlightening dialogue. Instead, she wound up alone.

She had heard rumors of his lengthy conversations with Tuttle, Upham and Lyon and itched to probe past the indifferent veneer he always presented.

Perhaps he wouldn't seem so threatening if she could just understand his mind.

She muttered under her breath, watching until the crowd obliterated him from view.

Rather than follow and force her company, she allowed one of the farmer's sons to lead her into the dance. She was a little stilted in poise and grace but her partner, the handsome and sought after Thom Liston, never noticed.

When the music came to an end, Eugenia found herself standing next to Meyer Lyon. She added her applause for the musicians, dipped Thom a curtsy, and took advantage of Miss Merriweather being absconded by another partner to face Meyer.

"Mister Lyon, I wonder if you could answer a few questions for me," she asked.

Meyer, following Miss Merriweather and her partner with his eyes, glanced down. "Of course, Miss Bailey. Let us get a drink and get out of the dancers way." He offered her his elbow gallantly.

She slid her fingers under his arm, grinning, and let him lead her between the bales of hay toward the refreshments. "I wanted to ask you about Nehemiah."

Meyer chuckled. "Let me guess. You want to know if there is any particular woman he has his eye on."

"Of course not! I mean—well—*is* there?" Eugenia hadn't intended to ask any such thing. Meyer piqued her curiosity with the thought there was a woman Nehemiah might be interested in. What kind of woman would he like? She knew all the single girls in town and she found herself impatient to know whether it was a dainty miss, a snobby one, or something in between.

Meyer glanced down, grinning like a he-devil. "If there is, she is the best kept secret in Malmsbury. As far as I know, he has not shown interest in any of them. Some men are like that, though. They keep their secrets close to the chest."

They passed a row of children bobbing for apples and stepped up to a long table. Meyer picked up a goblet and gestured at one of the wine casks.

She nodded, distracted with their conversation.

"Has he confided anything else to you of late? I know the last time we spoke, you did not know where his family was from, or even where Nehemiah was born."

Meyer filled the goblet halfway and handed it to her. He filled a tankard with mead for himself. "I know nothing new. He does not seem to enjoy discussing his past."

"Thank you." She took the cup and had a sip, rolling the taste of the wine across her tongue. "I cannot manage to get past 'Hello' or 'How are you' with him."

"Are you interested in Mister Trimble, Miss Bailey?"

She choked on her wine, coughing delicately. Rounding on him with wide eyes, she said, "Have you taken leave of your senses? Indeed not!"

"Really?" Meyer's dark eyes glittered with amusement. He led her toward the tug of war game about to start. "I wonder then, why you are so curious about him."

"I am curious about *every* new resident of Malmsbury."

"I seem to recall that you could not be bothered

when –"

"Mind yourself, Meyer Lyon."

"—when Ixworth Buxlowe arrived."

She scoffed and rolled her eyes. "I cannot even say his name without tying my tongue in a knot."

"If you had come to know him, instead of pretending he did not exist, you could have become familiar enough to call him Ixy, or perhaps Buxo."

"You are quite lucky I do not have a sharp object," she informed him archly.

Meyer barked a laugh, patted her arm in a brotherly fashion, and left her with the line of other women at the end of the rope.

Eugenia realized that once again, she had discovered no inroads or insights into the elusive Nehemiah Trimble.

The celebration lasted late into the evening. Food and drink were consumed in startling amounts, children ran wild, and the townsfolk engaged in contests that Dréoteth refused to participate in.

There was a watermelon seed-spitting contest that he found repulsive, a potato sack race, bobbing for apples and a pie-eating contest where the contestants ended up wearing more food than they ate. Half the time he was disgusted, wondering why he walked amongst these heathens like he was one of them. The other half he spent bemused and troubled.

At midnight, old farmer Thornton invited all the kids into the back of his wagon. Hay bales lined the wooden sides, used as seats and leaning posts.

Even from a distance Dréoteth could tell that one of the adults riding along was telling the children a scary story. Their faces were rapt, eyes wide, tension tightening the slim structure of their bodies. Some sat huddled together, clearly enjoying the thrill. He smelled their anxiety like he smelled the smoke from the bonfires. His senses were razor sharp, as any good predators should be.

He followed the wagon with his eyes while it made a circuit of the clearing and wound up staring across the distance at Eugenia Bailey.

Sitting next to Thea on a bale of hay, she locked gazes with him. None of the other women ever held his eyes so boldly. They always glanced away if he caught them looking, blushes on their cheeks, pretending like it never happened at all.

He stared until she grew uncomfortable and finally glanced away. Eugenia Bailey played a dangerous game. He didn't know if she baited him on purpose or whether she genuinely didn't recognize her folly.

Meyer Lyon joined him, providing a timely distraction, and they spoke at length about Tuttle's idea of opening a School of Higher Learning. The village was far too small for a University, they both agreed, but the School would be a step in the right direction. It could pave the way for such a venture in generations to come. Meyer always enjoyed discussing the possibilities with him, going so far to mention interest in a teaching position even though he owned and worked a rather large farm on the edge of town.

Dréoteth steered the topic away from subtle inquiries of his supposed job as a scribe, a convenient lie to allow him to mingle in society better. He *did* know how to read and write the English language, a task that had taken him some few years to learn, but he did not actively pursue a steady position. It gave him opportunity however, to get close to ancient tomes and tablets of some renown, which he enjoyed trying to translate when he could get his hands on them.

He was rarely around long enough for anyone to get suspicious about how he supported himself.

It was conversations like these that put doubt into Dréoteth's mind. Doubt about killing them. The longer he lived in their midst, the more he found himself morbidly attracted to human interaction. Some of them had intriguing ideas about the earth and the stars, things he had never given much thought to before now.

Meyer Lyon's intelligence was nothing to trifle with, either, and he took care to give nothing unusual away.

The citizens of Malmsbury started to stagger home in waves when a fine mist crept over the treetops, threatening to blanket the landscape and obliterate the low hanging moon. Dréoteth separated from Meyer with a final goodbye and a surprising promise to visit him tomorrow.

Most of the adults were inebriated to some degree and he saw several opportunities for hunting as he departed the clearing: one man staggering into the woods toward his cabin; two women arm in arm, laughing, paying scant attention to their surroundings; *Tuttle* and his jovial wife making their way to a wagon drawn by two horses that would take them to their farm on the edge of town. They made it almost *too* easy.

He saw Eugenia Bailey, her cheeks high with color, unsteadily waltzing in the general direction of home. He knew where her cottage was. He'd seen it once from the air. She earned his full regard for exactly thirty seconds before his mind was made. The nearest shadow belonged to a building lining the main street and Dréoteth sank into the confining darkness to hide his malicious intent.

He followed her by scent rather than sight, silent

now that he was actually hunting. His boots made no sound at all on the ground and his posture, should anyone have gotten a glimpse of him, was absolutely predatory. He didn't crouch or hunch or creep through the shadows, he *stalked.*

The fog grew thick and cloying around the buildings, reducing visibility to less than ten feet. Just before the gauzy mist swallowed her whole, he saw her glance back. He noticed the wariness in her astute gaze, recognized the first trickle of fear. Even with several goblets of wine in her system, this woman was still intuitive. Not for the first time, Dréoteth wondered if humans had an extra sense that allowed them to detect danger. Something they were barely even aware of, ingrained into the core so deep that they couldn't separate it from senses much easier to define and explain.

He didn't allow her to see him. Stepping away from the last building, he took three large, lunging strides and launched into the air. At first it seemed like he wouldn't do anything other than fall flat on his face.

But then, *then,* his lean body grew ultra streamlined. When his arms snapped out to the sides, they became wings. The change happened smooth and effortless, his olive skin growing scales, his maw filled with needle sharp teeth. Hard ridges protruded above the slits of his eyes, along his sinuous spine and around the oval shape of his nostrils. Smaller hooks ran the length of his tail, which ended not in the shape of a spade or something equally devilish, but a tapered point. The wedge-silhouette of his head looked sleek instead of blocky.

Dragons of lore were often described as bulky and large, but this creature was serpentine. Snake-shaped. Built for stealth and speed.

An iridescent blue sheen gleamed across his black scales whenever moonlight struck it just right.

Climbing above the foggy veil, he glided over treetops. Below, Eugenia was nothing more than a vague presence of heat with the fog between them. Guided by that and the sound of her running feet, he sliced down through the mist at a wicked, deadly angle. Under his belly, his talons curled tight and close, his long tail whipping behind him for turns and balance.

Something felt strange about the night. Eugenia couldn't say what made her glance back, or start running. Maybe it was the thick fog, the poor visibility, or the wine. The hair stood up on the back of her neck and goosebumps swarmed down her arms under the sleeves of her dress. It was a bad time to remember the dark whispers about what kind of threat lurked in Malmsbury: a crazed citizen, gypsies and curses, witches and spells.

She tripped over the gnarled knob of a root and went down with a thump and a gasp.

She felt the sudden rush of a brisk breeze but it wasn't like any wind she'd experienced before. It seemed too... contrived. As if something enormous had just flown past, low and threatening. The soft *whoosh* reminded her of wings, but even the biggest owl or eagle couldn't have felt large enough to blot out the sky. She couldn't *see* the sky, but the impression was the same.

Scrambling to her feet, breathless, she paused to listen. She looked for silhouettes in the fog that didn't belong, for shifting shapes, lumbering bodies. Her imagination was running away with itself.

The mist should have felt protective, cloaking her from prying eyes. Instead she felt blind and exposed.

Something was out there.

She knew it as sure as she knew her own name. Shirking etiquette with shocking swiftness, she snatched up handfuls of her skirt and started running.

Her cottage could only be another hundred feet, if that, ahead of her.

Almost there.

Keep running, don't trip, don't look back.

Just as she started to think she imagined the entire thing, something crashed into her from behind. She hit the ground hard, painfully knocking the wind from her lungs. Rolling twice before coming to a stop, palms scraped and abraded, she wheezed sharply and got to her feet again.

Instinct had kicked in; these next few minutes would decide whether she lived or died.

Convinced of it, she ran with a stitch in her side, pain shooting through her ribs and one ankle, so completely terrified that she couldn't even scream. She needed every breath, every ounce of energy to run the final forty feet. When her cottage suddenly loomed up in front of her out of the gloom, it startled her. She didn't stop until she barged in the unlocked front door, slamming it behind her. Desperate to brace something against it, she hobbled over to one of the heavy chairs at her small table and jammed it up against the knob.

Isolated from the rest of the town, and more importantly, help, she barricaded herself inside and listened for any sounds of menace. Wounded and afraid, her imagination ran wild over what exactly had attacked her. Was it the same thing that had absconded with the other townspeople? Was this the fate they met? Checking for blood on her nape and what part of her back she could reach, she discovered no blood and no rips in her dress.

Whatever it had been simply knocked her down, perhaps misjudging her size, or its own speed.

As the gloom thickened into the wee hours of a new morning, Eugenia Bailey thanked her lucky stars to be alive.

Chapter Two

Fall
The Night of the Festival

I cannot explain my own actions. For the first time ever, I have let one of them live. A human I do not even like. The woman whose eyes always seem to see into me. She was the perfect target on a foggy night, wandering alone and unaware, and I let her live. At the very last possible moment I retracted my talons and pulled up, snapping my fangs on nothing but air, leaving her rolling over the ground from the impact of my body. I am disturbed over my reticence. Never before have I had the slightest hesitation to end them.

Now she will raise the alarm, although I am positive she did not see me. The citizens of Malmsbury will be alerted and looking suspiciously at everyone and every thing. What will she say did it, I wonder? A bird? Did she hear my wings, hear the hiss of breath in my moment of indecision? If she was any less sharp minded or had diminished standing in the community, then I would expect her ranting might be dismissed by the elders. But she is not, and they will not be. Perhaps there will even be a hunt, like the mobs do for witches, with torches and swords and other weapons of destruction.

The thought almost makes me laugh. It also incites the beast in me and I have an almost irrepressible urge to take the whole town out right now. To leave my room with its single candle burning and incinerate every building, every human that breathes. To let them know true pain and suffering. I have done this before.

I sit here conflicted, licking my teeth, agitated in ways I have not been. These doubts are not me. This is not the way of Dréoteth. When did my loathing for humans turn into the kind of curiosity that makes me pause in the killing of them? Unthinkable. These indecisions are the path to annihilation. As much as I like to think otherwise, my kind are not invincible. We can be killed as humans can and given the motivation, they are capable of hunting us down.

Such unusual, pessimistic thoughts, these.

Dréoteth.

"It is the witches, I say!"

"A curse they have placed on us! Hunt them all down!"

"He lurks among us, one of our very own, probably standing right here listening to our plans!"

The strident accusations flew through the late afternoon air. Shouts, curses, assumptions and fear rippled through the community as word spread about the attack on Eugenia Bailey. Gathering under a clear sky and a bright sun, the citizens of

Malmsbury discussed the best way to rid the town of its threat. Several of the men were red faced and furious while mothers kept their children close. They were too wary to let them frolic freely.

Meyer stood next to Eugenia, who had arrived with a limp and bandaged ribs. He towered over her, jaw lined with whiskers, one hand resting on the hilt of his sword. The buckskin breeches and plain muslin shirt made him seem more warrior than scholar.

"Let us not jump to conclu--"

"Meyer, we must act *now!*"

Interrupted, Meyer raised a hand and tried again to calm the people. "And what do you propose to act *upon?* We have theories and suspicions, but no *proof.*"

Farmer Hufflestead jabbed the deadly sickle he carried upwards. "The attack came from the air. Only the witches have magic like that. Burn them!"

A rowdy cheer met his suggestion.

Meyer stalked into the middle of the clearing, pointedly looking at each face. He'd known these people his whole life. "What if you are wrong? What *if* they discover you are prepared to kill them when all you have are paranoid guesses and irrational hate? They will have cause to act harshly against us and *you* will have driven them to it."

A collective ripple of murmurs passed through the crowd. Farmer Hufflestead looked momentarily taken aback, both at Meyer's anger and the thought that any of them might provoke an attack by accident.

Meyer pressed his advantage. "I will seek them out in the woods and see if there is any deception in their words or their eyes. Before we pass judgment on *anyone,* let us first ascertain their guilt."

The ripple turned into a startled gasp.

"He's lost his mind!"

"Meyer, you cannot go into the woods!"

"Are you *mad,* son?"

"I do not want to see any more of our people disappear. The stories about the witches are old and probably exaggerated—how many of you *really* believe they used to snatch our ancestor's babies to use for sacrifices?" Meyer asked.

A handful of people had the grace to look abashed, and several others coughed or looked aside, unable to meet his gaze. Still others seemed certain they were responsible; the witches were an unknown element, the myth of a coven in the woods going back generations.

"Be sure not to look into their eyes," one man said.

"Aye, they are said to be nigh on horrible to look at as well. Have a care," said another.

"They are not gorgons," Meyer said, muttering under his breath. "I will take someone with me." He stopped before Nehemiah Trimble with his brows arched in question.

Dréoteth watched the proceedings with a concerned expression. Keeping up appearances just now was crucial. He'd shown up not long after the majority of the citizens had gathered, expressing what sounded like sincere apologies to Eugenia for her scare.

He'd been conflicted standing there regarding her wrapped ribs, gimpy ankle and her troubled eyes. Confliction was becoming far too familiar to suit him. He felt equal parts cruel and relieved; cruel because he had found it pleasant to strike such fear into her, and relieved that he'd changed his mind at the last second.

The hesitations annoyed him and these strange feelings unsettled him.

He traded speculation with Tuttle and Upham while the unrest grew, until the general buzz of conversation turned to shouts and threats.

Now, Meyer Lyon stood before him suggesting that he accompany the man into the woods to see the witches. Put on the spot, he could do nothing but incline his head and agree.

"Of course I will go," he said.

"Let us make ready," Meyer said.

Dréoteth nodded and turned from the group to go change. The day had gone much like he suspected it might. He hoped Meyer didn't plan on riding horses for any length into the forest or he would have a hard time explaining why the animals refused to let him anywhere near. He did not need attention drawn to him in that manner when the citizens were so volatile and restless.

With much on his mind, Dréoteth made his way into the Rose and Lion, empty now with the entire village in the clearing, and headed up the staircase. In his room, he changed into dark brown breeches and a fawn colored tunic, making short work of the transition. He chose boots with a little more wear on the heels and scuff marks over the toes. He wondered about the witches, of whom he knew nothing about and had not detected in his time here.

This could present a problem insofar that they might recognize him for the impostor that he was. Witches had talents humans did not understand, and that he'd only heard about once upon a time. According to legend, they had an ability to really *see* into the soul of a person. If myth were to be believed, these 'witches' would know immediately he was not what he pretended to be.

Standing before a witch intending to expose all

your secrets was tantamount to disaster for him, and he wiped away a grim frown before stepping out the door into the hallway.

The entire population of the town was still gathered in the clearing when he returned.

Meyer had added two daggers to the belt at his hips, giving the sheaths a tug to secure them. He accepted a kiss on the cheek and a murmur in his ear from Miss Merriweather, cupping her delicate jaw with a broad hand. He stared into her eyes, his own dark and serious, before turning away.

Dréoteth thought there was more between them than first met the eye.

He accepted a water skin that someone was passing out and attached it to his belt. Unlike Meyer, he wore no weapons. The citizens whispered and murmured amongst themselves, conjecturing and guessing and worrying. He caught several people giving furtive glances at other members of society, wondering, wondering.

Who had done it?

Not all of them were convinced it was the witches.

"Ready?" Meyer asked.

Dréoteth nodded, subtly glancing past the tall man for horses. He saw none. Small favors.

He met Eugenia's eyes for a breathtaking moment. As always, he fancied that she could see past the layers of his deception. She did not seem accusing, just curious, and he maintained his façade of concern for her, for the situation.

"Aye. Let us get on with it. If we are not back by nightfall, send scouts," Meyer said to the gathering.

"Godspeed." Tuttle stood resolute with his cane in his hand, appearing openly disturbed by the turn of events.

In a stroke of good fortune, they set out on foot. Dréoteth breathed an inward sigh of relief and flanked Meyer, heading for the trees. Behind them, the townsfolk of Malmsbury watched them go, some shaking their heads, others praying for their safe return.

"Have you any knowledge of these 'witches'?" Dréoteth asked. His tone implied that he had doubts about their actual existence, or whether they were truly what the citizens claimed.

"As rumor tells it," Meyer said, leaving the townsfolk behind. "They live in hidden cottages that no one has ever seen and move so silently that one does not detect them until they are right upon you. I do not know if that is a spell or some inbred talent."

Dréoteth forced a snort into the back of his throat. *He* would know they were there long before Meyer.

"They sound formidable," Dréoteth said.

"Aye, so the stories go."

"Are they rumored to attack strangers that enter their lair unannounced?"

Meyer, watching the debris-laden pathway, frowned in thought. "I have not heard it, but there was a tale passed down through the elder of Malmsbury that they cast a spell on an unwary trespasser, turning him into a crow. They say he is confined in the woods and cannot leave them, forever bound to be the witch's spy."

"A crow. Fitting. Now we will be suspicious of every bird we see." Dréoteth snorted.

"I do not intend to sneak up on them, so I care not if a bird betrays me," Meyer said. His mild amusement faded into a frown. "The people grow agitated. I fear if we do not find out what is causing these... disappearances and attacks... that they will take matters into their own hands."

"It is hard to strike out at an adversary they do not know nor see. I have a feeling that the witches will not be found unless they want to be," Dréoteth replied.

Meyer made a thoughtful noise and brushed a branch from his path.

Overhead, the canopy of limbs and leaves blocked most of the sun out. Only a soft glow, diffused and weak, penetrated the tall trees. The landscape seemed very raw and primal here, profusely overgrown and wild. Vines as thick as a man's wrist wrapped the trunks of the trees, draping like swags off the curves of the boughs. Ferns dotted the forest floor in greater numbers, brushing against their legs and giving off a green, earthy scent. Acutely aware of it, Dréoteth breathed deep.

There were no traces of passage, no footpaths to follow. If deer wandered here, and surely they did, there was no trail to give them away.

Stretching his senses out, Dréoteth tried to detect other forms of life in the bush. He smelled rabbits and birds and deer, but no humans.

Not yet.

Two hours of walking had taken them much deeper into the forest than Dréoteth would have imagined. He had a sense of great distance between them and the town, much further than it should have been otherwise. It was odd, and he wondered if there was magic at work here. Perhaps it was the sheer density of the foliage that skewed his perception.

Above them, a bird squawked. Both men glanced up but did not stop walking.

A crow sat high on a lofty perch, watching with its head tilted.

Dréoteth rumbled out a caustic laugh. "We are being spied upon."

"We should expect company soon then, aye?" Meyer said, amused.

"Only if you believe in legend."

Ten minutes later Dréoteth stopped and stared around them. To cover for his odd action, he asked, "Did you hear that?"

He'd heard nothing, but it gave them a moment to stand in one place so that he could figure out exactly what had drawn his attention. Something about the landscape, which was beautiful and ethereal in the gloom, seemed strange.

"I heard nothing but the wind in the trees." Meyer cast a suspicious look around, resting a hand on the hilt of his dagger.

"Perhaps that is all it was," Dréoteth said. He didn't sound convinced.

"You have passed onto private land." A quiet, feminine voice came from behind them.

Dréoteth turned three seconds before Meyer, posture tense but not defensive. Hands loose at his sides, he regarded the woman with narrowed eyes. He couldn't catch her scent, which puzzled him, and her utterly silent approach, a feat most unusual, elevated her above the status of a human.

A rustic cloak of dark red, replete with draping hood, hid her features from view. Shorter than the men, coming only perhaps to their chest, face lost in shadow. They could only make out the barest curve of her nose and chin, not nearly enough to judge anything by.

Meyer eased, sheathing the dagger he'd drawn.

"We have come to find the coven of witches who live in these woods," Meyer said.

Although he could not see her face, Dréoteth sensed something skeptical or cynical about her at Meyer's remark.

"You are not a very discreet man are you, Mister Lyon?"

Meyer's eyes narrowed. "How did you know--"

"We know all your names," the woman said. "After all, is that not a neighborly thing to do?"

"Then you have us, or me at least, at a disadvantage," Meyer said.

"I am Phae, and you are Mister Trimble," Phae said, indicating Dréoteth.

"Yes," Dréoteth said. He knew the woman was aware he was *not* human. This he gleaned from some sixth sense, as if he could *feel* her awareness of his inhuman blood. But she played along, for now, which piqued his curiosity despite the danger.

"You have come seeking information about the attack on Eugenia Bailey. She is lucky to be alive," the witch said.

Somewhere in the distance, the crow cawed.

Meyer twitched with surprise and frowned. "By Eugenia's own words, she *is* lucky. You seem to know more about this than we do. Perhaps you will enlighten us?"

Dréoteth's mouth thinned into a smile that was far from welcoming or encouraging. She knew about the attack. Any second, he expected her to launch into clever hints and clues meant to put him on edge and make Meyer suspicious.

Calm and collected, Phae pressed her hands, swathed in the mouths of their sleeves, piously together before her.

"The answers you seek have been within your grasp the whole time," she said. "It is only a matter of knowing where to look and who to ask. I can only tell you that I cannot provide the details you seek."

Dréoteth felt like she'd taken a direct stab at him with her words. It seemed she knew exactly who the culprit of the attack was, and yet thus far, she did not directly implicate him.

He wondered at her game.

"The people of Malmsbury are in danger," Meyer

said, admonishing her with his tone. "And you have answers, or ideas, but will not help us. I consider it your duty, Madam, to tell us what you know."

"Your people *are* in danger. More than you realize," she said, delivering her somber, shocking news like they were discussing the weather. "By the time you return, the entire village will be aflame and most of the people you have known all your life will be dead."

"What is this you say!" Meyer all but barked the words. It wasn't so much a question as a demand for clarification. Incredulous, his fist tightened around the hilt of his dagger. "Will one of the people light it on fire? Come! Tell us what you know!"

Dréoteth, alert and attentive, could not imagine what more dangerous animal than he lurked in the village. He had spent enough time there to know he was the only non-human masquerading amongst them. He scented the wind, but caught nothing other than the normal flora and fauna of the woods. No wisp of distant smoke. And yet he knew down deep in his bones that the witch spoke the truth.

Resilient and unaffected, she said, "It is a threat unlike your village has ever seen. Go now. Rescue any you can and keep an eye to the sky."

Her revelation surprised Dréoteth, not an easy thing to accomplish with his age and experience. He could only think of one adversary that attacked from the sky, capable of setting the whole town aflame: one of his own. Giving the cloaked witch a wide berth, he started running through the woods for Malmsbury.

Phae pushed back her hood with a flick of her fingers. A wealth of tawny hair rioted from her crown into the folds of the cloak, a few pieces blown across her chin by the breeze. Patiently, she reached up to brush them away. Smooth skinned, with nary a wart or scar in sight, she looked to be no more than twenty-five years old. A pair of gold-flecked, brown eyes kept watch on the trees where the men disappeared.

She could hear Meyer blustering through the underbrush like a bull on a rampage. He all but obliterated any sound the other one made.

"He is suspicious," a voice said behind her.

Phae did not turn to look at the woman who appeared to step right out of an ivy patch. "Yes. I cannot tell what he is, can you, Miriette?"

The second woman, wearing a cloak much like Phae, stepped up beside her. She pushed at the peach colored material of her hood, exposing hair as black as a raven's wing. They were of a same height, both slender with fine bone structure.

"Mm, no. But he is a predator and we would be wise to be wary," Miriette said, probing the growing shadows of the forest with a pair of lucid blue eyes.

"We should prepare," Phae said, turning toward the vines and the leaves. "I want to secure the hollow in case he returns."

Miriette followed suit. "Claudine was working on a spell when I left her."

There seemed to be no doors or entrances to the cottages hidden in the lush foliage of the hollow. Camouflaged by vines, bushes, branches and the trunks of the trees, they were built so smoothly into the landscape that the naked eye never determined unnatural breaks in the flow of the forest. Colors of autumn shimmered on the leaves, painting the landscape gold, orange and red.

Phae and Miriette disappeared around an enormous, twisting root while the

encroaching darkness converted the shades of fall

to cemetery gray.

"Trimble! Do you think she lies?" Meyer shouted, making a ruckus while he crashed through the thicket.

Dréoteth did not immediately answer.

Capable of running at much quicker speeds for longer durations, he tempered his pace. He didn't want to alert Meyer to his unusual ability.

"I think not. Although I cannot imagine what kind of attack could come from the sky," he lied, ducking swiftly under a branch.

Meyer grunted when he ran into the same limb.

Twigs snapped underfoot like brittle, broken bones. Others snagged their clothing, spindly fingers that hooked, pulled, caught and scratched.

"A trebuchet!" Meyer said. "That must be how they attack. The village is under siege!"

Dréoteth recalled reading about that contraption in the not too distant past; a wooden device that allowed attackers to launch heavy projectiles at a target with relative good aim. He hadn't thought of that before Meyer suggested it. Incoming rounds lit with fire could do the kind of damage the witch suggested and possibly explained her warning to keep an eye to the sky.

Stopping short, he glanced back at the sweating, out of breath Meyer. The difficult terrain and distance were taking a toll on the scholar. Although in good shape, Meyer was still subject to the limits of his endurance.

"The villagers would have noticed such a thing in the fields, along with the scores of warriors that must be accompanying it," Dréoteth said. After all, trebuchets didn't push themselves across the countryside.

"If they have only been there a few days, then the hunters and scouts might not have come across them yet. I know the parties have been hunting to the east, out past Edward Fitzhugh's farm," Meyer replied.

Dréoteth considered trebuchets and invasions. He was not well versed in the history of human war. To stand there and dawdle wasted time; he could think on the run. Turning from Meyer with a last, contemplative glance, he started through the underbrush.

The crow *caw-caw-cawed* overhead.

Dréoteth snorted to himself. Even if the bird was not the reincarnation of a man, he felt sure that it tracked their progress through the forest.

For an hour they ran, and another. He knew they went in the right direction but they could not find the edge of the forest. Darkness had conquered the land a half hour ago, plunging them into shadow. Several times he paused to get his bearings to make sure they hadn't veered off course.

Meyer came to a halt, breathing hard and fast. Frustrated, he said, "What trickery is this? We should have long come out of the forest by now!" Bending forward, he braced his hands on his knees.

Dréoteth stopped, turning just his shoulders to look back. He hardly seemed winded whereas Meyer all but panted for air. "I do not know. This *is* the right direction but we have been running for twice as long as it took us to find the woman."

"It looks like the same woods we passed through thirty minutes ago. That tree with the gouged trunk." Meyer pointed first at that one and then to another set of skinny trees like twins, side by side. "We have somehow doubled back. I recognize those two as well. Bloody *hell*."

Dréoteth wondered again if there was magic at

work, and if so, why. He doubted the witch cared whether or not they survived the attack. Perhaps he was wrong. Maybe they had encountered magic *going,* and their trip back was the true distance between the coven and Malmsbury. He didn't think it was beyond the witches to cast a spell to confuse any would be trespassers.

Imagining they recognized same trees and terrain might only be a trick of the night.

While they stood there, the sounds of the woods faded. Crickets abandoned their song and birds grew silent. A hush settled in. Dréoteth covered the oddity with motion. He set off at a stalk.

Meyer followed, muttering curses, obviously unsettled by the eerie delay.

Dréoteth had no comfort to give him, no explanations or excuses. He fought off the urge to lose Meyer and take his true form; he would be at the village in minutes rather than continue this inane bluster through the brush.

He could tell by the off-cadence of Meyer's stride that the man had developed a stitch in his side, but they pushed on, jogging instead of running.

Periodically, the crow squawked above them.

Suddenly, Dréoteth smelled smoke. Faint at first, then stronger on his second, longer inhale. He picked up speed, knocking limbs from his path, forgetting for a moment that he needed caution with speed around Meyer. He listened for the sound of leathery wings or the hiss of fire from a strafing dragon or even the missiles issuing from a distant trebuchet. So far he heard nothing but the faint crack-and-snap of flames.

Apparently the witch's prophecy was accurate.

"I smell smoke!" Meyer shouted, thrashing through the thicket and mowing over tender little plants on the ground.

"Just ahead," Dréoteth called, glimpsing a lick of fire.

Bursting from the edge of the trees, they came upon a nightmare; Malmsbury was burning. A red glow pushed back the darkness, enveloping houses and shops. Flames licked hungrily at barns and humans, leaving a swath of charred bodies in the middle of the road. Those still alive ran in mindless, confused circles, their clothing on fire, screaming for salvation that would only come with death. The strong scent of burnt flesh made Dréoteth peel his lips back and growl. He recognized the telltale signs of a dragon attack from the scorch marks on the ground.

His blood burned hot, demanding he change and take up the challenge.

Meyer, utterly shocked, slowed to a walk. The slack jaw, wide eyes and disbelief turned to fury between one heartbeat and the next.

"Mother of god," Meyer whispered.

The sight of a woman moaning and crying, writhing on the ground in her final death throes, galvanized Meyer into action. He ran like a man possessed, arriving just as she died. Cursing, he left her for another man, legs and shirt on fire, rolling him on the ground to douse the flames.

But it was too late.

Too late for so many.

Dréoteth recognized the names Meyer shouted as loved ones and friends. People the man had known all his life.

While Meyer frantically patted and rolled and doused and cursed, Dréoteth stalked through the village, looking for clues. Wary and alert, he stuck to the shadows, searching the sky with his eyes. As keen as his vision was, the billowing smoke made it all but impossible to see. He heard no more sounds of strafing, no whispery flap of wings.

His brethren could be anywhere.

It was not their way to linger after such destruction but he discounted nothing. He passed charred bodies and burning shops, the roofs caving and crashing, wood snapping with a fierce *crack*.

Illuminated in a red haze, the Rose and Lion stood at the edge of town, intact. Dréoteth did not appreciate the coincidence; it was the only place he'd lived since arriving in Malmsbury.

He walked in the front door, bold and fearless. The main room was empty as well as the kitchen. There were no villagers hiding here, no one taking refuge from the flames. Jared was gone as well as Eugenia Bailey. He heard no whimpers or rustles, only the distant sound of screams and Meyer's agony.

For some unknown, mysterious reason, the Rose and Lion had been spared. It sat apart from the main street but so did other farms and cottages that he was sure were almost all burnt to the ground. Perhaps a few stood, unharmed, at the very edges of town. He wouldn't know until he checked.

He took the stairs by two, listening at each landing for the sounds of life, for voices, for anything.

Nothing.

Any guests had been drawn outside into the roads and clearings at some point during the attack.

In his bedroom on the third floor, everything was as he'd left it. The only real thing of import was his journal and he found it under the armoire, undisturbed. Breathing deep, he did not detect any other scent but his. No humans—or dragons—had been here in his absence. He departed the Rose and Lion in search for Meyer. The sounds of the scholar's grief were disturbing.

He found Meyer crouched with his elbows on his knees, hands clasped and resting against his grim mouth, staring at a group of dead citizens on the ground. Some were women, some were children, all running for their lives when they died. Meyer's face was soot streaked and haggard. His dark gaze darted restlessly over the ruined, unrecognizable remains of the bodies.

"What manner of monster does this to helpless women and children," Meyer whispered.

The kind of monster standing right next to you, Dréoteth thought.

He rested a hand on Meyer's shoulder while the man agonized over the deaths.

"My friend—" Dréoteth said, and stopped. *Friend?* He did not make *friends* with human men. The thought persisted.

Meyer's easygoing attitude and jovial good humor made him comfortable to communicate with. He was an intelligent man with a fierce sense of loyalty and honor. Dréoteth was not bound by the same providence but they were not bad qualities in humans.

A part of his mind rejected the idea of having a human friend, *any* friend, with unsurprising vehemence. Yet he lingered here, reluctant to leave Meyer to deal with his loss by himself. He should gather his journal and depart the wreckage of Malmsbury for a new village far from here.

He *should,* but he did not.

"We should search the woods," Meyer finally said. He sounded desolate. "Maybe some of them made it to cover."

"Together or separate?" Dréoteth asked.

"We will cover more ground separate, but perhaps together in case whatever wrought this wrath returns. I hope it does. I will be the last thing it ever sees." He stood up from his crouch.

Dréoteth's hand fell away. He did not tell Meyer that he was wrong. Should he come face to face with the dragon, he would die like the rest.

"Come, let us go," Dréoteth said.

For three days they searched. They penetrated the woods in many directions but found nothing: no survivors, no witches, no dragons. Twice they walked directly through the heart of the witch haven without knowing it.

Meyer's voice grew hoarse from shouting. He refused to sleep, refused to stop, refused to spare one moment for himself. His clothes became haggard, soiled things with snags and tears from the underbrush.

Even when there were no replies, no signs of life, they continued to search until they had exhausted all possibility of hope. Dréoteth searched for clues about his brethren more than he searched for citizens of Malmsbury. He found nothing at all that gave him any information about the attack.

At night they gathered bodies and burned or buried them. Dréoteth hated handling the rotting corpses, hated digging their graves. This job was beneath him, nearly intolerable. He endured it because Meyer could not do it alone and he found himself strangely unable to say no when the scholar asked for help.

One particular day he discovered Meyer on a knee, proud shoulders bent with grief. Before him lay the twisted, half burnt remains of Miss Merriweather. Dréoteth watched Meyer mourn the woman and helped bury her in the graveyard with the rest of her family. He could not fathom the depth of emotion the scholar displayed. It made him contemplative.

When he destroyed entire villages he rarely felt anything but cold satisfaction. He was too arrogant, too *above* humans to care what the aftermath brought.

Yet here he was, hauling their burnt remains around and digging graves for their bodies. How above them could he be when he reduced himself to this? He suffered several bouts of silent fury while he tried to figure these complicated feelings out.

Meyer never noticed his preoccupation. All the better.

Five days after the attack, a drenching rain doused the last of the smoldering flames. Under the iron gray sky, Malmsbury looked like a smudge of grease on the ground, blackened with wet ash in piles where homes once stood. Jagged pieces of wood thrust up from the earth like rotten teeth.

That night in the lobby of the Rose and Lion, Dréoteth sat across from Meyer in a wingback chair, a glass of merlot between his fingers. The fire roared hot and bright at their side.

"Have you given any thought to what you are going to do?" Dréoteth asked. He had watched Meyer go through a gamut of emotions: anger, sorrow, desolation, resignation. Now he wondered what thoughts Meyer had, what actions he would find appropriate.

For him it would have been easy; simply gather his journal, pick a time in the dark hours before morning and take to the sky. He had moved between villages this way for centuries. This was the longest he had ever stayed in one town, the longest he had spent in the company of men.

He was puzzled and disturbed over his reluctance to leave Meyer alone. He owed the man nothing, had no ties to the land. There was nothing in Malmsbury but memories of death.

Meyer stared down at the whiskey he held, sloshing the liquor lazily around the bottom. "Some," he admitted. "I have thought of rebuilding it all, but what is the point?" He laughed hollowly, glancing up. "There is only the two of us and it would likely stay that way for years. We might pick up a random straggler now and then, but that is all. I loathe leaving because I was born here and because my entire family now lays at rest in the graveyard. What of you, Trimble? What are your thoughts? I know you once said you have no family to return to."

Dréoteth disliked queries about his supposed family, of which he had none. The lies fell easily enough from his tongue, but he feared tripping himself up on them if the layers became too tangled. "On to another town, I believe. There is nothing left to remain here for."

"The closest community is Faulkon's Cross, to the east. They have a vast population and it would be easy enough to assimilate. I know several scholars and a few farmers." Meyer lifted his whiskey and polished off the last swallow.

"How close is the next town after that?" Dréoteth asked.

"Twelve days west on foot," Meyer said. "Since we have no horses to ride." They had all scattered or died during the attack.

Dréoteth arched a sleek, dark brow. "Faulkon's Cross is...?"

"Seven days on foot."

"Then I say we set out for it at first light," Dréoteth said.

He had nowhere else to be, other than his distant lair in the mountains.

Beyond his noisome indecision about humans, he was curious to know how Meyer might settle into another community. It had been enlightening to see Meyer's grief process, even if he didn't understand it personally, and he wondered what happened now. Perhaps he shouldn't be so inquisitive –and then he remembered his old, redundant journal entries. The repetitive accounts of hunting and killing. Although that would ever be the most important and exciting facet of his life, he could not deny that Meyer's situation stimulated his mind.

Faulkon's Cross probably boasted at least a few artists and architects, all the more reason to go.

Maybe it was not such a mystery why he'd chosen to stay after all.

Meyer lifted his empty glass. "To Faulkon's Cross."

Dréoteth toasted their plans, and finished his drink.

Meyer stood at the edge of his property, staring at the remains of the modest house that he'd been born in and lived all his life. His parents had perished young, passing down the farm to their son, and Meyer had worked hard to see the crops thrive. Now it was nothing more than a few splinters of wood and a toppled tower of bricks that used to be the chimney. The landscape looked black and raw in the twilight, like hell itself had used it as a playground.

He scratched at his whiskered jaw, dark eyes panning over the destruction, and set out for the tree line. Most of the forest, except perhaps the very edges, had gone undamaged. His boots snapped dry twigs underfoot as he navigated the pine and spruce for a small hunting cabin his father had built years before. The structure appeared intact when he came upon it in a clearing, and he breathed an inward sigh of relief.

The sloping roof covered a single room that harbored a cot and a cold hearth. Meyer stepped inside after opening the creaky, lopsided door. Ignoring a nostalgic pang, he collected two sharp knives in their sheaths, a bow and arrows off the wall, and a knapsack that he stuffed several pairs of extra clothes into. They were not clothes he would wear into polite society but they would serve to see him through until he was back on his feet. Everything else had gone up in flames.

A hidden stash of coins went into his pocket. The last thing he grabbed was a miniature portrait of his parents propped in a niche on the wall. He looked more like his father than his mother with his broad brow and defined, hard jaw. She stared sweetly out of the portrait, delicate even in oil, rosy cheeked with a smile during a time when serious poses had been all the mode. What a stroke of luck that he'd thought to bring it here so many years back. He smiled and ran his thumb over the frame before slipping it into the knapsack.

Of his family, it was all he had left.

Dréoteth slept little. He was not a creature who collected trinkets and useless baubles, so it only took him a few minutes to stow his journal and his clothing into a pack that he sat near the door. Setting thoughts of hunting aside, in case Meyer came seeking him in the night, he paced a circuit in his room. When he'd worn some of the restlessness off, he stretched out, fully clothed, onto the simple bed against the wall. The upper half of his body was doused in moonlight from the window. Through it, he could see winking stars in a dark sky, and he allowed himself to get lost in contemplation until morning.

He wondered if his brethren had known he was here, and whether the Rose and Lion had been spared because of his presence within its walls. It seemed unlikely; dragons were not known for love of their own kind.

For love of *anyone,* or any thing.

It was not usually their nature to care. To make *friends.* He wondered, too, which direction the dragon had gone after the attack. It had moved on, he was sure, to new hunting grounds. What an irony it would be should the dragon choose Faulkon's Cross as its next victim. He doubted so, only because dragons tried to put many miles between one totally devastated town and the next.

He rose with the first slivers of weak light, gathered his pack and his water skins, and left the Rose and Lion for the last time. He glanced at the bar when he walked by; at least the nosy woman Bailey would not be cutting him to ribbons with her sharp eyes. A frown creased his brow at the thought of her death. Countless times he had imagined her demise with relish and anticipation. She annoyed him, badgered him, frustrated him. The absence of her pestering ways was a blessing. Wasn't it?

Briefly, he thought about Tuttle and Upham, whose bodies they had found among so many others. It was a pity he would never find out Tuttle's theories on astrology, a conversation they'd started once and had been interrupted from. A conversation they would never get to finish.

Dréoteth approached the graveyard and saw Meyer standing over the graves of his family, a look of regret and dismay on his face. He watched as the scholar kissed each of their headstones and murmured his final good-byes. He met Meyer's gaze and inclined his head like he understood. Those were emotions Dréoteth could only guess at.

From there, they set out for Faulkon's Cross, each man lost in his own thoughts.

Cresting a hill, Dréoteth glanced back at the scar on the earth that had once been a thriving town. That one of his own had put to utter ruin. He felt no crushing remorse, no great sense of loss. There *was* a peculiar disappointment that, upon examination, he cold not explain.

Crushed between the pages of the journal in his pack was the tiny dandelion Thea gave him, a gentle reminder of her childish whim.

Why he kept it, he could not say.

Hot.

Hot.

She couldn't breathe.

Her mother carried her through the flames and she saw the world on fire in snatches past her pale hair. Screams hurt her ears, her mother's included. She dropped her favorite doll into the dirt when a crazed man crashed into them, trying to escape.

"Greta!" she shouted, but her mother didn't stop.

Her fingers reached out for the beloved toy, the stitched eyes staring vacantly at nothing, until curls of smoke obliterated it from view.

"Greta!"

Held at a slant across her mother's body, so tight she thought her bones might break, she endured the heat and the pain with whimpers.

And then they were down. Thea rolled hard over the dirt, banging her elbow, scraping her knee. Across one cheek, something sharp and jagged had scratched her. She was just in time to look up and see a sinuous, long body, like a snake with wings, swoop in and snatch her mother up in its talons. Wickedly sharp, they pierced her skin like melted butter. Thea stared into its hateful eyes. Glowing blue, like the scales when the moonlight hit them just right.

"Mama!" Her tiny scream was lost in the horrible roar. With just one giant flap of its wings, the creature carried her terrified, bleeding mother higher into the sky. Billowing layers of smoke obscured them from view. Thea bobbled to her feet, looking frantically around for help.

Tuttle and Upham were burning. Gasping and coughing, she ran past their bodies, darting left between the tailor shop and the bakery. Like the rest of the children, she knew the shortcuts by heart. Fire drove her away from the city and into the forest. Another roar above the treetops urged her deeper into the shadowy canopy. She tripped over roots and dead branches, only to rise and run again.

She ran until she could not hear the crack and lick of flames. She ran until the thunder of the beast was gone. Scratched, sooty and shaken, she pressed her skinny body up against the rough bark of a tree trunk and stood still. Listening.

Her heart beat a frantic staccato in her chest.

She could only hear breathing, her own breathing, and the gentle passage of wind through the leaves.

No screaming, no chaos.

Her knees hurt. Her elbow hurt. There were tiny blood drops on her battered dress.

But she was alive.

In, out. Breathing. Living.

The images kept replaying over and over in her mind. Blue, glowing eyes.

The sheen of blue on black scales.

So pretty. So deadly.

Sharp talons, lethal talons, carrying her mother

away.

From around the side of the tree, something long and wet emerged to lick along her cheek.

Jaw to hairline, slick and slightly raspy.

Her gaze darted aside and there-- blue eyes, glowing eyes and blue-black scales on a long snout--

Thea woke up from the nightmare with a startled gasp.

Mama? Mama! The screams were only in her mind.

Maybe it was just a dream. Her mother would come rushing in any moment, soothing and crooning.

Too dark to see the room she slept in, she scrambled out of a soft bed and put her feet on the ground. She saw a sliver of light under a door and ran to it, throwing it open. The soft glow of mid-morning rays filtered into a living room from an intricate window, painting it yellow. Everything was delicate and pretty: from the floral, hand-stitched cushions on the divan, to the tasseled pillows, to the pale beams of carved wood on the arched ceiling.

Thea had never seen a house like it. Momentarily stunned out of her upset, she stared.

Plants stood in elaborate pots, growing thick and lush with broad green leaves and colorful flowers. The woodwork around doorframes and archways into other rooms was well crafted and quaint. Ivy vines trailed in open windows to spread out over the walls. The cottage seemed a part of the forest itself, built into the landscape.

"Good morning, Thea."

She glanced over in surprise at a woman standing near a striped, wide chair. Even to a child, the lady was beautiful. Her tawny hair fell in corkscrews down her back and she wore an ethereal dress of pale blue, filmy and gauzy with a sash that fit high around her ribs. Skinny straps made to look like ivy arched over her slim shoulders. She had a sweet face and kind, brown eyes.

"Mama?" Thea asked, hoping the gentle woman knew where she was.

"I am sorry to tell you that your mother is not here. I am called Phae."

Thea knew then that the nightmare had been real.

The fire, the creature. Her mother was dead.

Soulful sobs wracked her and the pretty woman came close to gather her up.

"Shh," she said. "Everything will be fine. Do you know where you are?" Phae asked.

Thea shook her head, terrified. Gone, they were all gone.

"You are in the woods. We will look after you sweetheart, do not worry," Phae crooned. The door opened and several other women entered, all genteel in manner, their cloaks flowing prettily from neck to ankle.

"Here now, look. This is Miriette, Ellery and Augusta," Phae said, easing the small girl around without removing the comfort of her arms.

Thea saw that the three women were as beautiful as Phae, as pretty as any from a fairy tale, and she wondered if she might be dreaming.

Miriette, with her black hair and blue eyes; Ellery, brown haired and green eyed, smiling kindly, and Augusta, auburn hair and hazel eyes making her stand out from the rest.

They greeted her with sweet, welcoming words, making a loose circle around her. Their hands petted and stroked gently over her hair, her cheek. Thea detected nothing but passive kindness from each, and she somehow knew that this is where she would stay.

These women, with their earthy scents and gentle nature, would become her guardian caretakers. Everyone else was dead.

Either from exhaustion or trauma, or perhaps a little magical nudge, Thea fell into a deep, dreamless sleep.

Chapter Three

It was day three of their journey. Night eased over the earth, spreading darkness across the landscape. Thousands of bright stars glittered against the sky, a bright three quarter moon casting a moderate glow over the ground. Leaves blustered by, end over end, ushered by a brisk wind. The hilly terrain hadn't changed much from Malmsbury, stretching across pastures flanked by deep forests in some spots, and dotted by rocky outcroppings in others. Mountains cut a jagged silhouette to the west.

Dréoteth slung his pack to the ground, hardly winded from an entire day of walking. He could have gone much further, his stamina and energy far above his human companion. His stomach had been demanding food for hours though and he knew he could put off hunting no longer. The meager supplies of dried meat and fruit that they'd brought were gone.

Meyer appeared more than ready to stop, brow lined with sweat, his shoulders slumped from the weight of his knapsack. Hearty and strong, Meyer nevertheless succumbed to the basic human need for rest.

"You should gather wood and build a fire," Dréoteth said. "I will go see what game I can hunt up." It would keep Meyer preoccupied while he was away. Dréoteth took a quick drink of water and capped the water skin before setting it down.

"Are you sure you do not want me to come with you?" Meyer asked, grunting with exhaustion as he set his knapsack on a craggy rock. He sat down and grabbed his own water skin, catching his breath.

"It will go faster this way. I have little doubt there is plenty of game to choose from here."

"I thought I heard a turkey not long ago. Good hunting," Meyer said, lifting the water skin after a drink. He set it down and lurched off the rock, turning away to start his search for kindling.

There was a terrible moment when Meyer put his back to Dréoteth that he had the urge to kill him.

It surfaced fast, that bloody hunger.

His blue eyes glittered, fingers twitching, and he pivoted away immediately. It was just his predatory nature, his dragon. These urges were common, if fewer and farther between these days.

Breaking into a run, Dréoteth sank into the shadows of the woods, increasing his speed once he knew he was out of sight.

Bursting into a small clearing many minutes later, he launched into the sky, wings snapping out against the air. The transformation was as seamless as ever. He took a slight risk in this but he felt confident Meyer would never be the wiser. Besides that, he was ten times a better hunter in his dragon than he was as a human.

Black scales glistened under the glow of the moon. He hunted well away from their campsite, flushing white tailed deer from the brush, killing several with vicious skill. Two he ate on the ground, tearing flesh from bone with his wicked teeth. His snarls and growls were too low to be heard beyond the small meadow.

When he'd sated his considerable hunger, he melted back into his human body and roped the feet of the last deer. He drug it behind him, following the scent of smoke back to the camp. There were no signs on his clothes that he'd engaged in a gruesome attack or that he'd fed while he was gone.

Meyer sat on the boulder with his pack, staring into the flames. He wore a distant expression that vanished when Dréoteth rejoined him.

He smiled broadly to see the deer. "You have a gift for the hunt," Meyer said.

"I have had a lot of practice," Dréoteth replied, not without a bit of dry humor. Indeed.

"We will hunt together next time," Meyer said, shaking off the last of the trance. "I am curious to see your technique, especially since you have no bow."

The two men connected gazes across the fire.

It wasn't quite a challenge that Dréoteth read in the man's eyes, but it was openly questioning. He never carried anything but a single dagger, and sometimes not even that, on a sheath at his hip. Weapons meant little to him.

His inner beast, edgy and volatile, started to stir. They didn't submit or cower to men.

Meyer grew uncomfortable under the steady stare and glanced away first.

Dréoteth dropped the rope and unsheathed his dagger, palming it with familiar skill. "Perhaps," he said.

The awkward moment eased as they began the tedious task of skinning their meal, but the incident was never far from Dréoteth's mind and he suspected it wasn't far from Meyer's, either.

They caught first sight of Faulkon's Cross at dusk on the seventh day. Topping a small rise, Dréoteth and Meyer had a perfect view of the outlying farms with the town nestled in the middle. Positioned in a broad valley and flanked by foothills, the town teemed with life. A thousand souls lived here compared to Malmsbury's modest two hundred and fifty.

There were many roads that criss-crossed at intersections, lit by the flickering lights of homes and shops. The sprawl of humanity stretched far into the countryside.

Dréoteth had his first reservations about attempting to seriously integrate into this large of a community. He had expected a far smaller population. More people meant more questions and busy streets with horses and dogs made for a precarious situation for a predator in hiding.

He told himself, not for the first time, that he didn't have to stay.

Meyer was more than capable of building a new life and since when had he become responsible for the man, anyway?

At the same time, as they started to descend along the path, Dréoteth was beset by the insufferable curiosity that plagued him. He wanted to see, on a larger scale, how humans coexisted together.

Dragons could never live like this.

He also wondered what artists might live amongst them, and what paintings hung on their walls. Which ones had stunning works that would fascinate him for hours on end?

Once, he had studied a painting for an entire afternoon in the home of a poor man that he had

killed simply to gain access to it. The colors had
been divine, the detail magnificent, depicting a
bloody battle scene between gods and monsters.
Unable to leave it behind, he'd taken it with him to
his lair to admire at his leisure. It had been the first
of many paintings he had acquired through
nefarious means to put in his mountain.

He'd been born to loathe humans, but he secretly
found their artistic talent amazing.

"You're thoughtful," Meyer said. He walked at a
quicker pace, anxious to reach one of the Inns in
town and book a room for the night.

"Mm," Dréoteth said, distracted. "As any
newcomer would be."

"You will like it here, I think. They have a School
of Higher Learning and a library that will astound
you."

"There are a lot of people." That seemed to be a
drawback for Dréoteth.

"All of whom will accept and welcome you. It has
been this way every time I have visited," Meyer said.
"There are, of course, heathens thrown into the mix
but Baron Herriott keeps rather good order here."

"Baron Herriott?"

Meyer smiled tiredly. "Yes. A rather eccentric man
with an unusual home who employs a stunning
amount of knights to keep his village safe."

"Interesting," Dréoteth said, and wondered if the
good baron had any worthwhile paintings to add to
his personal collection.

Fall
After the Great Fire

*We have been here for ten days. This town is not
like the last one. I remember observing it and its
people closely before I chose Malmsbury to live in.*

There are almost a thousand citizens here where the last had two-fifty or so. The streets are busy with people and animals, all of whom I must avoid so that they do not startle when they realize I am predator to their prey.

Meyer and I have taken rooms at an Inn for now, one much larger than the Rose and Lion. There are still only three floors but there are two buildings and a courtyard built nicely of stone. It took us seven days of walking to reach this village and I discovered nothing more along the way about the dragon that burnt Malmsbury to the ground. I saw no shadows at night, heard no telltale flap of wings. Meyer had I had a few tense moments after I returned from the hunt with a deer. I took no weapons but a dagger and rope and I believe he questions how I do it. He never tried to follow me to find out. A good thing, because killing him is not something I think I would enjoy.

This distresses me and I have contemplated this strange friendship with Meyer often. I am as conflicted as I was when I decided to live amongst them to begin with; although I do confess here in secret that once I had the urge to gut him. It was the same night he mentioned my prowess in bringing back game with no weapons.

I put that down to my predatory nature, a thing I cannot always easily control. It is not that we prefer the taste of humans to other prey. In fact I favor horses above all else. It is that our loathing of humans goes back so far into our memory that we know nothing else. It is ingrained, much as it is for a fish to swim in water or for a lion to hunt gazelle. Being around humans this much without killing them challenges me. What else do I have to fill eternity with?

Tomorrow I am to speak with a man here about an

old tome he wishes copied to a new book. I considered it because it is quite old and it is an easy way for me to have it in my possession without having to kill someone to obtain it. Fewer questions. In living amongst humans, I must keep up the appearance that I live as they do, anyway, and this helps with that. I suppose I could simply say that all my money comes from a family inheritance, but then they start asking about lineage and properties and titles. It is easier this way than to risk inviting too many questions into my past. Every time Meyer tries to broach the matter, I change the subject.

Our first four days here were spent repeating the news of the attack on Malmsbury, but it seems that the intense interest is finally starting to wane. I am grateful. Several townsfolk were starting to sound like they wanted to plan a hunt.

I feel a restlessness building. Perhaps tonight when the moon is low in the sky and the people are asleep, I will hunt.

Dréoteth.

He walked the main street of Faulkon's Cross with his hands in the pockets of his tan breeches. Today, the clothing felt confining. A dark brown coat buttoned over a white shirt that he'd left open at the throat. He felt trussed up and suffocated, and every time he passed gentry on the street with their high collars and tight vests, pompous and self important, he wanted to divert to the woods and seek his dragon. Sometimes, playing the role of a human tested his temper and his patience.

An overcast sky, the clouds dark and heavy, promised rain. He could smell it on the air, feel the oppression on his skin. The somber day didn't help his questionable mood. The gray atmosphere made it difficult to tell that it was only an hour before nightfall.

Every time a horse clopped by he was forced to duck into a shop until he was out of range of its scent.

He found himself in a small but curious bookstore one time, and in a mercantile the next. The proprietors always greeted him with a smile, but it wasn't the same smile he saw them greet the other townsfolk with.

Of course not.

He had only been here two weeks and was still a stranger. It wasn't just that, but the *otherness* he exuded. He walked different than other men, his lithe grace effortlessly predatory.

Humans, he decided, recognized the threat he presented on a sub-conscious level, down where their instinct lived.

It made men wary of him and it made most of the women submissive. Often he saw them lower their lashes and hide their eyes. Eugenia Bailey had been one of the few who challenged him, but even that little spitfire had backed down in the end.

A few were brash and forward, unable to detect the aggression and malevolence he was capable of. Either that, or they flatly ignored it.

One such woman approached him along the cobbled walk from the opposite direction. He'd just finished impatiently tugging at the collar of his shirt with a finger when she cut directly into his path.

He knew her name.

The whole *town* knew her name.

Lucille Fynch, with her high coiffure of blonde curls, snug dress trimmed in lace that dipped so low in the front it was scandalous, and brown eyes that flirted endlessly with men made sure no one forgot her.

"Mister Trimble! What a great pleasure to see you," she said. Her wide smile produced a dimple in her smooth cheek. Many men in town fought for her attention, for she was fair with porcelain skin and pretty teeth. Dréoteth was not unaware of her rare, perfect beauty, but human women were something to be tolerated, nothing less, nothing more. They were too frivolous and flighty and fragile to rouse his lust. As if he would lower himself to mate with a human female.

His thoughts amused him. Drolly, he said, "Mistress Fynch."

His sharp, pointed stare would have made other women falter or retreat.

Not so, Mistress Fynch.

Dréoteth couldn't tell if she had no inner instinct at all or if she thrived on the prickle of fear.

"I wondered," she said. "If you might be interested in being my escort tomorrow night for the Baron Herriott's ball."

"Am I mistaken in thinking it is the men who usually ask the women, Mistress Fynch?"

"Oh, I—" She stammered a moment. "Well, yes.

But you see—"

"Are there not a horde of eligible men at your disposal?" Dréoteth said, pressing the issue.

"Frankly, Mister Trimble, I am interested in having *you* as my escort." Lucille grabbed the reins and charged forward, chin lifting defiantly in the air.

Dréoteth's brows arched at her candor and her bluntness. "Miss—"

Suddenly, the sound of strident barking erupted to their left. He glanced aside to see four dogs of varying size and breed with their hackles up, teeth showing, making a half circle at his flank. Two of them seemed unable to decide whether to keep facing the threat or flee with their tails between their legs.

Their behavior started to draw unwanted attention. People on the street slowed down, staring and frowning, curious at the spectacle.

Lucille Fynch gasped, putting a gloved hand against her delicate throat. She played up the role of damsel to the hilt.

Dréoteth grit his teeth and stared the dogs down. This was exactly the kind of situation he wanted to avoid.

One of the dogs whimpered between barks and scuttled back five feet. Saliva flew from another one's mouth, foam gathering at the corners.

There could be no doubt at whom the dogs barked, though there seemed no outward reason for the extreme aggression.

Dréoteth wasn't antagonizing them or baiting them.

Lucille glanced from the dogs to Dréoteth and back again.

"I have never seen anything like it," she whispered. "What is the matter?"

"I cannot say," he replied.

Too many people were beginning to whisper, gathering in small clusters in front of shops and along the walk.

Dréoteth glanced up from the animals and met Meyer's gaze on the other side of the road. The man stood with a petite woman wearing a bonnet over her brunette hair in front of the bakery. He wondered if Meyer remembered the event at the Festival in Malmsbury, where the horses had shied and become skittish.

Now, Meyer regarded him across the distance with curious intrigue.

To diffuse the situation, before the entire town became suspicious, Dréoteth stepped briskly around the lady Fynch and turned down a narrow passageway between buildings.

The ferocious dogs were not brave enough to follow but their barking continued for another few minutes until Meyer stepped into the street and scattered them with a booming clap of his hands.

"Here now, tsssst!"

The dogs yelped and slunk away.

Rain began to fall, first in droplets and then a downpour; people ducked for cover in shops and under awnings, distracted from the strange event by the weather.

Lucille Fynch sighed in exasperation and sought cover like the rest.

Meyer covered Miss Bethany Archer's head with his coat. They stood at the door of her flat above the bakery, laughing as the storm raged around them. Thunder rolled like cannon fire through the heavens and lightning split jaggedly through the darkness, illuminating their faces three seconds at a time.

They were drenched to the bone, and neither

seemed to care.

"Thank you again for supper, Meyer. It was most pleasant," Bethany said. Under the yellow bonnet, her black hair stuck to her head and neck like wet ribbons. A pair of dark eyes peered up at him with a friendly gleam.

"Aye, it was. We should do it again. I will stop by in the morning for the promised pastry and see if your cooking is as good as rumor says," Meyer said, teasing her.

He had no doubt her baking skills were as extraordinary as she seemed to be.

"You will become quite smitten," she said, opening the door.

"Indeed, lady. Of that I have no doubt." He smiled devilishly and swung his coat back onto his shoulders. Two weeks into their acquaintance and he already felt like he'd known her a year. She was easy to talk to, easy to be with.

"Will you attend the Baron's ball tomorrow eve?" She asked.

"Will you be there?" He countered.

"Aye," Bethany replied, grinning.

Meyer couldn't see much past her petite shape to the flat she called her own, but what touches he detected were feminine.

"Then I believe I will as well. Until morning, Miss Beth." Meyer bowed gallantly and turned on a boot heel, descending the staircase while she peered out the door after him.

Meyer walked through the deluge toward the Mirmande Inn, where he and Trimble had taken up rooms upon their arrival.

Trimble.

The incident earlier in the evening came to mind and he wondered over it. Running a rough palm across the thin, dark whiskers on his jaw, he thought back to other eerie happenings when he'd been in Trimble's company.

How the horses at the fall festival in Malmsbury had startled and shied, Trimble's unusual skill in the hunt with nary a bow or a blade and how he had known without doubt that they had not become lost that day in the forest.

"This *is* the right direction," he recalled Trimble saying.

And how Trimble seemed tireless, barely winded at all when other men, even men in good shape, were all but passing out from exhaustion.

He'd noticed. More than once.

Three stories tall, with two buildings and a courtyard, the Mirmande Inn rose out of the gloom and the rain. The architecture was pleasant and square, with a carved ledge that ran around the perimeter just above the tall archway for the main door.

Meyer stomped debris from his boots and shook his wet hair before stepping inside. The man behind the long desk greeted him with a familiar nod and Meyer returned a smile, heading for the staircase.

He had a room on the third floor, across from Trimble, and as he drew abreast of his door, he paused.

Meyer considered knocking on Trimble's door to inquire about the dogs. It bothered him on a gut level that he couldn't name.

He wasn't sure why.

Tick, tick, tick.

He hesitated, staring at Trimble's room.

A moment later, he opened his own door and entered, shutting the world out behind him.

Baron Herriott's mansion rose majestically

against a dark sky. Tall spires capped round turrets, gothic archways stretching between. It was made of gray stone, with matching gargoyles perched upon baroque style pedestals flanking broad stairs. Centered in the shallow sockets of their eyes, rubies glittered and shined.

Dréoteth stood at the bottom of the steps, staring up at the double doors. Stained glass panels decorated the intricately carved wood; he could make out the shape of nymphs, animals and ivy vines.

This would be exactly the kind of home he would chose were he the type to settle down.

It was magnificent.

"If I did not know better, Trimble, I would say you are gawking." Meyer teased. He stopped beside him.

Dréoteth heard him coming long before he ever arrived. He glanced askance at the scholar, a faint grin stretched across his mouth.

"I did not expect to see this here," he admitted. Neither man mentioned the incident on the street.

"The Baron has eclectic taste, as his father before him. He was the one who had it built." Meyer glanced up at the intimidating façade of the structure. For the ball, he'd spent some of his precious savings on new clothes. Black, dark red and a snip of a white shirt were colors Meyer wore well. His boots were new and polished to a shine. Under his surcote, he wore a belt with two daggers sheathed at each side.

Dréoteth, in black, ash gray and white, shirked any frills at the neck. No man should wear ruffles, in his opinion. He heard more footsteps coming up on their flank and caught the scent of a female. He didn't need to look to know it was Bethany.

"Good evening, Mister Lyon!" Bethany called.

Meyer twisted his shoulders to see behind him,

and smiled at the picture she made.

The dark blue dress fit snug in the bodice with a modest neckline trimmed in cream. Bands of darker blue caught around her arms at the biceps and wrist, where the cuff rippled across her delicate knuckles. Caught back by tortoise shell clips, her hair cascaded in soft waves down her spine. It exposed her fresh face, cheeks pink from the chill in the air.

"You look ravishing, " Meyer said. "Have you met Mister Trimble, yet?"

Bethany stopped at the bottom of the stairs with the men and glanced at Dréoteth. "I have not had the pleasure. Hello."

"Nehemiah Trimble, may I introduce Bethany Archer."

"Mistress Archer," Dréoteth said, inclining his head.

She dipped a quick curtsy, smiling.

Dréoteth searched Bethany's eyes for wariness, but found none. Either that, or she was skilled at hiding it.

"Shall we go up?" Meyer asked, offering his elbow to the lady.

"I hear tell Herriott's got quite an evening planned," Beth said, sliding her fingers neatly under Meyer's arm.

"I will be up shortly," Dréoteth said, hanging back.

Meyer nodded and escorted Beth to the front doors, which opened from the inside. Two liveried footmen greeted them cordially, and closed the doors in their wake.

Dréoteth pocketed his hands, mouth quirking at a corner.

He could hear music inside and the distant drone of voices. Being enclosed with that many people would be a challenge, no matter how curious he was to see the rest of the estate. Feeling edgy and unpredictable, he slanted a look at the dark sky.

Hunting sounded better than dancing.

He licked his teeth, a muscle twitching in his jaw.

The swish and rustle of skirts in the evening told him someone else approached, but he remained as he was, examining the façade of the mansion.

"Having second thoughts, Mister Trimble, or were you waiting for me?" Lucille asked. She stepped up to his side, a cloud of sweet perfume clogging his senses.

He glanced over.

"Enjoying the fresh air before I go in," he said. Apparently, he was going to need it.

The full skirt of her gown, deep red with too much embroidery at the scooped neckline, brushed against his legs. Ribbons trimmed the long sleeves, and more embroidery decorated the hem. If there had been a little less extra adornment, it might have done her justice. As it was, Dréoteth thought she looked a spectacle, too trussed up and gaudy with her jewels sparkling at her throat and ears.

"Would you be kind enough to provide me escort?" One small hand reached for his elbow. Most men would have fought for the honor.

Dréoteth stepped ahead before her hand could touch down, ascending the steps without looking back. "I suggest you hurry," he said.

Lucille opened her mouth, gasping at the affront. Snatching a bit of her skirt in hand to prevent herself from tripping, she hurried in his wake. Walking in with him was apparently better than arriving alone, whether he aided her with his arm or not.

The doors swung wide, opening upon an enormous foyer and three long hallways that stretched to both sides and straight ahead. Beams of wood curved up along the walls and over the ceilings, reminding Dréoteth of a church he'd wandered into once upon a time. Molding of intricate design framed the windows and the seams on the walls. Elaborate Persian rugs added splashes of color against the monochromatic gray.

"Good evening," the doorman said. Their uniforms were done in deep blue and gold, the flat buttons glinting against candle light from iron sconces on the walls.

"Good evening," Dréoteth said. He all but forgot the woman at his side, following the straight hall toward a grand room at the far end. He could only see a sliver of it from here, along with several bodies milling around, but he knew that was where they needed to go. The sweet strain of a haunting violin wove through voices in conversation, adding an eerie element to the surroundings. They passed huge paintings on the walls, some of them portraits, the eyes of Herriott's ancestors seeming to stare straight into his soul. Of course he wanted to stop and examine each one in minute detail. He only gave them cursory glances on his way by, promising himself that he would find a way to study them up close, at his leisure.

"My heavens." Lucille had to hurry to keep up with him, her breaths coming short and shallow. "Do go a little slower, please?"

Dréoteth snapped a chiding look over his shoulder and did not slow his steps.

She huffed, quite determined to sweep through the tall archway at his side.

He could have outpaced her and ruined her ridiculous insistence to make a grand entrance. As it was she bustled four steps behind, chin high as if his indifference didn't exist.

The grand ballroom opened before them as they crossed the threshold, and Dréoteth paused. It was so sudden that Lucille kept walking until she realized he'd stopped.

"Mister Trimble?"

Here, the beams were carved of stone, meeting overhead like the skeletal ribs of a great beast. Between them, on the ceiling itself, murals had been painted. By a fine hand, Dréoteth could see, the colors astounding and complimentary to the architecture. The room was enormous, with more stone gargoyles on high ledges looking down over the gathered. Rubies gleamed in their eyes, tails circling their clawed feet. Three huge candle chandeliers, spaced generously apart, provided added illumination to the iron sconces on the walls. Candlelight flickered everywhere.

Trestle tables laden with food sat to the sides, out of the way of the dancers that swirled in a burst of color through the middle of the room.

Musicians played at one end, dressed impeccably in black. Other tables with benches for sitting sat close to the wall on the right. Men and women mingled in groups and as couples.

Meyer motioned to him from across the room where he was procuring a drink. Dréoteth inclined his head to let him know he'd seen him, but didn't immediately make his way over.

"Mister Trimble?" Lucille said again, trying to keep the exasperation out of her voice.

"What is it, Mistress Fynch?" Dréoteth glanced aside, meeting her eyes, annoyance ripe on his features.

He knew she was aware how many pairs of eyes watched every detail, judged every move. Personally, he hated it.

She smiled brilliantly, tilting her face up to his.

Putting on a show for the gentry. "Meyer and Bethany are just there. Shall we join them?"

He knew her game. Dréoteth was still learning the ways of men and women, but he didn't have to be told she was making a statement. He gestured her ahead of him around the revelers toward Meyer and fell in behind, giving him time to continue his examination of the ballroom.

More paintings hung on the walls, their gilt frames elaborate, striking.

He was reminded again why he tolerated humans, why he was drawn into their villages and skirted their lives. They had a talent for art and building structures that enchanted him. Dragons lived in deep caves that were beautiful in their own right, but *this.*

This was breathtaking. Someone's hands had shaped the stone and used colors to bring pictures to life. The small shires that he usually preyed upon rarely had elaborate buildings of this nature and never had he seen architecture so bold and commanding.

Lucille marched along in front of him toward Meyer and Bethany, passing out smiles and murmured greetings to men and women alike. She made it seem as if Dréoteth had escorted her, doing nothing to curb the whispers and assumptions people were making.

"Mistress Fynch," Meyer said. "Good to see you. A drink?" Behind him, there was a round table with bottle after bottle of wine and whiskey. Meyer had his own and Bethany cradled a goblet of merlot between her delicate fingers.

Lucille smiled at them both, kissing Bethany's cheeks. The women had known each other since they were children.

"What Bethany's having," Lucille said, all but

cooing.

Meyer chuckled to himself and set his drink down to pour her a goblet of red.

"Nothing for me," Dréoteth replied.

His distraction with the room did not go unnoticed by Meyer. "Impressive, is it not?" he asked.

"Very much so. I have seen a few books with depictions, but seeing it with my own eyes is different."

"You must have grown up in a rather small village," Lucille said, accepting her drink from Meyer.

"It was... rural," Dréoteth answered.

Meyer laughed and herded them away from the table toward a vacant spot with a good view of the dancers.

Dréoteth returned his attention to his company, noting the specific way Lucille smiled up at Meyer when she thought no one was watching, and how it made Bethany bristle.

Ah, societal intrigue.

Apparently Lucille wanted to assure both their attention should she fail with Dréoteth.

"How very glad we are that you two have come to stay in Faulkon's Cross. Isn't that right, Beth?" Lucille said.

"Indeed," Bethany replied, sipping from her merlot. She caught Meyer's glance and hid a smile behind her cup at the blatant wink he gave her.

Dréoteth pocketed his hands. Aware of the subtle game going on between the others, he decided to pay it little attention.

"Who is Herriiott?" he asked.

Meyer scoured the room, and pointed discreetly to a robust man speaking with a group near the musicians. He had receding dark hair, a long mustache and skin that appeared to be lightly scarred from the pox.

Dréoteth picked out these subtle things from a distance.

"He is one of the men involved with the School," Dréoteth said. "I recall passing him coming and going. Does he have an interest in it?"

"His father helped build it," Meyer said, hovering near Beth. "I never had the chance to meet the elder Herriott on my prior visits, but he did a lot for the community."

"He was as odd as his son," Lucille said. She set her goblet down on a small table behind them and impulsively extended her hand to Trimble. "Shall we dance?"

"Perhaps later," he said, with no intention of fulfilling her request. Dréoteth didn't dance.

Lucille looked mortified at being so thoroughly denied and snatched her hand back. She darted a look around to see who might have noticed besides Meyer and Beth.

Dréoteth knew it was an affront, rude by their standards, and just didn't care.

"May I interest you in a dance, milady?" Meyer asked Bethany. He finished the potent whiskey and set his cup down with the other.

Beth nodded enthusiastically and abandoned her goblet.

Meyer gallantly swept her small hand up into his and twirled her out amidst the other dancers. He guided her through the turns and the steps, moving seamlessly in and out of the complicated formations. He bumped shoulders with another man only once, and grinned his apology. Bethany precisely followed his lead, her slim body graceful and sure when she spun out and back on her toes.

Dréoteth watched them for only a moment,

noticing how smitten Meyer seemed with her already. Human relationships still baffled him. Before he could ponder it too long, he heard a huff from Lucille.

He glanced at her, blue eyes glittering in the candlelight. Dréoteth did not have the mass most of the other men had, but he was tall and his shoulders were broad. It was his presence that made him stand out, the dark menace that made people whisper behind their hands and stare when they thought he wasn't looking. He seemed untouchable, unattainable, which made him a target for women like Lucille.

He arched a brow.

"You have no intention of dancing with me, do you?"

"No."

"Why not? Everyone else is—"

"Not *everyone.*"

"Only the old and addled!" she said, exasperated.

"If you are so adamant, then ask another."

Lucille gasped. "I cannot *ask* a man to dance."

"You asked me."

"That was different. I—"

"You what?" He stared aside from lidded eyes.

Flustered, Lucille fidgeted with the folds of her skirt.

"I am not here to coddle you," he said.

She gasped, outraged. "No one ever said you need coddle me, sir!"

Dréoteth smiled like he knew things she didn't, and stepped away without another word. He circumvented the dancers and headed for the hallway, his boots barely making a sound on the floor. A few women watched his exit, whispering behind their hands.

Lucille's face turned bright red, and she stalked

after him, making much more noise with the rustle of her skirts.

Dréoteth passed through the open front doors and out into a starry evening. He knew she followed but didn't glance back. Taking the steps to the ground, he struck out across the dirt path that the carriages used.

"*Mister* Trimble!" Lucille rushed to catch up, careful not to trip.

Dréoteth didn't stop.

"How dare you walk out on me. I *demand* an apology!"

He halted so suddenly that had she been closer, she would have bumped into his back.

He turned only his head, pinning her with a malevolent look.

"Have a care how you speak to me, Miss Fynch." His quiet words rang as a warning.

Lucille stopped a handful of feet from him, chest rising and falling with her panting breaths, apparently humiliated beyond reason. He could tell by the high color of her cheeks and the indignant set of her shoulders. He wondered if he was the first man to ever tell her no.

"Perhaps you should have a care how you treat people! I was proper and polite and did not deserve —"

"You will accept whatever treatment I decide to dole out, and like it," he said. Arrogance made his posture taller, imposing.

Lucille wet her lips, fists tight in the material of her skirt. Turning abruptly away, she stalked toward the long line of carriages across the grass.

"Brahm!" Against all decorum, she shouted for her driver.

Dréoteth followed her with his gaze until she was halfway to her carriage. He stepped on, careful to keep away from the horses even though hunger burned in his belly.

Her carriage flew by along the road some minutes later. The horses tossed their heads and fought the bit, but the driver spurred them on and soon, they were out of range of his scent.

Dréoteth wanted to take to the air and follow her coach. He wanted to wait until she was alone and stalk her, make her skin prickle with fear. He wanted her to know, *really* know, what it was like to be hunted. He wanted to pierce her perfect flesh with his needle sharp teeth, draw her blood to the surface and lap away her life one lick at a time. Slowly, so she knew exactly what he was doing to her.

A growl built in his chest and he let it surface. There was no one else around to hear. What right did she have to demand anything from him? He was not her escort for the evening or her companion. He owed Lucille Fynch nothing. These were the wily games humans played that grated on his nerves. The men could be as bad as the women, depending on their motivation.

From a stand of pine to his right, birds burst from the branches and into the air.

Away from him.

Away from the threat.

Often he smelled animals and heard them in the night, creeping or darting in the other direction. Rabbits, foxes, raccoon. There wasn't one species that didn't fear him.

His path took him to the outskirts of town and he walked the streets in silence, letting his anger fade. He passed small cottages and shops, wondering what manner of humans lived or worked there. Were the women like Lucille? The men like Meyer? What ones were artists, or builders? The School of Higher

Learning, a rather small but well-appointed structure of pale stone, loomed out of the darkness to his left. Many interesting books lined the walls and he was pleased to have temporary access to them all.

A single light shone from one window near the door. The rest were dark. He continued walking, eventually coming upon the Mirmande. He'd thought this building quite unusual when they'd arrived. Herriott's mansion made it look like a hovel.

Entering through the doors, he avoided eye contact with the desk clerk and made way to his rooms.

Later, when the town settled and the mist rolled in, he would hunt.

Chapter Four

"It only stings a little bit now," Eugenia said.

Miriette bathed the skin with a cool cloth. "It heals well, love. You will always have the scar, but better that than your life."

The long scorch mark, from her elbow to her shoulder on her right side, was one of three severe burns she'd endured in the attack. The other two were also on the right, along her hip and thigh. Those burns healed as well as this one had, much to Eugenia's relief.

Two months had passed since the attack on Malmsbury.

Miriette had found her face down in the forest and brought her here, to their haven. With tender care and dedication, Eugenia Bailey, would thrive.

The rumors she'd always heard about the witches that had run rampant through Malmsbury were completely false. They were not ugly and dirty but graceful and beautiful. Their gentle temperaments made the strain of recovery easier.

She lived with Miriette in her cottage and had come to love the tranquil forest that surrounded them. Snow made everything white, hanging heavy on the boughs of the pine and spruce. Winter struck early in the season, dipping the temperatures down below freezing. As cold as it was outside, the inside of the cottages were pleasantly warm. A small iron stove sat in a corner, leaking heat through the modest rooms. Other unusual pedestals with glossy, black rocks stood at every corner, chasing away the chill. Eugenia was fascinated with it, with their magic.

Miriette laughed when she caught Eugenia staring at one.

"Here then, cover your arm. What would you like to learn today?" Her eyes twinkled merrily.

"I would like to learn how to make those stone warmers," Eugenia said. She glanced from the black rocks to Mirette's face, grinning.

"That takes a little more magic than you know just yet. How about learning another posset?" Mirette said. Her manner was always soothing and calm.

Eugenia groaned, pulling her sleeve up past the burn when Miriette took the cloth away. "I have learned ten possets by now! Those hot rocks are fascinating."

"Aye, as you have said." Miriette looked vastly amused. "A posset," she insisted, rising to cross to a trunk under the window. It had symbols and carvings over the entire surface. The latch was a small knot of rope that no one but Miriette or one of the other witches could undo.

Lifting the lid, Miriette withdrew several satchels tied round the top with twine.

Eugenia laughed in delight. She enjoyed all her lessons, regardless of what they were. The women had been utterly giving and friendly, willing to teach her skills to survive. Not all of them included magic.

The most important lessons had been to learn that life was still valuable and that she would recover body and soul, given time.

She rose from the padded chair, dressed in a loose robe of white that wouldn't stick to her burns, and moved across the room to the round table in the small dining area. [1]Like the trunk, the table had many engravings and runes carved into the surface. Each of the four chairs was different and unique, some with a higher back, some with paintings of birds, and others that were stout and cushioned with material.

Miriette's cottage was much like the others, quaint and comfortable. Eugenia had felt at home immediately upon awakening from her tragedy.

Eugenia sat down while Miriette picked separate pouches out from one of the satchels, her long hair trailing over the arm of another chair. Miriette made little piles of leaves and strange dark berries and dried chunks of a green plant. A rustic looking little pot was set between them, and she started adding particular amounts of certain things, naming them off.

"This is Thistle, Loganberries—"

The front door burst open and Thea ran in. "Miri, 'Genie! I hit the target! Come see!" She was dressed in tiny britches and a tunic, a belt circling her bitty waist. She had a bow in her hand and smudges of left over pastry from the mornings breakfast on her chin and her cheek.

They laughed as the youngster barged onto the scene. Eugenia had been shocked to discover the girl had also survived and they had grown close under the care of the women. She had known Thea's whole family and tried to help through her grief.

They left the posset making on the table and followed Thea out into the snow. It was a wonderland of white, glistening and pristine, with a few pathways shoveled here and there to make passage between cottages easier. Against the thick trunk of a tree, a round target proudly displayed an arrow that penetrated the surface at the very edge.

Phae stood at a safe angle to the target, a placid, pleasant smile on her lips. She had foregone the robes and pretty dresses for britches of fawn and layers of soft shirts the color of the earth.

Thea ran over to gesture wildly at the target and her arrow.

"Look how good I am getting!" The youngster announced.

Eugenia followed Miriette, who was dressed much like Phae, and examined the target closely.

"A beautiful shot," Miriette said.

"I believe you have done better than I!" Eugenia said, laughing. She had been injured too badly to do much bow and arrow practice. Her attempts lately needed... a lot of work.

"I am going to be the *best* archer Malmsb—" Thea stopped. Her chin trembled and she cleared her throat, starting over. "In Malmsbury."

According to Miriette, the town no longer existed. No one had the heart to tell Thea how thoroughly it was destroyed, least of all her. Even now, Eugenia struggled through her own bouts of sorrow.

"You are well on your way, dearling," Phae said.

"The *best*," Eugenia agreed.

The witches encouraged them to mourn, but they did not let them spend every hour of every day wallowing in misery. Diversion came in the shape of teaching and exploring, and both she and Thea had eaten up the attention.

"Let us see you try another," Miriette said.

Thea ran through the snow in her moccasin boots to the quiver of arrows, loading another one carefully between the bowstrings. A quick learner, she practiced every day.

She focused and concentrated.

Zing.

The arrow thwacked into the target three inches closer to the bullseye than the other.

Thea jumped up and down, celebrating. "Look, look! I did it again!"

Phae laughed and went to hug her, providing more than just someone to watch and support. She offered warmth and caring and understanding.

Gleefully, Thea hugged her tight. Afterward she ran to Miriette and Eugenia, throwing her arms around their waists.

Unselfishly, they returned the affection.

"Perfect, sweetling. You make me anxious to try my own skill soon," Eugenia said. The little girl was an inspiration.

"We should shoot together, 'Genie!" Thea shortened her name up all on her own. Nia had gone by the wayside in favor of childish exuberance.

"Go on, keep practicing," Eugenia said, encouraging the girl to do more. Thea, happy to practice under the praise of the older women, ran back to the target.

Eugenia watched her go before glancing away to the trees in the direction of Malmsbury.

Sometimes she stared for long minutes, wondering. The terrors she'd experienced there left deep scars; nevertheless, she was curious. Miriette had informed her that it was nothing more than ruin, and as hard as she tried, Eugenia could not pull images of the destruction to mind. There were flickers of fire in her memory and the screams of dying people. Everything else was hazy and vague.

"Do you have questions?" Miriette asked.

"I am drawn there sometimes," Eugenia admitted. "I wish to see it with my own eyes. All I remember is flames and explosions and screaming and pain. You said there were no survivors beyond Thea and myself, but I wonder if my cottage still stands, if Honey, my cat, made it to safety."

In the beginning, Miriette had encouraged them to stay in the woods, away from the wreckage, especially protecting Thea because of her age and vulnerability. Their wounds and the danger had kept them close to the cottages for weeks.

"Would you like to talk a walk?" Miriette asked.

Surprised, Eugenia glanced at her. "Now?" Wariness crept into her voice. She hadn't expected that.

"Yes, today. It will not be an easy thing to see," Miriette said.

"Aye," Eugenia said, after a moment's consideration. "I want to see it." She thought her leg was up to the journey and the exercise would do her good.

"Just give me a second to change," she said, and after another glance in the direction of Malmsbury, she made her way to Miriette's cottage. It had taken her longer to figure out how to enter than it had Thea, who took to the hidden haven with an enthusiastic amount of childish wonder.

Eugenia went inside and changed into a sturdy pair of brown britches, cautious of her burns and injuries. She pulled a deep green tunic over an ivory muslin shirt and stuffed her feet into soft boots. After she'd laced them up the front, she stepped outside. Her stomach tightened with anticipation and nerves.

Miriette was having a private word with Phae, undoubtedly discussing how to keep Thea distracted.

They left on their 'short walk' scant minutes later, leaving the snowbound haven behind.

Even blanketed in white, Eugenia noticed that the landscape outside the hollow was not quite as pretty. The comfort and warmth receded, the ethereal beauty fading the further they went. The trees were as tall, the pines as lush, but the magical quality was gone.

They walked for less than a half hour, Miriette guiding the way. Twice, Eugenia felt a strange sensation against her skin, and a brief dizziness overcame her. It almost seemed as if the forest had expanded and settled, like it was a pair of giant lungs breathing in, breathing out.

A crow squawked noisily in the branches above.

Eugenia grew vaguely winded after twenty minutes of walking. Her leg ached and she had a pain in her side. It was manageable and she smiled to let Miriette know she was fine. Just a minor discomfort.

They reached the edge of the forest in a shockingly short amount of time, Eugenia thought. She paused when Miriette did, meeting the woman's eyes. She read the caution in her expression.

"It will be all right," Eugenia said. She wasn't entirely sure she spoke the whole truth.

Miriette hesitated only a moment before leading Eugenia out of the trees.

Eugenia, fortifying herself with a deep breath, followed.

A sharp gasp pierced the otherwise still day at the wasteland that had once been her home. Her hands flew to her mouth, too late to stifle a choked sob. The buildings and homes were gone. Not just blackened shapes with the roofs caved in—but totally gone.

The whole center of town, flattened like some giant had stomped its foot there, was a charred streak of black. This time last year, had she stood in the same spot, she would have seen *Canterly's,* the shoemaker and the tailor's shop.

Snow blanketed the ruins but even the thick layer could not snuff out the scorched ground. The black ate the white, evil consuming the just and the good, and Eugenia felt rife with despair.

She stumbled forward and darted suspicious glances at certain mounds that she worried might be bodies.

Oh god.

Miriette followed at a slower pace, keeping an alert eye on the surroundings.

Eugenia could hardly tell where the main road had been. She found it soon enough and walked along what had once been the heart of the village, dismayed at the devastation.

Something in the distance, out of place for its solid walls and intact roof, caught her eye.

"Miriette! The Rose and Lion! It still stands!"

Eugenia ran down the snow-covered road, ignoring the stabs of pain in her sides. She rushed up to the doors of the Inn and threw them open. No scorch marks darkened the outside, and the interior looked unscathed. "Hello? Is anyone here? Jared?"

Her shouts seemed loud in the silence.

Everything looked almost exactly as she'd left it. Jared had moved a crate against a far wall and had left a stack of towels folded neatly on the counter. For such a bulky man, Jared was incredibly neat. With a pang, she realized he was probably dead.

She went behind the bar, smoothing her palm over the surface. Full bottles of wine and scotch sat in straight rows, ready for customers who would never drink it. Bumping through the swinging door into the kitchen, she scanned the room only to find it empty.

Coming out, Eugenia saw Miriette in the common room, hands folded passively before her, a concerned frown on her brow. She looked quite uninterested in the Inn.

"Come child. There is naught here. We should go," Miriette said.

"I thought to perhaps find a clue—"

"There are precious few, and those are buried with the dead. Except for what you and Thea saw." Miriette met Eugenia's eyes and turned back to the door.

"I still do not understand what it was, or what I saw." Eugenia followed Miriette outside, hesitant to leave without inspecting every room, every niche.

She suspected Miriette knew exactly what had attacked Malmsbury, but wouldn't say. Eugenia had glimpsed something black in the smoky night, a shadow that was too hard to define in the panic and poor visibility.

"In time, the answers will come," Miriette said, beginning to lead her toward the trees.

Although the witches could be cryptic, Eugenia discovered they never lied. Disheartened after the initial rush of hope, she followed in Miriette's footsteps until a striking thought hit her.

"The cottage! Maybe Honey is alive!"

She dashed past the back of the Inn and around a clump of tall bushes. Several broad trees blocked her view. Her heart pounded at the thought her home might be spared. The belongings she owned were meager, but what she did have, she cherished.

Honey above all.

An ominous swath of black on the ground alerted her that something was amiss. Hobbling around the trees, she saw the long mark leading up to the cottage—or what had once been her home. A hundred feet ahead, splinters of wood thrust up from the ground and a few stones lay crumbled in the vicinity of the hearth.

Several trees had been scorched and all her beloved plants were nothing but snow-covered ash. A keening noise replaced the beginnings of a sob that she caught against her palm. Prepared for the worst, the devastation still shocked her.

"Honey! *Honey!*"

There was nothing to salvage in the home, not one scrap of clothing or any cherished keepsakes. She couldn't bring herself to scour through the debris for signs of the cat. She jumped when Miriette gently touched her arm.

"She's gone," Eugenia mourned.

Impossibly, a small, timid meow rang through the air from deeper in the forest.

Eugenia gasped and glanced from Miriette to the woods. "...Honey!"

The cat bounded out of the brush, darted around the remains of the cottage, and ran for her.

"Oh Miri, she made it!"

"She has great perseverance," Miriette said, a smile in her voice.

Eugenia gathered the feline up, checking her for signs of injury. Honey appeared undamaged and purred for the attention.

"Oh, my sweet girl, did you miss me?" Eugenia crooned. Honey head-butted her under the chin.

Eugenia glanced at Miriette, relief stark on her face—until she saw the way Miri had paused, looking around them at the cold day, eyes narrowed, posture stiff.

"What is it?" Eugenia asked. She was unnerved by the alertness Miriette displayed. Glancing around, she saw nothing immediately suspicious.

Honey's ears went flat, a low growl replacing the purr.

"We must go," Miriette said, and turned abruptly for the forest. She moved with quickness and determination, skirting the wreckage.

Goosebumps swarmed over Eugenia's skin under the layers of warm clothing. She hurried to follow Miriette, deciding against setting Honey down. The cat would trail behind them all the way back to the hollow under normal circumstances, but there was something out there and she wouldn't risk losing Honey twice. Every few feet she glanced back, trying to detect a threat.

Nothing.

Miriette had a knack for finding the path of least resistance through the undergrowth, the heavy boughs barely brushing them in passage.

Suddenly, Miriette stopped walking and glanced to their right. Eugenia nearly bumped into her. She glanced the same way but saw only dappled shadows.

Miriette reached back for her hand and they took three fast steps forward, reciting a spell in a language Eugenia had never heard. The world melted around them, the landscape sinking into shades of gray. Everything seemed to liquefy, the trees warping into shapeless streaks. There was no sky, no ground.

Nothing but the odd pewter bubble that surrounded them.

Eugenia's heart beat loud and frantic in her chest, the only sound in all that silence. She suffered several moments of severe disorientation and vertigo, but before she could complain or tug on Miriette's hand, the earth righted itself again. Trees reshaped and the forest stretched out around them. Color exploded across her vision at the same time the sound came back; birds trilled, the rush of water from a nearby stream burbled merrily, and the wind made its whistling presence known through the treetops. They were back in the haven, she realized, and gasped in surprise. Honey had hunkered down in the crook of her arm.

"Miriette! What happened?"

Miriette released her and walked deeper into the hollow the witches called home. "We were being hunted," she said.

"Hunted?" Eugenia shivered, and glanced into the woods.

"Yes. It cannot find us here. Come along, let us find the others."

"But what *is* it, Miri?"

She received no reply.

A handful of days later, Eugenia found Ellery practicing with her bow. The woman was an incredible archer, neatly piercing the bullseye every time. Four arrows stuck out of the dead center, and Eugenia smiled her praise as she approached.

"Spot on, as ever."

Ellery glanced over, lowering the bow. She wore a long robe of pale blue, the hood settled back against her neck. The garment didn't hinder her movements. She smiled and pressed a dainty kiss to Eugenia's cheek.

"Practice, dear one, practice. Have you come to join in?" Ellery offered her personal bow to Eugenia.

"Actually, Miss Ellery, I have a question."

Ellery tilted her head and lowered the bow to her side. "Go on."

"I am ever curious about the creature that attacked Malmsbury. Have I imagined the blackness of it, the enormous size?"

"What did Miriette say?" Ellery asked, her gaze kind but shrewd.

Eugenia shuffled her feet in the snow and had the grace to look sheepish. "She would not say what it was."

"Perhaps there is a good reason for her silence." Ellery let that sink in before offering her bow once again. "What you should concentrate on, as young Thea does, is bettering your aim." She winked, and Eugenia laughed.

"Aye then. Let me have a crack at it." Eugenia hid her disappointment. What weren't the witches saying? Why the secrets and silence? What were they protecting them from? She took the bow from Ellery and picked a fresh arrow from the collection.

Ellery stepped over to remove hers. There were countless little black marks in the red painted center.

Eugenia wasn't sure she would even hit the target. Her technique needed a lot of work.

Gamely, she notched the arrow and pulled back the string, pinching an eye closed. Ellery stood well to the side but she had no fear of being accidentally hit. Overhead, a crow started cawing madly and Eugenia paused, glancing up.

"Do not let distractions get in the way," Ellery said, laughing.

"It always knows the exact second to make a fuss!" Eugenia said. Amused, more at herself than the bird, she lifted the bow and concentrated on the bullseye. She let the arrow fly. It smacked into the side of the tree, several inches from the edge of the target.

The crow *caw-caw-caw*ed again. Eugenia swore it sounded like laughter.

Thea stared up at her ceiling. Little pale blue and silver stars hung from threads of all different lengths. Some were as small as her thumbnail, others as large as her palm. The curved silhouette of a man with wise eyes and a secretive smile made the shape of half moons that dotted the starscape. Curling streamers in varied colors bobbed and swayed, supporting tiny dolls and figures on the ends. One doll sat on a whimsical swing; another was a puppet on strings. They had sweet faces and angel eyes and little red lips curved into bright smiles.

Phae was the architect of the splendor, her talent for painting faces unmatched amongst the witches.

Gauzy, dark material sprinkled with sparkles covered the ceiling itself, giving an ethereal backdrop to the hanging toys.

Thea's gaze went distant, her mind conjuring scenes of destruction and death, one finger relentlessly twisting a silvery strand of hair.

She heard her mother screaming, saw the fire.

She saw the hated, glowing eyes swooping in to finish them.

"Some day," she told the stars and the man in the half moons. "I am going to get revenge."

"It is better to put it from your mind, sweetling," Phae said from the doorway.

Thea turned her head on the fluffy pillow, the ringlet pulled tight. When she let go, it bounced back into shape. "I cannot. I want it to die for what it has done."

Phae smiled. She had such a winsome, comforting smile. "Is it worth *your* life to try?"

Tonight, Thea couldn't be comforted or distracted from her dark thoughts, even at the reminder her own life would be in peril. She nodded. *Yes.*

"But think how much the others and I would

miss you," Phae said. She came into the room and leaned over the bed to kiss Thea's brow. "Try to sleep now."

Thea wrapped her arms around Phae's neck and hugged her tight. She loved the woman already. "I will. Good night, Miss Phae."

"Good night, Thea."

Phae straightened, smoothing her hand over the girls flaxen hair. She studied her small face, and then turned to leave the room.

Thea watched her go, flipping onto her side. The bed, unlike any she'd ever slept in or seen before, felt like the softest feathers. She closed her eyes, trying to sleep, but her mind was too busy. Ideas and plans and plots interrupted her mental star counting.

After a half an hour, she scrambled out of bed and peered through the crack in her door. Opening it enough to slip through, she crept out to the living room and knelt before the long bookcase against one wall. Candlelight flickered off the ancient looking tomes, illuminating the spines for her to read. Finding the one that she wanted, she hugged it to her thin chest and rose.

Snow fell outside the panes of the window and she stopped to peer out, an atmospheric glow making the landscape achingly pretty. Fat snowflakes swirled from a black sky, landing on a blanket of white that was so pristine it glistened.

She glanced up at a stray noise and hurried to her room. Phae was nowhere to be seen. She didn't want her to know she had chosen *this* book to read. This book, with the strange symbols on the front and the odd markings carved inside the cover, was supposed to be off limits.

Thea crawled back into bed, making the dolls and stars sway overhead, and pulled three candles closer

on her bedside stand. They gave off more than
enough light to read by.

Chapter Five

The first day of spring dawned clear and sunny. All the snow from the long, hard winter had finally melted. The nights still had a bite to them, but today promised to be warmer than any so far.

Meyer could feel the heat through the layers of his brown tunic and beige breeches. He welcomed it. Grinning broadly as he strode along the center street in Faulkon's Cross, he greeted passerby with a jovial "Good morning!" or a polite bow of his head. Several men wondered at his unusually upbeat mood, and women flirted shamelessly.

"That Meyer. What a charmer," one said.

He heard, and boomed a rakish laugh, dashing a wink in her wake.

"Mister Pennington!" Meyer called out to the local barber, who was just about to step into his shop. "Have you seen Trimble about?"

Mister Pennington rubbed his three chins and shook his head after a moment. "Not today. You need a haircut!"

"Soon, I will let you have your way with the blade," Meyer promised, grinning. He left the barber behind. Just as he was about to turn a corner and seek out the School of Higher Learning, he saw Trimble step out of a small pub on the other side of the street.

"Trimble!"

Dréoteth stopped short, smiling subtly when he saw Meyer. Glancing for oncoming wagons or horses, he crossed the road to Meyer's side. A crisp shirt of white tucked down into dark breeches, his boots black and dusty. The belt had no ornamentation other than a plain silver buckle. Unlike other men, he had no weapons attached. "Meyer, what has you looking so enthusiastic?"

"I have news!"

Dréoteth arched a brow. "What news?"

"Bethany has agreed to become my wife!" Meyer clapped his hands on Trimble's shoulders, and looked him right in the eye. "I want you to stand up with me. It is to be the end of next week."

Dréoteth stiffened at the clutch of hands. Meyer thought he had just surprised the man.

"To stand up with you?" Dréoteth asked.

Meyer's euphoria backslid a little. He stared at the man, still grinning, waiting for the punch line. The end of the joke. Something. When Trimble continued to look at him in confusion, he elaborated.

"Yes, you know. Stand up with me. Bear witness. You are my best friend, are you not?" Meyer asked. He let his hands fall away, back to his sides.

The lazy clop of hooves heralded a horse and rider at the far end of the street.

Dréoteth gestured Meyer along another avenue, away from the main thoroughfare. "I confess," he said while they walked. "I have never been to a ceremony. I know little about the workings of weddings."

Meyer regarded him closely, wondering at the guarded expression on the man's face. Maybe he didn't want to stand up. Could he be shy? Meyer hardly thought so. "It takes no special skill. All you have to do is stand there and witness our vows. If you do not wish to, I will ask one of Bethany's brothers—"

"No, no. I am pleased to participate. Is this one of those things that I will have to wear formal attire to?"

Meyer laughed, hooking his hands in the broad belt circling the outside of his tunic. "Yes, it is one of those occasions. You have never truly been to a wedding?"

"Never." Dréoteth smiled. "If this will make you happy, if this is what you wish, then I am honored to go."

"Bethany will be pleased. She is quite fond of you." Meyer kept his attention on Dréoteth more than the pathway they walked. Shops and businesses were lined up one after the other. Neither man paid them any mind. He didn't dare say that Beth had confided she thought Trimble likeable but a little strange. Meyer, aware Trimble was a different man than most, didn't hold it against him.

"As I am of her," Dréoteth replied. He sounded convincing.

"We will have fittings with Mister Kline in the morning. Say eleven, when we break at the School?" Meyer paused to face Trimble.

"Yes, at eleven. Should I meet you there?" Dréoteth asked.

"I believe so. Now then, I have things to do before supper with Beth's family. I will see you tomorrow." Meyer grinned broadly, almost boyishly. Long strides took him away down the busy road until he disappeared amidst the throng of merchants and shoppers.

Dréoteth had never seen such madness. The days leading into the wedding were some of the most hectic he'd ever witnessed and it wasn't even his ceremony. He learned more about this odd ritual than he cared to, and barely withstood the ceaseless fittings and measurings that were required for his clothing. He stood with his arms out, then down at his sides. Front and back and stretched forward. It tested his patience to the limit more than once but he clamped down on his control and got through it.

There were several celebratory luncheons that Meyer invited him to, and he went because it was expected of him. The women giggled and gossiped and talked about colors and cloth and jewelry until he thought his head would explode. Beth treated him kindly, warming to him despite his sometimes-standoffish nature, and presented him with a basket of baked goods after an especially trying day of rehearsing.

He took the sweet pastries and muffins back to his room at the Mirmande, sniffing them warily. His diet as a human form consisted mostly of meat and raw fruit. These sugary breads with fillings and powders made him all but nauseous to even smell.

They went into the trash without another thought.

In between the fittings and dinners, he worked on copying the tome into a new book, delving into the mysteries it represented with relish. When he wasn't hunting and in his dragon, the contents of the tome took his mind from the complexities of the humans and their strange behavior.

The whole town was abuzz with the news, and he couldn't go anywhere—not a shop or a store or a stall—without hearing of the coming nuptials.

He was happy for Meyer on one level, glad to see the man moving on from the tragedy of Malmsbury.

On the other, he wanted to take him aside and tell him to forego these notions of marriage and all the chaos and just *live*. He reminded himself time and again that their way wasn't the way of the dragon and kept his mouth closed. Jovial and exuberant, Meyer seemed on top of the world.

The unpredictable spring weather almost put a halt to their outdoor ceremony, but the thunderclouds cleared the eve before the wedding, and it went on as planned.

He stood up there behind Meyer, feeling quite conspicuous and on the spot, and he wondered if anyone noticed his discomfort. The crowd annoyed him to the point of distraction, and by the time they had all gathered in the clearing for a feast and celebration after the wedding, he'd had enough.

Taking the time to wish Meyer and Bethany congratulations—he knew that much at least about proper decorum—he left the masses and melted away into the forest, relieved to be away from the press of bodies and shrill voices. He took to the hunt with a vengeance as darkness fell, miles from the nearest human, and spent the entire night in the wilderness.

He rested along the broad trunk of a fallen tree after he fed, legs stretched out. The sound of the wind through the trees and the bubbling creek not far away began to ease the tension that had built and spread across his shoulders.

In the distance he heard birds trilling and chirping and somewhere else, a bullfrog droned a low mating call. He was too far away to disturb them.

When he emerged from the woods early the next

morning, he felt a measure better than when he'd gone in.

Spring
The Year of Revival

I have attended my first wedding ceremony. Meyer took Bethany to wife, and I stood as his witness. The entire affair is so overdone and ridiculous, that I found it hard to stand there and watch. More than half the town turned out to see it, perhaps because it was another excuse to socialize and gossip. Sometimes I think humans cherish their melodramas more than anything else. I heard many whispers during the vows that either interested me or disgusted me. Someone near the back had a scare the evening prior while they were out hunting. It was not me; I do my own hunting far from here. I missed a few words, but this man (I could not look to see his face, that would have given me away and distracted the entire congregation) had an encounter with something that stalked him through the forest.

He suggested bear or wolf, but heard nothing more than the snapping of a few twigs and rustling branches.

What annoyed me were two other women making catty bets on whether Meyer Lyon would take a mistress or not. I have no respect for these ceremonies or rituals or beliefs, but I was irritated that these women would conspire before the vows were even sealed with the requisite kiss.

Meyer has purchased a farm for he and Bethany, which did not surprise me. As well as teaching, he is a skilled farmer and warrior. I have seen him in what they call sparring matches and rarely does he lose. Slowly, he is making a new life for himself here.

During the long winter, I grew restless. I wanted to leave Faulkon's Cross and go somewhere warmer. I do not dislike the cold, but I cannot be outside as much as I prefer because people might ask questions. My body generates enough heat that I do not have to worry about the temperature, as the humans do. So when I hunted, I flew farther and spent more of my night in my dragon. It helped take the edge from my ceaseless pacing. I have not had the urge to hunt any of the humans in Faulkon's Cross, and I cannot figure out why. I have not hunted them since the night I almost attacked Eugenia Bailey. It puzzles me.

I wonder how long I can last. How many years I will be able to take living amongst them. I keep myself apart far more than Meyer does, always on the fringe instead of in the middle.

It suits me to keep them guessing.

Summer came, and summer went. Copying the tome, no matter how fascinating, became tedious and tiresome, and Dréoteth sought the solace of the woods often. Meyer was busy being a husband and tending his farm between teaching assignments. They did not see each other more than two times a week but their companionable friendship flourished. The fall harvest descended and the festival was crowded with revelers. Dréoteth caught a glimpse of it before he sank into the woods, missing the event entirely. Restlessness gnawed at his insides, driving him into the wild where he spent three days hunting and thinking. His return to Faulkon's Cross was a brooding, solemn affair, and he found he could barely be civil in polite society.

Winter slammed the countryside hard and early, and lasted through a final, heavy snowfall late in April. Dréoteth took advantage of people being housebound and left the Mirmande in the dead of night, taking to the skies in the frigid air. He stayed gone for days, once as long as a week, expending his pent up energy with perpetual activity. It infuriated him that he wondered what the humans were up to. Even with his mouth full of blood and his prey dead in his talons, flickers of his other life passed through his mind.

Later, he had sat upon a boulder far above the town, glaring at the tiny glimmers of light from the windows of their homes. Inside, they slept, unaware that a predator observed them. How he hated their innocence, their dependency on each other. Clustered together in bands and groups, all vying for power and higher social standing.

Yet a part of him yearned to hear their music again, to see the masterpieces they painted. He was drawn inexplicably into their midst, irritated and relieved at the same time. It tore at him, like a saw scraping back and forth across his nerves.

Another year passed in much the same way. The times Dréoteth saw Meyer were fewer, but the scholar always drew him in with his charming smile and avid interest. Even Bethany was happy to see him, inviting him out to the farm for dinners and conversation. He was more comfortable there and relaxed in ways he never would be in the city.

The beginning of fall nipped at their heels, the weather teetering back and forth between sweltering warmth and a cooler bite to the air. Excitement swept through the citizens of Faulkon's Cross; it seemed to be their favorite season.

Dréoteth, in a simple pair of buckskin breeches and a crisp shirt of white, strolled along a less busy street to avoid horses and hounds. It was still early in the day, the sun round and gold in a clear sky.

One shop in particular always drew his attention

whenever he passed this way, and he approached the easels set up outside with paintings of landscapes and flowers. There were portraits of people, their eyes fixed and staring, their mouths set in pensive lines. He wondered what they were thinking, what they were feeling.

Under the shade of the awning, he stood with his hands clasped behind his back, intently studying the exquisite brushwork.

This was what made humans indispensable. They had the capacity to create stunning things with their hands. For an isolated, horrible moment, Dréoteth felt inferior. What could *he* create? He was too wary to even touch an instrument or a paintbrush, preferring to watch from a careful distance.

The thought shocked him. Inferior—to *humans?* His nostrils flared defensively, a muscle flexing in his jaw. He must be mad, even pretending to sugges—

"Trimble! I see you have found Elizabeth Brown's shop once again," Meyer teased, strolling up behind him.

Dréoteth glanced at Meyer, a wry smile on his mouth. "So I have. She is most talented with a brush and oil."

"Aye, she is. One of the town's best." Meyer admired a few of the paintings, grinning jovially. "Perhaps you should ask her to paint your likeness."

Dréoteth stared. "What?"

Meyer pointed to one of the portraits. "A likeness. Of yourself."

"I heard you," Dréoteth said. He frowned in thought, both insulted and intrigued. "I have no use for something like that."

He turned and started walking, clasping his hands behind his back.

Meyer fell into stride, undeterred. "Whyever not?

Many people have portraits done. I should like to have one of Bethany and myself someday."

"That is you and Bethany."

"What makes you any different? You have long admired the world of art."

"Because I am—" *A dragon.*

Meyer arched a brow, patiently waiting for him to finish.

Dréoteth snapped a look aside and saw his friend's curiosity. About to reply, they were both bumped into by a woman who came hurrying from the milliner's shop.

"Oh! Pardon me—" The woman all but bounced off the combined wall the men made.

"Here, are you all right, Miss?" Meyer asked. He helped steady her with his hands and released her when she found her balance.

Dréoteth tried not to be annoyed, and offered no assistance. Her scent, however, pricked his senses.

At the same instant, she glanced up, flashing an apologetic smile. It turned into a gasp of shock.

Meyer's mouth fell open. "*Eugenia Bailey?* Is it really you?"

Dréoteth's lips thinned. The fiery hair and inquisitive eyes—it could be no one else.

"Oh... I... how did you... but you were all dead!" she said. Her gray eyes shifted frantically between Meyer and Dréoteth, like she thought they were ghosts.

"Not all. Trimble and I were in the woods and came back to utter devastation. Is it really you? How did you survive?" Meyer, intent and astounded, loomed and stared.

Eugenia seemed to cast about for answers, opening her mouth only to close it and try again. She had several false starts, Dréoteth noticed.

"A woman named Miriette found me badly

wounded," she said. "She helped me recover."

"We searched those woods for days," Dréoteth said. "We found nothing and no one." He hadn't caught scent of any unknown woman, either.

"You must have searched in the wrong place. She has a cottage deep in the forest and I spent a very long time recovering from my wounds."

"Wounds?" Dréoteth asked. She looked whole and hale, her auburn hair caught back with a clip and shining red-gold under the sun. A smattering of freckles dusted her nose and cheeks, her skin otherwise unblemished and smooth.

"Yes, I was burned quite badly." She made a gesture to her right side.

"Amazing!" Meyer said. "Did anyone else escape with you? Were there other survivors?"

Eugenia's lips parted, and she looked from Meyer's hopeful gaze to Dréoteth's wary one. "... no. I'm sorry, no. Miriette found me alone."

"Where are you residing? You must come stay at the farm with Bethany and I," Meyer said.

"At the Mirmande. I could not impose, Meyer. I am not staying in town but a week or so," she said.

Meyer was taken aback. "A week or so? Where will you go after this?"

"Back to Miriette. I find I am fond of the solace." She bit her lip for a moment.

Dréoteth eyed her hard, glancing at the lip bite. Her reply didn't quite ring as sincere as it could have.

"My wife and I are often in town. She owns the bakery there on the main street. We should get together before you leave," Meyer said. He touched her elbow like he was hesitant to let a part of his past take leave.

Eugenia smiled, brushing a wayward red curl from her jaw. "I would love nothing more, Mister

Lyon."

"Trimble here also stays at the Mirmande. How about meeting for supper tonight at the Inn?" Meyer said.

Dréoteth, caught in a web of Meyer's making, stood there and let him railroad the woman into dinner.

"Are you sure? I... well yes. That would be wonderful. Say seven? That will give me time to finish my errands," she said.

"Perfect. Until then, Mistress Bailey." Meyer bowed over her hand.

"I will see you both later. Mister Trimble," Eugenia said, meeting his eyes.

Dréoteth locked gazes with her as she stepped between them, turning his head to watch her scurry off. She was as delicate and bold as she'd ever been. He knew she was trouble.

"Can you believe that?" Meyer said, watching until she'd disappeared from view. "What luck!"

"Yes, she was very lucky to have survived the attack. I wonder if she saw anything," Dréoteth said. He mused silently over the encounter, hands still behind his back. They continued walking along the street.

"I will be anxious to query her more this evening. I cannot fathom that she will not be living here permanently."

"She seems to like solitude," Dréoteth said. He didn't believe it for a minute. Eugenia Bailey had thrived on the bustle and chaos in Malmsbury.

Meyer grunted, rubbing his fingers through the dark scruff on his jaw. "I would have wagered a field of crops that Miss Bailey preferred this." His hand fell away from his face and gestured absently to the teeming town. "I must return to the School, Trimble. We will see you at seven?"

"Thanks to you, yes," Dréoteth said. He smiled wanly at Meyer.

The scholar boomed an unrepentant laugh, clapped him on the shoulder, and strode away.

Eugenia Bailey closed the door to her room at the Mirmande and leaned against it. She tried to catch her breath, one hand flattening against her forehead.

Meyer Lyon and Nehemiah Trimble... *alive!*

If she hadn't seen it with her own eyes, she wouldn't have believed it.

The open window ushered in a mild breeze. Enough daylight streamed inside to see by. The furnishings were spare, bulky and sturdy, better suited to a monastery than an Inn. It was a far cry from the inviting warmth of Miriette's cottage. She realized she had become spoiled in her years at the hollow.

She started unlacing the front of her day dress, marching to a carved, wooden pedestal nestled against the wall.

Removing the garment, she stood in her chemise and soaked a cloth in the cool water of a small basin. The looking glass above it showed her freckled cheeks were rosy with color and her eyes fairly sparkled with health and energy.

Her first trip back into society since the fire and she found two people she'd long thought dead. Dabbing the cloth against her forehead and her throat, she wondered what to do. Miriette had given her blessing for her to come, offering protections and advice.

Eugenia only meant to stay a week or two, gathering supplies and items on a list for her and the others, and then she would return to the hollow.

She missed the women and Thea, who had pouted and sulked for a week when she learned of the excursion.

Seeing Meyer had been wonderful, and she was desperately curious to know about the woman he had apparently taken to wife. The desire to sink right back into the workings of the town flared hot and undeniable.

Nehemiah Trimble was another story.

She didn't know what to think of his dead on stares and his infuriating silence. He was as intimidating as ever, his blue eyes sharp and hawkish. Sometimes she thought he could see right down into her very soul.

"Blasted man," she muttered.

Carefully selecting a thin gown of pale blue with flaring sleeves past the wrist and cream embroidery on the bodice, she slipped it over her head and dealt with the fastenings up the front. It had a hood that she left down for now. Her burns had healed well, though her skin was discolored and patchy in certain spots along her right side.

Picking up her brush, she drew it through the long length of her hair, the curls bouncing back into soft waves. Re-clipping the front, she let the rest cascade around her shoulders.

She couldn't wait to tell Miriette and the others about Meyer and Trimble. There were a hundred questions still rioting around her mind about their survival and journey to Faulkon's Cross. She remembered vividly the last day she'd seen them in Malmsbury, when they'd entered the woods to find the very witches she now lived with.

Transferring a few coins from the pocket of her other dress into the blue one, she checked herself in the looking glass one more time before departing for dinner.

The Mirmande Inn housed a tavern on the lower floor, adjacent to the entrance lobby. Stone flooring of gray gave way to white walls and thick, curving beams across the ceiling. Tables and chairs were scattered in no apparent pattern, some nestled into corners for a modicum of privacy. Candles flickered in sconces and a hearth blazed at one end.

Dréoteth, arriving early, chose a table near a window with plenty of seating. A goblet of wine sat at his elbow, untouched. He regarded Eugenia as she stood framed in the archway of the tavern, not drawing attention to himself out of the eight or so other patrons taking their ease. It was only a matter of moments until she spotted him anyway.

Somehow, against all odds, she had survived. Dréoteth realized he wasn't too surprised. Eugenia Bailey showed a strength of will uncommon in women. He had always thought her boldness might be her undoing someday.

She saw him and he registered her brief hesitation before she came over. He sensed her unease.

"Mister Trimble," she said.

"Miss Bailey." He didn't stand up to receive her, or hasten to tend to her chair. Those customs were degrading to men, in his estimation.

"I see Mister Lyon and his wife are not here yet." She glanced at a vacant chair, but did not sit down.

"We are both a trifle early." Dréoteth watched her squirm, silently amused at her quandary.

Taking initiative, she swished her skirts smartly and saw to her own chair across the table from him.

"Being punctual is a virtue," she said. She sat primly, spine straight, shoulders square.

Dréoteth, predatory even in repose, stretched one

of his legs under the table. He wore black breeches and a black coat, the snowy shirt beneath undone at the throat. He hated the snug fit of some of the clothing, always preferring to loosen the material there.

"And you are a woman of virtue." He said it as a statement rather than a question.

"Of course, Mister Trimble. Any woman of quality should be." She lifted her chin, staring him down.

He smiled, barely a curve of his insolent mouth, refusing to let her stare rile him. "I am surprised you would consider a life of solitude and loneliness in the woods rather than an exciting one in the city. Perhaps you do not long for a husband and children, as most other women do."

Dréoteth correctly read the startled look in her eyes that meant he'd hit very close to a personal truth. It pleased him to know that all his time amidst the humans, studying them, hadn't been a complete waste.

"I... " She stammered, pausing.

"Trimble, Miss Bailey!" Meyer saved the situation, calling out from the archway. He had his wife on his arm and he walked her over, making the introductions quickly. Bethany smiled at Dréoteth before turning her gaze on the redhead.

"Bethany, may I introduce Miss Eugenia Bailey. Miss Bailey, my wife."

Beth, wearing a pretty dress of deep burgundy and black, tipped Eugenia a polite nod. "Very pleased to make your acquaintance, Miss Bailey. Meyer has told me much about you."

Eugenia stood and returned the brief nod. "My pleasure, Madam. I am most anxious to hear about your meeting with Meyer and your courtship."

And so it began.

Dréoteth drolly watched the women immediately

start chattering away about luncheons and flowers and romance. He glanced at Meyer and rolled his eyes, remembering to be playful about it rather than show his bored irritation.

Meyer laughed and ordered everyone food while the women talked, engaging Dréoteth in talk of work, the farm and the upcoming festival.

It started a whole new round of intense excitement from both women, and before Dréoteth had cleaned his plate, Bethany had coaxed Eugenia into staying for the event.

He noticed that Eugenia glanced at him often, when she thought she was being discreet, and once they met and locked eyes. He read the same deep, searching stare from her that had once nearly made him lash out.

Tonight, he exhaled through his nose and stood up. The chair scraped sharply against the floor, making his ears hurt.

"Ladies, Mister Lyon, I must depart. It was a pleasure, as always." It had been far from pleasurable, but he forced a smile as Meyer and the women rose.

"Mister Trimble. It was very nice to speak with you again," Eugenia said.

They'd hardly spoken at all, but Dréoteth smiled indulgently and nodded. He suppressed a growl of impatience and stalked away after Meyer and Beth said their cheery good-byes, apparently unaware of his mood. He swore he felt Eugenia staring a hole in his back.

He shut himself in his room, away from humanity. Dragging a heavy chair over to the window, he threw open the shutters and slouched into the seat, balefully glaring out at the dark sky.

He wondered, not for the first time, why he endured it. Their incessant chatter had grated on his very last nerve until he thought he might snarl them into silence. Perhaps it was Eugenia's presence that made his temper short. Bethany's company of late he found no fault with, and grudgingly had come to tolerate rather well. Now and again, she had even coaxed a laugh out of him.

He sat there well into the early hours of the morning, eerily still, conflicted and thoughtful.

"Hush your pretty mouth, lassie, 'fore you make me put a gag in it."

"Get your hands *off* me!" The woman's voice echoed to the end of the alley. Dréoteth, passing by on the other side of the street, paused.

He knew that voice. He crossed the road, stepping into a triangle of shadow. He followed it alongside the wall of a building, his steps too quiet to hear. Ahead, halfway down and behind a rickety stairwell, he saw two figures struggling. One, much smaller than the other, was obviously a woman. His keen vision picked out the tiny waist and the ripple of a skirt.

The man covered her mouth with his and pushed her hard against the wall. She fought him, her screams muffled, small fists battering his chest. A sliver of moonlight glinted off her auburn curls.

Dréoteth recognized Eugenia's scent, and closed the distance with purpose. Anger uncoiled inside him like a striking viper, surprising him.

Twenty steps from intercepting them, the man suddenly reeled back, holding a hand against his eye with a shout.

"She-devil!"

Eugenia kicked the man's knee. "Indecent pig!"

Dréoteth closed in, snaring the man up by the collar of his battered coat. Shoving him back against the other building, he got in the man's face. He didn't recognize him, but that didn't matter.

"I believe the lady told you to leave her alone," he said. Menace dripped from every word. The man was taller than Dréoteth by two inches, and outweighed him by fifty pounds.

Dréoteth handled him like he was a child, bracing him effortlessly with one hand.

Eugenia gasped, eyes wide.

"Le'go of me. That hellion deserved it!"

Dréoteth tightened his hold, and the man started struggling in earnest, unable to breathe.

They made it too easy, these humans, Dréoteth decided. "When I release you, you will exit the other end of the alley and be thankful I allowed you to live. Never touch her or look at her again. Am I understood?"

"Y... y.. yes'sir." The man wheezed, gulping air when Dréoteth took his hand away. He stumbled away, looking back just once, until he was gone from sight.

Dréoteth turned to look at Eugenia, nonplussed over the brief, physical confrontation. He was still annoyed that the man had cornered her. She appeared roughed up, her dress askew, her hair mussed from its pins. Three days had passed since dinner at the Mirmande.

"Th... thank you, Mister... T... trimble," she said.

"There is no need for thanks. Are you injured?"

"I do not think so. The nerve of that man!"

"Does that happen often?"

"Not to me. I cannot say for other women." She sniffed, indignant. Her fingers pushed and prodded loose strands of her hair back into the pins.

Dréoteth watched her shaking hands impassively. "What are you doing out at such a late hour?" he asked.

"Bethany offered to let me stay in her flat above the bakery, so I moved my things up there earlier this evening. I realized that I must have forgotten or dropped my mother's shawl at the Mirmande, so I was going back there now to search." She lowered her hand, unsuccessful in righting her hair.

Dréoteth regarded her throughout, identifying only the truth in her explanation. "I will walk you the rest of the way," he said. He didn't think too long or hard over the reasons why he felt the need to see to her safety.

"That is very kind, Mister Trimble."

Dréoteth guided her from the gloomy alley and onto the dusty, hard-packed road. The Mirmande was only a short distance down on the other side.

Moonlight gleamed off his blue-black hair, casting half his face into shadow.

He walked at a pace that didn't require her to hurry to keep up. Feeling the weight of her gaze, he turned to catch her watching him. This time, she didn't seem to be trying to see inside him so much as trying to figure out why he'd intervened. Clearly, he could have simply walked on and left her to her fate.

"Is Miriette one of the witches in the forest?" he asked. The question was probably not the one she expected to hear.

Eugenia gasped, giving herself away well before she stammered an answer. "Wh—oh, I... " She hesitated, perhaps thinking better of lying. "She is, yes."

Dréoteth maneuvered around an empty, wooden cart, still looking at her profile. "We searched and never found any cottage," he said.

Eugenia fidgeted, picking up her pace. Her steps came quick and small, hurrying her forward. "Well, they *are* gifted, are they not? They have ways of keeping their homes hidden."

"How many witches are there?"

Eugenia blanched. "Mister Trimble, I think it most inappropriate to divulge all their secrets." She cut a sharp, almost knowing look up into his face. "Many people have secrets," she said.

Dréoteth chose to be blasé this time in the face of her leading remark, instead of becoming riled by it. Eugenia Bailey was as intuitive as he'd given her credit for.

"I concede you that," he said. To say otherwise would have been a blatant lie and they both knew it. "What secrets do you think I hold, Mistress Bailey?"

To his surprise, she laughed. It was a velvety sound, soft and pleasant.

"As many as any other ma—oh look. Here we are," she said, coming to a stop at the front doors of the Inn. "Thank you for the help in the alley and for escorting me here."

Dréoteth arched a brow curiously, but didn't press her for the statement she didn't finish. "You are welcome. I will walk you back to the bakery after you search."

"Oh no, that is not necessary," she said. "I will keep to the main roads and not use the alleys."

Dréoteth stood there, indecisive. He stared at her fey face, the long length of her dark eyelashes.

"As you will, then," he said, reaching past her for the door. It brought them into uncomfortably close proximity and he felt her inch back to give him room to pass. He stared down at her with a mocking grin in his blue eyes, letting her know he understood his presence overpowered her.

Her eyes flickered indignantly and he laughed, stepping into the Mirmande.

Unless she caught it to follow inside, the door closed of its own accord in his wake.

Even through the wood, he heard her huff in exasperation.

$$Chapter\ Six$$

Two weeks passed. Bethany and Meyer invited Dréoteth and Eugenia out to the farm several times for dinner and began preparations for the festival that had the entire town in a tizzy. The time was well spent, the company comfortable enough and enlightening.

Dréoteth realized he took mild delight in making Eugenia stammer and stutter when he asked questions he knew she didn't want to answer. He'd found a way to turn the tables on her, to some degree. It helped break up the monotony of the women's constant chattering and gossiping. It also helped to keep him focused and distracted.

Sometimes, Eugenia found a clever way around his tactics, answering a question *with* a question. Instead of replying, he changed the subject completely. He decided after several visits that the only way she could annoy him was if he allowed her to. It was a minor epiphany.

Meyer and Beth genuinely enjoyed having them over and laughed often at the banter.

Dréoteth could *almost* say that he was enjoying

himself.

This afternoon, he sat near the window in his room at the Mirmande, dark head bent over his journal. The quill scratched over the ivory page, gaze intent on the words. Three candles sat in brass holders on the table, melting wax dripping lazily down the sides.

A rapid *knock-knock-knock* at his door interrupted his concentration. He rose from his chair, setting his journal aside, and paced silently to open it. He already knew Meyer stood on the other side.

"Trimble! I have news!" Meyer said, striding inside without invite. He looked fit to burst with excitement. His tan breeches and brown tunic showed signs that Meyer had recently come from the fields. Bits of dust streaked his boots and his knees.

Dréoteth closed the door in his friend's wake, following the man to the small sitting area he'd just left moments before. There were only two fat chairs with thick cushions and footstools to match, the table between.

"The last time you came with that announcement, you had just proposed. Come sit and tell me," Dréoteth said, gesturing to a seat.

Meyer would not be contained. He pivoted around to clap Dréoteth on the shoulder with one strong, meaty hand. "I am to be a father. A *father,* Trimble! The child will come in the spring."

Dréoteth almost forgot to look surprised. He realized after exactly three seconds of silence that this was news he needed to be excited over, too. He smiled, returning the clap of the hand to Meyer's shoulder. Dréoteth was typically the type not to touch others, but every so often he and Meyer traded these shoulder claps and they were harmless.

"What news it is, too. Congratulations are in

order, I believe. Should we toast to it?" Dréoteth asked, stepping over to the small trestle table against the wall. He popped the cork out of the wine and poured two goblets.

He handed one off to the exuberant Meyer before facing him and lifting his own.

"To family," Dréoteth said.

Meyer, smiling deep and wide, tapped his goblet against the edge of Dréoteth's.

"To family. And *friends."* Meyer said. His emphasis along with the direct look he gave Dréoteth made his meaning clear.

Dréoteth smiled and tilted his head in ready acceptance, taking a long drink of the wine. Friends. He could hardly credit that he was a friend with a human man.

Meyer, too restless to sit, paced through the room toward the window. The shutters had been thrown open and a crisp fall breeze buffeted the scholar's face. Meyer's hair, grown now to just past the tops of his shoulders, was shot through with a few gray strands at the temples. Subtle, but Dréoteth noticed. Around Meyer's eyes, the fine lines started to deepen, like the ones around his mouth.

The signs of aging were unmistakable.

"Always I longed to have children, spawn a family. My first wife could not bear them, but I never resented her for it. Fate works in strange ways, does it not?" Meyer said. He glanced away from the darkening landscape to Dréoteth, grinning.

"It does. I am pleased you are happy," Dréoteth said. For this man, he was sincere.

"Thank you, Trimble. What of you?" Meyer took a sip of his wine, leaning his shoulder against the windowsill. "Do you not ever think of having your own family?"

These were dangerous waters. Dréoteth

proceeded with caution. He looked thoughtful over the question rather than wary.

"If I am honest, I have never desired to have family or settle down in one place too long." He rolled the goblet between his long fingered hands and then lifted it for a swallow.

Meyer seemed puzzled and curious, but not judgmental. "Really. Most men do, but I suppose it is not for everyone, hm? Have you siblings?" In all their conversations, the subject of brothers and sisters had never come up.

"I am the only one," Dréoteth said. "The only one left, as well. My family perished during a sweep of the plague a long time past." The lies fell so easily from his lips.

Meyer grunted at the news. "Aye, many were lost then. Tell me something, Trimble," he asked, looking out the window again. "Have you any ideas about what caused the fires in Malmsbury?"

The question took Dréoteth by surprise; they had not discussed the attack in years, and when it came up before, he'd played the part of ignorance well. "I am no closer now to knowing than I was when it happened," he said. "Why?"

Meyer stood in silence for a moment before answering. "There are times when I wonder if this town will be attacked like the last. Being the closest to Malmsbury," he explained. Meyer glanced across at Dréoteth, concern in his eyes.

Dréoteth thought perhaps it was the news of becoming a father that had inspired Meyer to new, protective heights. Even he could recall the small lumps of burning children on the streets of Malmsbury, and it was no hardship to guess where Meyer's mind went with it.

"I think not. Whoever it was, I believe they would have come back sooner to attack this town if that was their intent. Why wait so long?" His quiet words were filled with false conviction. Dréoteth was not positive that Faulkon's Cross was safe.

Meyer listened, finishing his wine. "Of course. You are right." He smiled across at Dréoteth and walked the goblet to the table, setting it down. "Are you going to come to the Festival on the morrow? You missed the last one," Meyer reminded him.

Dréoteth finished his wine and set the goblet beside Meyer's. He inclined his head, amused at the reminder. "I will be there. Do you think I would miss the great tug of war between women and men?"

Meyer outright laughed. "Absolutely not! The women only won last year because we men felt sorry for them."

"Perhaps *you* felt sorry for them," Dréoteth said.

"You might too, if you ever joined in," Meyer said. He wore a rakish grin.

"Games--" Dréoteth paused, reconsidering his initial answer. "--of that nature do not appeal to me. I enjoy watching, though." He tempered his reply with a wan smile, suggesting he liked the struggle the men went through over whether to let the women win or not.

Meyer knew it and laughed. He headed for the door as darkness engulfed dusk in greater gulps. "Precisely. I will see you tomorrow. Good-night."

Dréoteth inclined his head, following at a slower pace in Meyer's wake. He opened the door, swinging it wide. "Tomorrow. Give Bethany my congratulations."

"I will," Meyer said before disappearing down the hall.

Dréoteth stood there as Meyer's footsteps faded away. Closing the door, he strolled back to the wine bottle and poured himself another glass. A child. Family. These were things Dréoteth could not easily understand. He, like all the rest of his brethren, were born to a woman in the same way as humans. Except they were most assuredly *not* human, and their mothers did not care for them in the same manner. They provided food and protection deep in the heart of giant underground caves, raising their young independently, almost secretly. Grown male dragons often killed younglings of their own kind if they found them, and sometimes the females as well. Reproduction was a treacherous thing, and rare. Finding females became harder and harder, either because they had grown so skilled in hiding or because too many had been killed off.

The females taught the young how to feed, how to kill, how to fight. They were fierce on their own merit, to be fair, and always abandoned their offspring after the first change to prevent their own accidental death. There were no families. No celebrations of birth or death. They were born, they spent a life hunting, and eventually, after eons, they died.

He could not fathom having a parent as excited as Meyer. Their relationships, the sleeping in the same house and raising young together were strange to him. After all these years he was accustomed to seeing it, but it was not natural. Not in his eyes.

Contemplating it all, he picked up his goblet and took it back to the table. Opening his journal, he poured his thoughts onto the page one scratch at a time. When he finished the entry, he stowed the leather bound book in its usual hiding place under the dresser and left the room.

He needed to hunt.

She could see its eye, just one eye, through the underbrush. The fawn, curled in its camouflaged nest, didn't move an inch. Instinct told it to remain utterly still and Thea contemplated her chances of getting closer. She wanted to touch it, to stroke her fingers over the spotted fur. From a distance it seemed so soft, so gentle, with enormous dark eyes and a sweet face. The only reason she could see it was from the pale glow the moon cast down, dappling the forest floor with pockets of light. One stray cone of illumination happened to shine right on the thicket.

With a sudden leap, the fawn darted from the cover of brambles and brush, scrambling through the woods to get away from its stalker.

Thea didn't give chase. She knew that it would only scare the fawn and her chances of ever getting close would be lost. Standing up, she brushed the knees of her britches off and sighed. Not quite into her teens, she was tall for her age with the same tangle of blonde curls that she'd had as a child. The pale green of her eyes had seen suffering and death, but they were not always haunted.

Tonight, an animated curiosity chased the shadows away. Lithe and lean, she looked like a young gazelle, long legged and slightly gangly. Her clothes were earth colored and hand stitched, a craft she'd been taught in her years with the witches. Her sewing left something to be desired, but her hunting skills, she thought, were exceptional.

Being this far away from the hollow after dark made her edgy. She started picking her way back through the trees, careful not to trip over roots and branches. She'd wandered farther than she realized in her quest to find and pet the fawn. The night was quiet, calm, with only the hoot of an owl and cricket song to keep her company.

These woods had become very familiar in the years she'd called them home. She knew the direct area around the hollow like the back of her hand; the territory stretching beyond that she only knew in sections. The further she went away from the haven, the less familiar the landscape became. Here though, where the doe and fawn nestled in the bush, Thea was comfortable and secure. She did not have the special connection with the animals that the witches had, not yet, but she was learning.

Suddenly overhead, a *swish* of air disturbed the treetops. A sound she hadn't heard since she was a child made her blood run cold; the distinct *flap-flap-flap* of leathery wings. Startled, she gasped and looked up. She was in time to see a dark body pass between the trees and the moon. As it arched up and away, veering to the left, she saw the sheen of blue shimmer along the scales. Frequent nightmares kept the memory of the attack in Malmsbury excruciatingly fresh.

This was the same creature.

Swallowing a scream, she dashed through the underbrush. Ferns bent underfoot and twigs snagged at her clothes. She shoved at branches and leaves, her panting breath mirroring the frenetic beat of her heart. Gnarled roots stuck up from the ground like arthritic fingers; she tripped over one, her shoulder rebounding painfully off a tree. Was she supposed to go left? Right? She darted one way and then another, panic clouding her senses. All the training she'd done deserted her for the moment; she could only think of escaping the fire and the talons and the death that was sure to come.

Overhead, the flicker of movement caught the dragon's attention. A pair of sharp eyes picked out the motion and honed in, gauging the general direction it was trying to escape. There were many heat signatures dotting the ground, but this was the only one making a run for it. His hunter's instinct shifted into high gear.

Swooping upward, his wings went vertical when he circled to come around behind it for another pass, leveling out as he skimmed the treetops. It was a beautiful maneuver, a ghastly pirouette of death. The dragon worked on instinct, using low altitude and fear to try and flush his prey into the open. There were several clearings big enough for him to slice toward the earth and snatch it up in his claws. Birds trilled and squawked, bursting into startled flight when he invaded their territory.

He was almost on it. Coming up quick, he smelled the fear in the air, knew it was *human.* Forced to glide by with only several layers of branches and leaves between them, he soared upward and tilted his wings, making a tight turn. On the hunt, he lined up another pass, skinny tail lashing the air.

He could almost taste the blood and the flesh.

Narrowing his glowing eyes, streamlined for attack, he marked the darting prey and pealed a deep roar from his belly.

Suddenly, his prey seemed to vanish into thin air. Where there had been a terrified, running human, now there was nothing. Wheeling around to the left, wings stretched long, he came at a cross pattern in an attempt to flush it from hiding.

It must have gone to ground, cowering under a bush, hoping to confuse and lose him. He sensed no heat and its scent was gone.

A furious growl rolled past its teeth.

Still and calm, the forest gave up none of its secrets.

Easier to rage in this form, the growl turned into a vicious, night shattering roar. He left the forest of

Malmsbury in frustration, his animal mind turning from the complexities of a disappearing human to other, more predatory things.

Thea ran like the hounds of hell were at her heels. She almost screamed when the dragon roared; fear kept her silent. Her arms and legs felt numb. Her lips were ice cold. Thrashing through the under growth, panting shallowly, she desperately sought shelter.

Safety.

She needed Miriette and Phae. Like they'd materialized out of her most ardent wishes, Miriette stood calm and serene on the path ahead, waiting. A thin robe of sage green pooled around her slender body, the hood drawn up over her dark hair.

Miriette would not allow the dragon to harm her.

Too afraid to speak, she flung herself into the woman's arms. Stronger than she looked, Miriette caught her and held her tight.

"It has gone now. All is well, Thea," Miriette said.

Tears streaming down her face, Thea clung to the earthy smelling witch like she was her mother.

"I thought it was dead. I thought it was gone all these years," Thea said through hiccups and small gasps.

"They are tricky to kill darling, and live long lives. Have no fear, they cannot get to you here," Miriette said. The shield of illusion she had cast to confuse the dragon worked flawlessly.

"Was it a dragon, Miri? Was it? I saw scales and it roared."

"Yes, it was a dragon."

"Was it the same one that—"

"I do not know, dearling. There are not many of them left in the world."

"It must have been. It killed Mother." Thea sobbed, heartbroken.

Miriette soothed her with wordless sounds of comfort and understanding.

From the gloom, Phae appeared. She blended in almost perfectly with her darker green cloak, the hood pushed back. Her eyes found Thea's, and the girl saw compassion and protectiveness there.

Movement several trees over brought Ellery into view. Smiling, ethereal in a robe of dark red, she closed the distance and touched her fingers gently to Thea's cheek.

They rallied around her, providing security when she needed it most. Standing in a loose circle, they all glanced upward when the sound of distant thunder rippled through the heavens.

But it wasn't thunder.

It was the dragon.

Thea shivered.

Dréoteth funneled his fury into a new hunt. Miles from the ruin of Malmsbury, he glided high above the ground, covering a great distance in a short time. His eyes narrowed when he saw a tiny village nestled up against the base of a rocky ridge. In a fit of immediate and irrepressible rage, he swooped down, cutting skillfully through the air.

He opened his maw, ready to spew forth fire and split the night with a deafening roar. Villagers would spill out of their huts like frenzied ants, giving him his choice of victims.

At the last possible second, he snapped his heavy jaws closed and swerved up from his strafing run. Several thatched roofs came loose of their bindings at the wind gust he created. Pinwheeling away from the homes, he snatched an unwary cow from a meadow. They were easy to pick off and no challenge to hunt. Boring.

The cow bawled once and succumbed to the dragon's sinuous strength a few minutes later, providing a decent if unexciting meal. Its flesh ripped apart with almost too much ease, blood soaking into the ground in large puddles. He took four more before he sated his hunger and his anger.

Dréoteth the man walked back into Faulkon's Cross several hours later, neat and clean in his breeches and overcoat. The hour was so late that no one but the night clerk at the Mirmande saw him. He retreated to his room without a word, closing himself away to brood over why he had chosen to spare the small village instead of burn it to the ground.

He wondered, too, about the strange disappearance of the human. Could it have been one of the witches? He'd hunted in the forest near Malmsbury, but not directly behind it, where he thought the witches lived.

Then again, he had never come across any haven or cottages, despite that Eugenia said they were there. The witches magic clouded his mind, he thought, making it that much more difficult to figure out the exact location of their nest. He could have been right on top of it or a few miles away.

So who was it he had chased through the trees?

He got up to retrieve his journal and took it to the table near the window. There had always been something calming about writing his thoughts. Snatching up the quill, he dabbed the nib into the inkpot and put his experience to paper.

Pensive, Dréoteth approached the festival with his hands in his pockets. His mouth thinned at the happy, lively atmosphere. Under the material of his plain, dark gray tunic, his shoulder twitched. Black breeches tapered into hand worked boots with the soles beginning to wear down from use.

The scent of roasting pork floated thick on the breeze. Children ran pell mell from one end of the clearing to another, shouting and taunting their playmates. Contests were well underway and he stayed on the fringe of the gathered, keeping a cautious distance from the horses hitched to wagons in anticipation of the hayrides.

Meyer's booming voice was easy to pick out of the rest and he saw the dark haired man with Beth at his side, smiling proudly as he announced the news to their friends. Beth blushed and smiled alongside her husband, accepting congratulations graciously.

He did not immediately make his way over.

Instead, he preferred to try and overcome the dark mood that had descended upon him at the end of last night's hunt. Sometimes it was this way for him, fighting against the inner urgings that whispered darkly to wreak destruction on everything in sight.

Beth saw him first and she left Meyer's side to come fetch him. The rose color gown went well with her dark hair, the hem swishing over the grass. Her cheeks had spots of color from the excitement.

"Mister Trimble! How good it is to see you here. Meyer relayed your congratulations and I wanted to come thank you personally." Coming to stand before him, she upturned a fresh smile, upbeat and enthusiastic.

Dréoteth paused, turning toward her as she arrived. He struggled to remain passive and neutral when he smelled the changes of pregnancy on her body. Instinct demanded he gut her, even if she was not a dragon. Males of their species were known to take the lives of both mother and child.

His fingers fidgeted inside his pockets.

Inclining his head at her gratitude, he forced his attention to other things. "Of course. I would have it no other way. You are feeling well?" Weren't men supposed to ask a woman that in her condition? He wasn't sure.

She blushed furiously and cleared her throat, making him wonder if he'd blundered.

"Yes, I am doing quite well. Will you come join us? Meyer will be over here shortly to abscond you either way." She laughed, a sweet sound of sincerity.

"Meyer *does* like to have his way," Dréoteth said. He smiled, amused, and impulsively offered his elbow to her the way he'd seen Meyer do.

His nostrils flared slightly and a muscle flexed in his jaw.

Bethany, looking surprised, accepted with a tiny laugh. Her skirts brushed against his legs as they made their way to Meyer.

The group of people he stood with were unfamiliar to Dréoteth.

"Trimble! It is about time you showed up," Meyer said. He stepped forward to accept his wife into the crook of one arm while extending his other hand for Dréoteth to shake.

Dréoteth shook, matching Meyer's smile if not for exuberance, then for sincerity. Despite his inner conflict, he realized he was glad to see Meyer and Beth happy.

"I knew you would be flapping your mouth for some time and impossible to talk with anyway," Dréoteth said, earning laughter from the circle of people around them.

Meyer grinned roguishly and did not deny it.

"Let me introduce you," Meyer said. He made the rounds of all the people and Dréoteth accepted with a typical, subdued bow of his dark head.

All in their early twenties and middle thirties, each man had a woman on his arm. It did not escape Dréoteth that again, he stood out as the only one without a female companion. Now, as ever, he was not moved to correct this.

One of the men, Sean Farthington, had other ideas. Tall with broad shoulders, he had hair the color of wheat and a rakehell grin. He had a reputation for blunt rudeness that not everyone in town appreciated. Dréoteth recalled hearing the name several times in passing conversation.

"So, Trimble, when are *you* going to choose a lady for the taking? I hear tell that Miss Fynch is smitten with you as well as Miss Shannon." Sean's brows arched high, green eyes filled with malicious mischief.

Mistress Shannon had a reputation of her own as a racy, sometimes willful woman that had already taken a lover. Or three.

Dréoteth understood that he needed to underplay the situation, as he always did, so that their attention would move on rather than focus on it.

"I am in no hurry. When the right one presents herself, then I will consider courtship."

"Most men of your age have five or six kids by now," Sean said, pushing the issue. He had everyone in the circle's attention; they all glanced from Sean to Dréoteth expectantly.

"They may have another five or six, or ten if that is their desire. I will not be rushed into marriage I do not feel ready for." Dréoteth sounded droll and unbothered. The tactic worked well, for several of the other men nodded like they thought him wise to pick carefully.

Meyer clapped him lightly on the shoulder. "Trimble is patient and wise."

Bethany feigned affront. "Just what are you saying, Meyer Lyon?"

A ripple of low laughter swept through the group.

"Or perhaps it is not *women* you prefer, eh, Trimble?" Sean said, posturing arrogantly. He thought he had the upper hand.

The shocking, dramatic statement brought a sudden hush over the small gathering. One of the women covered her lips with her fingers. There were few offenses worse than suggesting a man preferred another man, especially in front of a crowd.

Sean's wife, a large boned woman with close-set eyes and skinny lips, elbowed his ribs.

Meyer's expression grew annoyed, his fingers curling into a fist.

Dréoteth stared Sean down. A hard, unrelenting stare that made every single person uneasy. He took a step forward, lethal and predatory. He seemed capable of cutting Sean down with nothing more than his unamused glare.

"You have exactly five seconds to rescind your blasphemy," Dréoteth said. He was beyond enraged, speaking in whispers, hanging onto his control by incredibly thin threads. That a *human* would dare to suggest it to him publicly was more insult than he could handle. Amongst his kind, such a thing was unheard of. He had discovered long ago that some men and women alike shared preference for the same gender, but it was not so in the world of dragons.

Had Dréoteth not learned a shred of patience all these years, Sean would already be dead.

Alarmed, Sean's wife gripped her husband's elbow tighter.

Sean looked Dréoteth up and down with an insolent sneer. He took a threatening step forward, shaking his wife's hand from his elbow. "Or what?"

Meyer chose that second to step in. He put his big body between the men, glaring at Sean for trying to start trouble. "Here now. Stop this. Sean, you know better than to antagonize—"

"What. He cannot speak for himself?" Sean taunted.

Dréoteth's stare never wavered and when he struck, it was with a swiftness none of them were expecting. One moment he was two feet from Sean and the next, almost before anyone could blink or breathe, he was *on* him.

Dréoteth took Sean down so fast that the man had no time to even put up his hands in defense. A feral growl ripped from Dréoteth's chest, his fingers curling hard against the jugular, ready to rip Sean's throat wide open.

Meyer hooked Dréoteth's elbows and bodily pulled him away, grunting with the effort. Dréoteth allowed him to at the last possible moment. He yanked his arms out of Meyer's hold, glaring at Sean, his face a mask of ill concealed rage.

"Beware ever crossing my path when you are alone," Dréoteth said. "It will be the last thing you ever do."

Sean scrambled up the second Dréoteth was off of him. He looked flushed and furious. His chest rose and fell with the force of his panted breaths, blossoms of red erupting on his throat from the force of Dréoteth's grip.

"Sean, get yourself gone, fool," Meyer said. He snapped the words aside, again putting himself in a position that wasn't directly between them but a blockade nevertheless.

Sean smeared his wrist across his mouth, and let his horrified, embarrassed wife guide him away from the confrontation.

The other couples whispered to each other, the

women holding onto their respective men's arms.

Dréoteth snapped a dark look around at the eyes of the remaining men, challenging any one of them to take up Sean's argument. His hands balled into fists and released, a vein standing out sharply in his temple. He recognized the signs of submission by how they averted their eyes or made their posture humble, probably without even realizing it.

He read the same expression on almost every face: *would Trimble have killed Sean if Meyer hadn't interfered?* No one dared ask, and he did not offer the truth. An awkward pall fell over the group, and Dréoteth felt the weight of their stares when he turned to Meyer.

"Enjoy the rest of your evening," he said. He simply could not stay a moment more.

Without waiting for Meyer's reply, Dréoteth pivoted on a heel and stalked away. He heard the whispers behind him turn into concerned murmurs; it infuriated him further that these humans would dare pass judgment only after he'd taken himself from their company.

He had no doubt that the blame would fall with Sean for instigating it, but he was sure that come morning, the other citizens would watch him warily, uncertain of his honor. He wasn't exactly in their good graces to begin with, unlike Meyer, who had won the whole town over. Their differences were glaring: Meyer was charismatic and jovial, always willing to help those in need; Dréoteth was reserved and distant, a puzzle with too many pieces.

Yanking open the door to the Mirmande, he stalked to the stairs, flatly ignoring the desk clerk. Taking them by twos, he reached the third floor and flung the door open to his quarters. It slammed hard behind him.

He paced the perimeter, thrusting a hand

through his jet-black hair. There weren't enough vile curses in his repertoire to adequately express his dislike for Sean.

Dropping into a sleek crouch, he fished out his journal from under the armoire and slapped it onto the table to write.

Fall
The Year of the Golden Talon

Rage rolls through me and I cannot control it. A man from this town by the name of Sean committed an offense that he should die for. I know if I do so, if I give in, I will jeopardize my standing with the community. I have spent years building trust between Meyer and myself and he is the only human I consider a friend. Such as I have them.

Is it worth it? Would I suffer later if I burnt this whole town to the ground? Would I miss his and Beth's company? Do I care?

I demand satisfaction for the insult Sean wrought, even if it means I must leave here and never return. My fingers itch to become talons and flay his body open all the way to his soul.

I need to be out of this room, away from confinement.

He barely made a scratch of the quill on the paper instead of his name and shoved back the chair to stand. Snapping his journal closed, he tucked it into the waist of his breeches and left the Inn, threading his way toward the back of the building so his departure would go unnoticed.

Two horses shied when he hissed in their direction, snapping their leads. They galloped away from the post and into the city. Before the echo of their pounding hooves faded, Dréoteth stepped into the forest.

He never looked back.

A half-mile from Faulkon's Cross, Dréoteth's skin turned to scales, black and gleaming. His nose and jaw elongated and talons replaced his fingers. Between one step and the next, he went from two legs to four and lunged into the air, teeth snapping sharply. Every breath burned. Growls scattered wildlife in all directions, the air thick with their shrill warning cries and flapping wings.

As soon as night fell, the slaughter began. He destroyed meadows of cows, herds of horses, and several deer that he hunted with a vengeance. Fierce and furious, he gave no quarter. With every death his control slipped further, until he was all beast, ripping and tearing and shredding his way from one group of animals to another.

He came upon the same small village he'd once spared, but this time the inhabitants were not so lucky. Lining up for a straight shot, he strafed the huts and the crude buildings, listening with relish to the screams and the prayers that would never be answered. He didn't stop until their pitiful cries faded and their houses were nothing but ash.

The silence descended, thick and absolute, as if the world was a gigantic heart, and this was the space between beats.

He flew away from the scene of his destruction, sated by the annihilation of innocents. Hundreds had paid for the mistake of just one.

Each flap of his leathery wings took him closer to the jagged outline of the distant mountains. During winter, the caps would be covered in snow. Deep in the womb of the earth, an enormous cave waited. Their kind knew how to find the safest caverns, a built in instinct. Like hunting. He had found it years ago and made it his own.

Thick stands of pine and spruce suddenly gave way to a clearing at the base of the mountain, and he glided down to the ground, his talons extending. When they actually clutched the earth, it was his booted feet that jogged forward a few steps, his dragon receding in favor of his human form once more. He walked another ten feet as the momentum of the landing eased. Clothes intact—a trick they all learned from the first teachings—he brushed his sleeves off even though not so much as a speck of lint dirtied the material. He had no great love for cotton and linen confinement, tolerating it for society's sake.

The heavy scent of wooded forest and fresh earth was strong here. Nearby, a creek slithered through the landscape, burbling over a bed of smooth, small rocks. He smelled raccoon, deer, bear, foxes, rabbits and hundreds of other animals, all of which had scattered when he'd drawn closer to the clearing. Distantly, birds chirped and squawked, never daring to come back to their nests while he was in the open.

He sought a craggy crevice behind a large boulder and green bushes that helped hide the entrance, disappearing into the darkness of a winding tunnel. He didn't need light to see by.

There were many twists and turns, some of the passageways between the jagged walls narrow enough that he had to slink through sideways. The dull thud of his boots echoed off the stone, and he knew by taking a deep breath that no human had passed through here since his last visit.

Sloping down, always down, the tunnel took him deeper until a weak glow alerted him to the end. After a final hairpin turn to the left, it yawned into an enormous, atmospheric cavern. The change from close and confining to this was astounding. Or it would have been, if he hadn't seen it a dozen times, and wasn't used to the fact such places existed.

Humans would have marveled at the stalagmites thrusting down from the ceiling, the misshapen cones sparkling with chips of marcasite. It threaded through the entire cave, along with numerous other minerals that cast their own glint and shine. Fresh water slithered from an opening in the rocks to a gaping tear in the earth, forming a pool.

To the right, a large, mostly flat area provided a place to rest. Even in his dragon, there was three times the space he needed.

Unhurried, he walked to a crude rock that he set his journal down upon. The surface was smooth and even enough to support a small pot of ink and a few quills.

Against the right wall, hundreds of oil paintings leaned. They seemed out of place here against raw nature with their gilded, ornate frames. Foreign faces stared out of a foxhunt, or a portrait, expressions frozen in time. Some were landscapes or depictions of flowers. Others were god-like scenes, with intense, blue skies, fluffy clouds, and humans with cloth draped in artful places.

He stared hard at them while he pulled off the tunic shirt. He threw it to the ground and shucked his boots next, careless where they landed. His breeches skimmed down powerful but lean hips and he kicked them aside.

Naked, his olive skin stretched taut over his honed muscles, the teeth of his spine in sharp relief and quite prominent down his back.

He stared in particular at the foxhunt painting.

Not for the first time, he wondered who the men on the horses were. Lords or nobles of some sort by the cut of their clothing.

Pompous and arrogant men.

Men like Sean.

A snarl ripped through the cavern and he took a swipe at the painting, claws extending from the ends of his long fingers. Jagged tears cut through the canvas, through the horses and the staring eyes of the humans.

The ruination of the masterpiece gave him no pleasure after his immediate ire was spent. He was too appreciative of the talent, a talent no dragon man would ever own.

Grim and dark, he stalked away from the painting toward the pool, comfortable in his nakedness. It was his natural state when he wasn't covered in scales and killing teeth. Crouching, he cupped handfuls of the cool water and drank, washing away the residue of blood on his tongue. His reflection made him scowl, and he threw harmless droplets from his hand onto the surface so the ripple would warp his image.

Exhaling a hot breath through his nose, he rose and turned toward the immense flat area, his bones and muscles reshaping into the sleek dragon. He curled in on himself, the sinuous tail wrapping more than half around his body. The relentless frustration that plagued him lately was not so dire and strong in his animal mind. He escaped here, heaving great, deep breaths, his eyes closing to blot out the sight of the shredded painting.

Finally, the dragon rested.

Chapter Seven

When Dréoteth opened his eyes, he knew that a long time had passed. It was a sense that they all had, guided by some internal clock that never steered them wrong. Rumbling, he raised his head. The cave looked as it always did, his clothes in the same spot, his journal untouched. The painting sat tilted and torn where he'd left it.

Dréoteth couldn't exactly say whether three months or three years had gone by, but it was longer than overnight. It was longer than a week that he'd fallen into the deep sleep dragons sometimes needed. Their bodies all but shut down, requiring little sustenance to keep them alive.

Stretching his legs and his tail, he moved into the center of the immense cave and extended his leathery wings. The light flap he gave them stirred the air harmlessly.

The transformation back into his human form took only seconds, the shape of the dragon melting down into something smaller and lean. He went to the pool and sated his thirst, drinking long and deep.

Besides the gurgle of water from the stream, the only other sound was his breathing. He could not be more aware of his extreme isolation. In decades past, this had always been a balm; dragons needed no one. They were solitary creatures who lived to hunt and feed. In earlier eons, he had rarely taken his human form, preferring the strength of his dragon to the somewhat susceptible shape of a man. Over time, as populations grew and his curiosity about men peaked, he shifted often.

Now he was a man more than a dragon, moving amongst the herds undetected. He told himself it was to better know his enemy. That knowledge was power and a powerful dragon could never be defeated. He convinced himself it was part of adapting to his surroundings, that learning the ways of humans was a natural step in his evolution.

Diving into the water, he rinsed away a layer of psychological dust. He felt refreshed after he climbed out, even if he hadn't been dirty, and let the air dry his skin. Running his fingers through his black hair, he gave it a shake and stalked toward the haphazard array of clothes on the floor.

The silence seemed to mock him.

Tucking the shirt into the breeches, he snagged his journal off the stone, gave the painting a troubled glance, and left the cavern. Sliding the leather bound book into the waist of his breeches, he traversed the tunnel, detecting no new scents of humans or trespassers. He felt the mantle of evening before he ever stepped outside.

In the clearing, a handful of deer grazed at the very edges of the trees. When they caught his scent, they darted away in great, frantic leaps. Other nocturnal nightlife slithered and scampered away to safety.

Evergreen, pine and spruce lined the field, adding a potent, fresh smell to the air. He appreciated the rich, earthy scents after being underground. He struck out in the direction of Faulkon's Cross, stretching muscles that had been dormant too long. He could have flown in his dragon, and he would eventually, but the exercise felt good.

His thoughts inevitably turned to Meyer and Beth. He wondered if the woman was round with child, or if Meyer was already a father. Had they passed judgment upon him for his heated words and subsequent disappearance? Perhaps his absence suggested guilt.

In the distance, an owl hooted.

He was not driven to hunt yet. His metabolism had slowed considerably, the last meal he'd gorged on absorbed at a trickle. The effect would reverse the longer he was awake and aware, and only when he felt the first pangs of hunger would he shift and ferret out a meal.

After another deep breath, he understood the season to be spring. He smelled it in the new shoots of green grass, the fresh layer of leaves on the trees. Every season smelled different and again he pondered the length of his sleep. Winter had been approaching when he'd gone below ground.

Meyer had told him the night before the festival that Bethany was due in the spring. He might arrive to find the couple with a newborn.

He took to his dragon when his body felt sufficiently nimble, shifting effortlessly, soaring above the treetops under a clear, starry sky.

For a moment, he thought about Sean. The image of the man's face came to mind unbidden. He was not stirred to fresh fury at the recollection of their confrontation and promptly forgot him. Any anger that had driven him to obliterate life so violently had been purged during his long slumber.

It was an hour before dawn when he recognized the terrain near Faulkon's Cross. He landed in another small field well short of the city to avoid any chance of being seen. After the transition, he chose to enter from the west, allowing him to see the long main road that ran down the middle of town.

His first hint that more time had passed than he'd realized came as he set foot upon the street. Before it had been dirt and now there were cobblestones. Several shops filled previous gaps in the landscape and others that had been run down showed signs of renovations and improvements.

The changes were stark. Surprising.

More than one season had gone by. The late hour meant the street was clear of people, and he found his steps leading him to the Mirmande to see how it fared. With his hands behind his back, he saw the recent updating to the exterior and new statues by the doors. The landscaping looked more mature. A new bookstore had been erected directly to the left.

He did not bother to go inside the Mirmande and see if his old room was as he'd left it. He'd taken everything important to him when he'd gone, so he did not mourn the things he'd lost. As twilight touched the horizon and started to spread creeping fingers over the land, he turned away. Irrevocably, his footsteps led him into the forest.

Taking every shortcut he knew, he made his way through the dense trees toward Meyer's farm. It was a mile outside of town, but he knew the position well. As his boots flattened baby ferns and snapped dead pine needles beneath the sole, he wondered what he might find when he arrived.

A contemplative frown creased his brow.

Should he stay away? Let the unknown number of seasons turn into eternity? This was his chance to break free of the town, of the friendship he'd nurtured for years. He knew, of course, that it could not last forever.

Dragons lived eons. Meyer would only live into his late forties or early fifties, if he were lucky. At some point, he had to say a permanent goodbye.

Approaching Meyer's property, he walked to the edge of the trees and stood in a long shadow as the twilight gave way to dawn.

The homestead looked *almost* the same. Bushes were fuller and bigger, the landscape more mature. Several of the fields had been sown for crops and Meyer had added a new barn with another pasture. The horses, at least, were in their stalls and would not give his presence away. He wondered if Meyer still taught at the School of Higher Learning as well as farming his land.

He could say this for humanity: some of them had unflagging energy.

Patiently he waited, knowing it would not be long until the couple stirred to tend their farm and their child. He was sure by now that the baby had already been born.

A mere half hour later the back door banged open and Meyer emerged. Instantly Dréoteth recognized the solid build, the distinct, brisk gait. Meyer could have worn formal attire, farming clothes, or leather armor and a sword and every guise would have seemed natural. Meyer had not made his life about just one calling. He was as talented with words and grammar as he was with a blade or a plot of land. Today he wore clothes meant for a day in the fields, the colors two tones of brown.

What shocked Dréoteth was the *age* that Meyer wore so distinctly. Dark overall, his hair now had a startling amount of silver threading through at the temples. Twice as much as last time he'd seen him.

Deep lines carved his skin on each side of his mouth and at the corners of his eyes. He still carried himself with pride and power but the signs were there.

Meyer was approaching his middling years.

Just behind him, a small hand caught the door and a little boy ran out after him. Dréoteth had never been good at judging the age of human children, but he thought the child must be five or six at least.

"Da, wait! Wait for me!"

"Well come on, slowpoke. I have meetings later and a paper to read at the School," Meyer said, glancing back. His fatherly pride was more than apparent.

Bethany opened the door after the both of them, and tucked into the crook of her arm was *another* child in swaddling clothes. Her belly was round with a third.

"Remember to stop by the Smith's and –"

"Get the fabric you ordered. I know!" Meyer jovially cut Beth off, winking at her over the top of the little boy's head. Beth, a handful of years younger than Meyer, had tiny lines advancing across her face. He saw no gray in her hair yet. It was just a matter of time.

Dréoteth watched, amazed.

Never had his slumbers had quite this much impact before. There had been no friends to watch grow and age over the years. He'd never stayed in one place long enough to bear witness to the inevitable changes of life. Always the passage of years for him was painless, like breathing. One day turned into two, and two turned into ten. The years inched by in that eternal way where the seasons came and went so quickly that they could have been hours instead of decades. It was this way for his kind, living so many thousands of years that a handful was nothing. A few drops of rain in a deluge.

He felt a pang under his ribs that he could not account for. It made him uneasy, this peculiar, somber sense of having missed too many things.

He swallowed tightly, angry with himself, torn between memories of all that had happened over the past decade and the urge to leave immediately.

Put all this behind him.

Time felt strange to him just now.

For another few minutes he stood there, transfixed, before he receded deeper into the woods. Daylight was streaming over the landscape but the shadows hid him well. When he met up with Meyer, he did not want his children anywhere near.

It was time to say good-bye.

Dréoteth timed his appearance from the woods impeccably.

Three hours after watching Meyer and Beth on their back porch, he stepped onto the small dirt road that led into town just before the scholar and his horse passed by.

The animal immediately spooked, lurching sideways out of control. A shrill scream split the air and his hooves kicked up small clods of earth. Meyer fought to control him, holding tight to the reins.

He saw Dréoteth and all but wrenched his neck to hold eye contact as his steed swung around to the right.

"God's blood, man! Where have you been?" Meyer dismounted when he'd moved the horse back up the path several yards, securing the reins to a branch. He strode back toward Dréoteth, the disbelief easy to see on his face. The disbelief turned to wariness when the realization struck that Dréoteth looked *exactly* as he had the last time he'd seen him.

Dréoteth read the expressions like pages from a book: shock, suspicion, curiosity. He thought about lying, making up some wild tale of witches and woods and spells, but in the end he chose a wayward version of the truth.

"I did not expect to stay gone when I left town that night after Sean," he said. He slid his hands into the pockets of his breeches, elbows casually bent. "I left to cool my temper and found myself embroiled in a situation not of my making. I had no way to send word." It occurred to him that his words could be construed as apology. The thought disconcerted him.

Apologizing to a human.

What was next? Hugging?

Meyer crossed his burly arms over his chest, frowning. Finally, he said, "Embroiled? Were you attacked—Trimble, you have not aged a *day.*"

It came down to these unexpected moments; Dréoteth could try and jest his apparent youth away, but they both knew he would be doing it to avoid the truth. Meyer was too sharp to misunderstand him. All he could do was silently incline his head in agreement.

Yes, he had not aged a day.

Perhaps Meyer expected him to deny it, to make some excuse. He seemed appalled and more suspicious than before.

"What is this?" Meyer said.

Although he whispered, Dréoteth heard him clearly.

They searched each other's eyes.

"A thing I wish not to explain," Dréoteth finally said. That, at least, was the whole truth.

"Why not? Have we not shared all manner of secrets between us? That is what friends do," Meyer said. He pressed for information like there might be some logical explanation for the things his eyes told him that his mind denied.

Dréoteth shook his head. "I cannot, and I will not. Do not ask me again. I came to tell you good-bye. As you said, you have been a friend, an unexpected one, and I wanted you to know that I valued it." The confessions were honest, guileless. These were things he actually did feel, and he realized at the very last moment, that he was not ashamed of them. As complicated as he could be, as torn as he felt about humanity and his small part in it, he knew those words to be utterly true.

Meyer, and Beth at the end, had gifted him with rare insight into the detailed workings of humans.

Meyer took a brave step forward. "Aye, as have I," he said. "There is no reason for you to leave. Stay and talk to me as we did in younger days."

"There is every reason. Do not make it difficult. Let us part on good terms. Like gentlemen." Dréoteth was anything but.

He could pretend for the sake of these final minutes in Meyer's company, the same way he'd pretended in Malmsbury and Faulkon's Cross amongst the citizens. It was much less a sacrifice than some of the other things he'd endured.

He extended his long fingered hand into the space between them for a final shake, an action he had never precipitated nor engaged in before. His intent was clear.

They locked gazes. Meyer did not immediately reach for Dréoteth's hand. The moment stretched thin. The sun beat down upon the dusty path, the forest eerily silent around them. Too silent.

"You leave me curious, Trimble. Now and forever I

will wonder. But if this is the only way, then I thank you for the years of friendship." He clasped Dréoteth's hand, shook it heartily, and released him.

Dréoteth parroted the motion, taking a step back when they were through. He inclined his head. "For men like us the not knowing is the worst part."

He commiserated with that.

"Be well, old friend." Dréoteth turned and slipped back into the trees. It seemed inconceivable that this was really the end. His gut tightened and a muscle in his jaw flexed.

He wondered what Meyer and Beth had named their children.

The lack of footsteps told him Meyer had not moved from his spot. He was probably watching him disappear into the forest, thoughtful and confused.

The sharp sounds of hoof beats on the path a few minutes later alerted Dréoteth to Meyer's departure, and he stopped to turn and stare through the forest. There was nothing to see but limbs heavy with pine needles and leaves and fat trunks covered in rough bark; he looked nonetheless.

When the sound faded away, Dréoteth exhaled a breath, surprised to find himself tired.

Goodbyes were harder than he thought they would be.

Crouched in a triangle shaped shadow at the corner of a building, Dréoteth watched people stroll by on the main street of town. He was not easy to see for the apple cart that sat not far from his knee and for the complete stillness of his body. Only his eyes followed the movement of legs and bodies. He recognized a few of them, never calling out or directing attention to himself.

The glint of sunlight on a mane of red hair drew

his gaze, and he was unsurprised to find himself staring at Eugenia Bailey. A basket over her arm, she looked to be straight from the farmer's stalls in the marketplace. She too had aged, though in the soft way some women had, the crinkles at the corners of her gray eyes adding character. The changes were minor compared to Meyer, perhaps because she was so much younger than he to begin with.

Turning down a side road, she marched away from the heavier foot traffic toward some unknown destination.

Curious, he rose and followed her, leaving a small distance between them. Avoiding other citizens, he tracked her to a less populated series of streets where the small shops were spaced further apart. She stopped at one with an awning over the door and a table sitting outside in the shade. An old woman wrapped in too many layers of clothes for the weather sat behind the array of embroidered scarves.

Eugenia paused to examine the selection, the scent of fresh baked bread and fruit coming from her basket. She greeted the old woman with a smile and ran her fingers over an emerald green scarf, tracing the unique floral stitching at the edges.

Dréoteth stepped up right behind the redhead and touched the scarf—a deep blue that reminded him of his scales—right next to the green one. "I think this suits you better," he said.

Eugenia yelped in surprise, snatching her hand away from the material, turning with wide eyes to see him.

This close, he could better see a few more discreet signs of aging. Still young, still pretty by a human's standards, but she had not escaped the passage of time unscathed.

"*Mister* Trimble! Is it really you? I—" she paused.

Dréoteth knew she was thinking the same thing Meyer had. He cut in before she could think to finish her thought. "Yes. You are still here."

Eugenia blinked rapidly. "Where else would I be?"

"In the woods, with the witches?"

She cleared her throat, cheeks pinker than when she'd been looking at the scarf. "I live in Faulkon's Cross now," she explained, staring at him. "Where have you been all this time, Mister Trimble?"

"Busy," he lied. "I came back long enough to say good-bye to Meyer and Beth."

"You are leaving again? But why?" Eugenia regained her composure, smoothing a few stray strands of hair that had escaped the pins holding it up.

"It matters not. I—"

"Of *course* it matters, Mister Trimble," she said. "Meyer and Beth will miss your company terribly." She averted her eyes quickly, like there was more to the statement, something that she caught before it could slip free.

Dréoteth wondered what it was. "They have survived well enough without it these last years," he pointed out. "You—"

"Eugenia! There you are." A man strode toward them from the other direction, sword at his hip, his cadence brisk. Fair haired with a mustache and clipped beard, he glanced between them and cupped Eugenia's elbow in his hand when he arrived.

"Oh!" Startled, she swung a look toward her name and then between the two men. "Mister Trimble, allow me to introduce Mister Herriott. Mister Herriott, this is Nehemiah Trimble."

Dréoteth, who had watched the man approach with slightly narrowed eyes, assessed Herriott— whom he guessed was some relation to the Baron—

shrewdly. "Mister Herriott," he said.

"Ah, yes. I recall your name. You left town unexpectedly, is that right?" Herriott asked. Although his manner was cordial enough, Dréoteth recognized wariness in his eyes.

"I did. You are the Baron's...." Dréoteth let it trail, expecting Herriott to fill in.

"Son, yes. Miss Bailey, have you considered my pro—" Herriott started to ask Eugenia a question. She interrupted him.

"I have not. I was just trying to talk Mister Trimble into staying in town a little longer. Meyer and Beth Lyon will miss his companionship." Eugenia spoke quickly, diverting the conversation.

Dréoteth had the same sense about Herriott and Bailey that he'd had with Meyer and Beth during those first days of courtship.

So Bailey had a suitor. He wasn't sure why he was surprised. Before either of them could speak, Dréoteth stepped around them, meeting Eugenia's eyes one last time as he passed.

"Be well, Miss Bailey. Herriott," he said. He caught a flicker of something in Eugenia's gaze, too complicated for him to figure out or understand.

Disappearing around the first corner he came to, he departed the town for the forest, wondering over the things Bailey thought but hadn't the courage to say.

Chapter Eight

Dréoteth walked the woods for hours. He skirted the city just out of sight, able to hear the sounds of horses and children and construction in the distance. Life went on for humans as it did for dragons, though Dréoteth's path was a solitary one. Theirs was not. Even now they gathered and congregated, painted and baked, laughed and gossiped.

Well. He would not miss that part of human nature at all.

Everything in the forest that breathed beat a hasty retreat at his presence. He was acutely and ironically aware that humans were the only other creatures that did not flee his immediate vicinity. How could they? They did not know better.

His thoughts were deep things, spanning more than his friendship with Meyer and Beth. In recent decades, he was prone to examine the centuries of his life in depth and contemplate the long years left to come.

Never before had he considered it anything but exciting to live through the cycle of seasons, hunting at will, traveling great distances to far off places most humans only dreamed of.

Just then, in a pessimistic snit, he was not looking forward to starting over. He was not looking forward to finding a new town or making acquaintances or having to fit in. Perhaps he needed a longer break than a handful of years that whipped by in a blink.

He breathed deep, pulling in the scent of a nearby creek and wildflowers that dotted the landscape. With no reason to hurry back to the mountain, he took his time navigating a path away from Faulkon's Cross.

Suddenly, he stopped walking.

His ruminations were interrupted by a smell that didn't belong.

He followed it, narrow eyed, for perhaps fifty yards. He moved with stealthy grace, barely making a sound.

The forest gave way to a small, secluded clearing. A cone of sunlight shone brightly down upon tender shoots of grass and plants with broad leaves the size of a man's palm.

Death lurked nearby. Not old death, with bleached bones and black sockets for eyes, but the thick gouts of red blood and shredded flesh of *new* death. He followed his nose to a mangled bush and found the rotting carcass of a deer.

He growled at the other scent mingling with the slaughtered remains.

Dragon.

His kind.

It was unlike any other in the forest.

He darted a look around the clearing, half expecting to see a man watching him from the shadows.

He saw nothing.

Looking back at the deer, he judged the carcass to be several days old. The only thing he could tell about his brethren was that it was male.

What was it doing in Faulkon's Cross? How long had it been here? There were no signs of attack on the town, but it was hunting and feeding in the vicinity. He wondered if any of the citizens had gone missing recently. Maybe it waited for some other reason to wreak its devastation.

But it was coming. Oh yes, an attack was certainly coming.

Dréoteth turned immediately away from the carnage and stalked into the cover of the trees. He prowled the perimeter of town, searching and seeking, finding nothing more than the lingering scent of his brethren. There were no more kills, no lairs, no clues. He wondered if the dragon had dirtied himself with humans, blending into society's fringe in order to hide.

He could not count the unlikely possibility out.

What he didn't know was why it waited to strike. Dusk had given way to night hours ago, a perfect time to attack while the humans were disabled by darkness and disoriented by sleep. He wondered if it was the same one that had burnt Malmsbury to the ground. Perhaps it had planned another attack on Faulkon's Cross all those years ago, letting the hysteria and panic ease before razing this town like the last.

Baiting the humans into inattentiveness.

It was not above a dragon to play these kinds of games.

Dréoteth paused behind a white church with a high rising spire. Small panes of stained glass adorned two walls and both front doors.

The outlands produced nothing. Now he was forced prowl the streets for his brethren. He had to be here, lurking *among* them. Hiding right in their midst, as he had done—was *still* doing.

Their kind, especially males, did not get along. They rarely existed in the same vicinity longer than it took them to find separate roads away from each other. They did not kill on sight, but provocation into battle took little.

He wondered whether he should warn Meyer and his family. He felt strangely protective of the Lyon clan and did not stop just then to contemplate his feelings over it.

Torn and indecisive, he cut past the church to the main street. The thoroughfare was much less busy at this hour. He counted one wagon and a smattering of men, some of them in a hurry to get to their destination and some not. In another hour, maybe two, the roads would be clear until morning. He doubted the dragon would hole up inside a building, any building, and fully expected to come across him somewhere in town. Avoiding the men as well as the horses, he stalked along the path in front of the shops. His gaze pierced the shadows between buildings and homes, muscles tense under his clothing.

Men and women and children had probably walked right past the imposter, as they did with himself, never knowing.

Never suspecting they were being hunted from three feet away.

An hour passed. And another.

Nothing.

Suddenly, from the other end of town, he heard screams.

Stepping into the street from an alley he'd used as a shortcut, he narrowed his eyes and tried to pinpoint the exact location of the disruption. His senses were honed to a fine point, adrenaline threatening to make his claws extend from his fingers. Sometimes, when they knew battle was close, their bodies began to make the change to their beast automatically.

People were running pell mell, confused, some running toward the screams and some running away. The shouts drew citizens from their homes out into the open, their silhouettes like death shadows in the night. Dréoteth had no trouble picking them out.

Standing in front of one of the buildings, he had a perfect view of the eruption of flame; it blazed down the middle of the road, engulfing the people and anything else in its way. Windows blew out from the heat and the pressure. A gaseous scent choked those too close to the flames and sizzled their eyes in their sockets.

Dréoteth made out the large shape of the dragon at the other end of the flame. It pulled up after its strafing run, soaring overhead with its wings tilted into a turn, bringing it around to align for another pass.

Cast into an orange glow, the main street of Faulkon's Cross started to burn.

Dréoteth sank back into the shadows, running along between two structures, and launched himself into his own dragon when he was out of sight of the townsfolk. There was no time to wait, no time to be picky about his transformation.

His wings slapped the air, pulling him higher, even as the other dragon came in again, spewing fire over houses, over the innocent. Dréoteth was surprised to think of them that way.

Humans screamed. Agonizing, terrified screams that usually swelled him with dominance and triumph.

This night, it infuriated him.

Clouds scuttled across the moon, making the dragons all but invisible.

Dréoteth used his other senses to track his prey, following the vague swish of wings in the air and the heat that emanated from the dragon in thick waves. The sudden, erratic change in the gout of flame warned him that the dragon knew he was coming.

In a strange twist of irony, he realized that he was about to commit an act of protection for a human. The longer he was in his dragon, the harder rational thinking would become, but he understood the complexity of what he was doing just before his keen vision picked out a wicked, sinuous silhouette ahead.

Like Dréoteth, the male had black scales that had a translucent blue sheen when any kind of light hit it just right. He was slightly larger than Dréoteth with a longer wingspan. The dragon's eyes gleamed green instead of blue. These details were minor; what counted were the ages and the battles they had been in before this unlikely meeting.

Skill and experience mattered.

Dréoteth had been alive a long time.

Circling, they came at each other with roars and talons extended, clashing hard enough to shake the heavens. Their scales were like armor, deflecting much of the initial damage, their sharp needle-teeth going for the throat. Dréoteth broke apart before they could become dangerously entangled, regaining his height and balance. In periphery, he saw people scattering, frantic to get under cover.

Dréoteth came straight on again, dominant and aggressive, colliding hard with slashing claws and twists of their sinuous bodies. He rolled the other dragon over and caught one of the wings, rendering it useless. They plunged to earth, the green-eyed dragon's roars loud enough to drown out all other sound from below. Freefalling, Dréoteth fought for supremacy, forcing the other to land first.

Crashing into the ground behind a cluster of buildings, Dréoteth heard and felt one of his opponent's wings snap. The other dragon was substantially injured, a gust of fire-breath whooshing out its mouth. Dréoteth latched onto the throat with crushing force just beneath the hinge of the jaw. The scales were thick but not as hard as the rest of the body, and though his teeth sank in, he had to claw its head at a hideous, upward angle until the bones cracked.

The sound ricocheted through the night and the dragon beneath him went limp.

The fight had been fast, furious and brutal.

Dréoteth's superior fighting skill made it a quick kill. The scent of dragon-blood filled the air. A few hapless citizens, desperate to get away from the fire, ran into sight beyond one of the buildings. He saw their wide, shocked eyes, and before they could really get a fix on him, he roared, spewing a stream of flame into the sky to encourage them to flee.

They did, with fresh cries of alarm and screams that ripped through the night. He knew they were not sure exactly what they'd seen, other than large shapes and a pillar of fire they couldn't explain. Perhaps they thought his roar came from the fury of the flames instead of a beast.

These were how the rumors of dragons had been born throughout time. Snippets and glimpses of shadows and fire.

He could not leave the body for others to find, or he would be forced to torch the entire town, leaving no one alive. Any surviving citizens that found an intact dragon body would raise the alarm and call for a hunt. Their well-deserved paranoia would spread like a disease, until groups of men were formed to do nothing more than that—drive them into extinction.

Hooking his talons into the dragon, he lurched into the air with the dead in tow, slicing away from the town with the intent to dump the dragon in a far off place where men would never find it.

To his right, *another* eruption of flame distracted and surprised him.

It came from the direction of Meyer and Beth's farm.

Two. There were *two* dragons.

Dréoteth let go of the one he carried and it crashed through the trees, landing with a shattering thump.

That this second one was strafing so close to Meyer's domain enraged him and he closed the distance with impressive speed, releasing a deafening roar to get its attention. He wanted it to focus on him and the oncoming fight instead of Meyer and Beth's home.

The swerve of its head his direction came just before Dréoteth slammed into it on the side, sending them both sprawling through the air. Tails lashed and teeth snapped, their wings flapping hard enough to bend the treetops below. Twisting and rolling, they flew apart, winging away only to make tight circles and come dead on, eyes glowing, the promise of death in every furious roar.

The midair impact shook the night, bodies violently twisting and twining. Tumbling through the sky over Meyer's intact house and an empty field, Dréoteth went for the throat.

He latched on, but had the wrong angle.

His wings beat shallow and quick, keeping them aloft.

Shoving the dragon away, Dréoteth gained height and cut an impossibly small circle, attacking before the other could recover. Their roars sounded like the loudest thunder, startling birds from trees a half-mile away.

From behind the clouds, the moon sliced into view. Just for a moment, their scales glittered iridescently, black to blue.

The other dragon rolled onto its back just as Dréoteth attacked, knocking their balance off. Overcompensating, Dréoteth found one of his wings pinned. Arching sharply, he freed it, using a talon to shred the leathery wing of his brethren. Tangled, they plummeted toward earth.

Fire that the dragon had spewed burned several acres and part of the trees. The flames illuminated their serpentine tangle and they crashed hard into the middle of the field.

Somewhere, a woman screamed.

The dragon beneath him, stunned, snapped teeth at his throat. Dréoteth jammed his claws into the mouth and broke the jaw with a sickening snap. The body went limp beneath him and he ripped the throat out, growling his victory around scales and dragon-blood.

He bled, too, in thick, black rivers, but he was not mortally wounded. Already energy rerouted itself to start the careful, precise process of knitting his injuries and stemming the blood loss. Dragons had an incredible capacity to heal.

Amidst the death and destruction, blood and fire, another scent broke over Dréoteth's senses.

The scent of a human. A man he knew well.

He swung his sleek, wedge-shaped head around, blue eyes narrowed. His wings, partially extended, made him look bigger. Threatening.

Meyer stood between his home and his burning fields.

They stared at each other for long minutes,

dragon and man.

Dréoteth had killed two of his own for this man and his family.

For *humans*.

For all of Faulkon's Cross?

He knew that Meyer could make the shape of him out against the night, lit by flames. They were close enough for direct eye contact and there was no hiding what he was, or what lay dead beneath him.

Now there was a witness, and witnesses had to die.

Beyond Meyer, from the direction of the house, he heard a small voice.

"Daddy, *Daddy!*"

Meyer's son.

Beth screamed again, herding the kids back inside the homestead.

Dréoteth never looked away from Meyer, and Meyer never looked away from the dragon.

Suddenly, Dréoteth hooked his claws into the dead dragon and lurched with effort up into the air. He roared at Meyer, discouraging him, winging away with his prize into the night.

Meyer stood, transfixed, watching the dragons – yes, they were dragons—fight over his land. Fire blazed somewhere behind them and all he could hope was that it ran out of fuel before his entire farm was lost.

At that moment however, he thought of nothing but the surreal creatures in a duel to the death. He met the blue gaze of the victor across the landscape and something familiar sang through his gut.

Why would he feel familiar with a creature as foreign as this?

Rumor had persisted for ages about dragons but

Meyer had always dismissed it as folly.

Of course.

They were not *real.*

Now that he faced them down, he discovered that they *were* real and that he felt like he knew something more about them than he was supposed to. At least the one who snarled and roared as it hefted the dead dragon into the air.

Meyer turned and ran to the barn, his mind busy with the danger and the niggling feeling that there was something he was overlooking. Taking a shovel, he brought it with him over the fields, running toward the streak of fire across the ground. It was there he spent the rest of the night, digging a swath through the grain and grass, trying to cut the fire off before it hit the trees closer to the house. He'd already lost half his crop. He didn't want to lose his family too.

Dragons. *Dragons.* These were the creatures that burned Malmsbury to the ground. *They* had killed countless friends and loved ones and now they were back for Faulkon's Cross.

Just as he'd feared.

Breathing hard and sweating, he swore silent revenge as he frantically shoveled a firebreak that probably wouldn't stop the flames from ravaging everything he owned.

This time, though, his family *would* get out alive.

Thea watched the attacks from the cover of the trees. Fawn colored breeches, soft as butter, and a multi-colored tunic over a deep green shirt helped her blend into the foliage. To cover her pale head, she'd drawn the hood up on the tunic.

Crouching in the underbrush, she observed the creatures that had so ruthlessly gutted her beloved

Malmsbury. Two dragons, not one, belched fire from their terrible maws, setting houses instantly aflame. They were at opposite ends of town, lost against the black sky until streaks of fire gave their positions away.

Instead of running in fear, she watched for weaknesses, learning their moves, their technique. There would be no retreat to the hollow, no tears and sobbing for what had been lost.

Maturity made her stronger, wiser.

These dragons had killed her family, her friends.

They had almost killed her.

Only a fool would not respect their awesome, violent power but she planned to use it to her advantage.

Somehow.

Revenge glittered in her green eyes, and her fingers tightened around the curve in her bow. It had been a gift from the witches of the hollow, carved with runes and strange symbols. The arrows, the special ones she reserved for the dragon, were tipped in poison and magically enhanced. She'd cast the magic herself with Phae looking proudly on.

She was surprised to see more than one. The strategies she had envisioned and planned over the years would have to be expanded to include this second beast.

Into her middle teens, she was lanky and tall but graceful. Her chin curved delicately, shaded by a light cleft, her jaw well pronounced and strong. High cheek bones and almond shaped, pale green eyes were offset by silvery blonde hair—hair that was drawn back and hidden so she wouldn't stand out in the shadows like a sore thumb.

On an oak branch not far above her head, a hawk lurked. It watched with a sharp set of beady eyes, turning this way and that to get better angles on the dragons and the girl below. It was the only bird within a half-mile radius of the volatile confrontation.

Thea had trained him herself with Phae's help. Over time, she had grown to love and trust her feathered friend. They became inseparable over the years and last summer, Thea had started sending him on scouting missions for the dragon. She knew Phae and the others were aware—one couldn't keep secrets from them—but they never chastised her or forbade her to seek information.

It was how she'd ended up here, tonight, watching both beasts wreak their terrible havoc.

Shockingly, *another* dragon joined the fray. She drew in a startled breath.

Three dragons. How many more? Were they all converging here and now, to destroy Faulkon's Cross as they'd done to Malmsbury?

Anger burned like acid in her chest.

"Jasper," Thea whispered. "Follow them."

Through the limbs and leaves, she glanced at the hawk. The bird tilted its head to the side and down. Jasper lifted off and tracked the dragons when they disappeared past the treetops.

Before she could move, two of them reappeared and clashed hard mid-air. They were not far from her hiding spot. Illumination from the flames glinted off their writhing, black scaled bodies. She watched their tapered, wicked tails lash and thrash as they clawed and rolled.

A gout of flame erupted from one dragon's mouth, searing a path straight down toward the ground—straight toward *her.*

There was no time to move. No time to run.

Screaming, she put her hands up over her head like it might help ward off the flames. Ten feet in front of her, tree trunks exploding from the heat and ferocity, the fire seemed to hit an invisible bubble where she crouched, passing harmlessly over and around her.

A deafening roar filled her ears and heat threatened to blister her tender skin. Sweat popped out on her brow, her throat. Everywhere.

It was hard to breathe.

The fire raged around her, scorching everything in her immediate vicinity.

Peering upward, past the lick and lap of flames that never touched her, she saw the enormous, sinuous bodies of the dragons locked and tumbling like a meteor about to impact earth.

The flames sucked away with the passing of the dragons. She panted and wheezed and wrenched a look behind her.

Miriette, Phae and Claudine stood there amidst the flames, untouched. They made a surreal vision standing there so calm while the inferno swept around them, *over* them.

Phae followed the dragons with her eyes. A rare expression of distaste and annoyance crossed her face. Thea knew she was displeased with the beasts. Phae glanced back and inclined her head subtly, granting permission like she knew exactly what Thea wanted to do. After all these years of raising her, it was a good bet she did.

Eugenia was in town somewhere, possibly hurt and afraid, and Thea wanted to help her as much as she wanted to help the citizens of Faulkon's Cross. She could not take on two dragons engaged in their own surprising war, but she *could* offer aid to those in need.

With the scent of burning flesh and foliage in the air, Thea broke cover and ran through the charred forest for town. It mattered little that Faulkon's Cross wasn't her home. The people needed help and the children would need comforting and food and shelter.

Eugenia was undoubtedly suffering a setback—or perhaps the plucky woman was doing the same thing Thea intended to do herself.

Thea's insides hurt to think anything might have happened to her.

Bracing the bow on her back, she dashed into the melee, immediately finding several injured people and many buildings on fire worth trying to save.

She helped as many as she could. The survivor's injuries were grievous, hideous, and more than once Thea had to swallow down her anger and indignation. Her clothes became covered in soot and stains, her skin streaked red and black. Every moment she expected to hear a different kind of roar rather than the kind the fire made, feel talons digging into her back. With every injury, every death, her resolve grew stronger. She worked side by side with strangers to save their lives, their homes.

She understood their shock and their fury personally. And when they asked her name, she always gave it honestly, selflessly.

Thea.

She knew the witches were in the forest, watching over her and helping in their own way. Small fires suddenly doused as if someone beat them down with a blanket and a woman's skirts, on fire, seemed to burn themselves out before it ever touched her skin.

It made Thea bolder, knowing her guardians were close by.

She found Eugenia, cheeks streaked with dirt, red hair a mess, helping a woman with a burn on her leg to the shelter of the church. They hugged briefly in relief, their gazes saying more in that moment than words ever could. Together they supported the lady into the confines of the Lord's house, where others were gathering to start sorting food, blankets and water amongst the survivors.

Whispers and rumors raged even now about the cause of the destruction.

An hour before dawn, leaving Eugenia with the collection of frightened townspeople, she hopped aboard a wagon filled with men heading out to a farm where someone needed aid. Flames threatened to engulf the house and all of the crops. She wanted to help save it, spare the home for the farmer and the family he most likely had.

It made her feel better to be busy, to be doing something, but in the back of her mind she processed the clues she'd gleaned from the attacks and filed them away to pick apart later.

Thea smeared her wrist against her cheek, spreading soot unknowingly to her hairline. Someone passed a water skin and she drank thirstily. The one she carried with her she'd passed out to a woman and her four terrified children.

Exhausted and sore, she rested on the bumpy ride, accepting an apple from a grungy man to her right. They communicated with tired but determined smiles and nods, saving every ounce of energy for the work yet to come.

"Bloody saints, look at that."

The wagon came to a stop just behind the charming farmhouse. Beyond, where the fields stretched toward the trees, a man feverishly dug a trench that did not look nearly wide or long enough to stop the flames that licked ever closer to a large patch of dry grass. Dark haired, his shirt stained with sweat and dirt, he shoveled wads of earth out of his way.

"Grab the tools, men!" The driver, as grimy and

dirty as the rest of them, jumped to the ground and tied the horses to the stump of a tree.

Thea snagged a shovel and climbed down, ready to battle the blaze. She left her bow and arrows in the back of the wagon, trusting that they would still be there when she returned. The tunic she'd peeled off long hours before when she felt too overheated to function, her undershirt unbecomingly stained.

The sun, barely over the horizon, cast its rays through the trees and into the sky.

She wondered, briefly, what happened to the dragons.

Why had one been attacking another?

Questions rolled through her mind as she trotted between one burly man and the next. Diligently, she picked a spot and started shoveling. Lean and strong, she bent to her task with a vengeance. Her years with the witches had honed both her body and her mind.

She saw the farmer, his face covered with days old, dark whiskers, greet them all with a curt nod and get right back to work. There wasn't one second to spare.

They all felt it, that desperate need to get a handle on the fire before it was too late. Thea knew the witches were in the woods, watching.

Helping.

No one else noticed how the breeze whipped up against a specific tree already aflame, keeping it from jumping to another. It happened again on the ground, the fire contained to a patch of dry grass. Every time it tried to jump to fresh kindling, the wind switched, blowing it gently the other way.

Thea had not yet learned those specific talents, the scope a little beyond her ability.

The men never complained about her doing what traditionally was considered men's work, but brought her water and gave her breaks in rotating turns with the rest of them.

The farmer's wife, Bethany she learned, brought food and refreshments. She had a rambunctious little boy at her side, a toddler in her arms, and looked to be due any day with another. Thea was slightly concerned for *her,* so obviously far along in her pregnancy, and every time she saw the woman come waddling out with trays, she dropped her shovel to run and help. Bethany thanked her sweetly every time.

They worked tirelessly, the ragtag group of men and one lone girl, pressing through fits of exhaustion and muscle cramps.

Night came, and night went.

Shortly before noon the following day, they trapped the fire in half of a field and it burned into nothing more than smoldering embers that they doused with buckets of well water. Just to make sure.

A rousing cheer went up, and Thea thrust the shovel into the air in triumph. They'd done it.

They'd beaten the fire.

The dragons would not claim *this* land, *this* farm.

They would not claim these precious lives.

She jabbed the spade into the ground and started to unravel the bloody cloths tied around her blistered palms. Many of the men had done the same sometime during the night. She heard the farmer start making his rounds, shaking hands and giving thanks.

His shirt soaked through with sweat, hands grimy and bleeding from hours on the handle of the shovel, he approached the pale blonde girl and bowed when he stood before her. Thea eyed the silver shot through at the temples of his dark hair. Scruffy and grimy, he had kind eyes and a ready smile.

She had a vague sense of déjà vu.

"My lady," he said. "I thank you for your tireless help. You, along with the others, have saved my farm."

Thea nodded, smiling tiredly. Her pale hair, lacking the hood to cover and protect it, had come completely out of its braid and sat in mutinous disarray around her face. She was as dirty as he was and didn't care. She doubted he did, either. "You are most welcome. I am Thea."

She saw something spark in the man's eyes.

"Thea of Malmsbury?" He asked.

He startled her, and she inclined her head. Wary. "... aye. How do you know that?"

"We thought everyone had perished! Look how you have grown. You were but a child the night Malmsbury burned. Trimble and I, do you recall Trimble? We went into the woods that day and returned to find it aflame. I am Meyer Lyon."

Thea regarded the aging but still strong, well built man before her. He was imposing in size, his clothing well made but that of a farmer. She did not recall him specifically. But the name Trimble rang many bells.

Ah *yes.*

Trimble she had dreams about. His face was forever locked into her memory, like the dreams of the dragons. Always with Trimble it was the same dream; standing in a meadow of ash, handing up a little yellow flower. The yellow was the only color, the one vivid spot amidst a landscape of gray.

"I remember Mister Trimble. Vaguely, but I do remember," she finally said. "I am sorry that I do not remember you."

Meyer smiled and brushed away her apology with a flick of his hand.

"Did your mother make it? Eugenia Bailey survived the attack as well. She lives here in Faulkon's Cross. What a striking coincidence," Meyer said.

Thea felt a stab of old pain, regarding her mother. She shook her head. "She did not make it."

The redhead had told them all about the initial trip into Faulkon's Cross so many years ago, but not who she encountered. Eugenia had since moved into the town with Miriette's blessing, coming back to visit the hollow in the spring and summer months.

Apparently, Eugenia hadn't told the men about her, that she had also survived, and she guessed it was a protective measure.

"I am glad to hear she made it out alive," she said of Bailey, taking the safe route with her reply. She hesitated to mention Phae or Miriette or any of the others. Meyer seemed too distracted with the current tragedy to put the pieces of the puzzle together regarding her and Eugenia.

"I am sorry to hear about your family. I remember them and liked them well," he said. "Let us hope Miss Bailey was uninjured in this latest attack. Forgive me, I must see to my wife and my children. I hope we can speak again in better circumstances."

He started to retreat, an exhausted smile on his face, but Thea stopped him with a question.

"Mister Lyon. Do you know what caused these tragedies?"

He paused and glanced back at her over the broad, dirty span of a shoulder. There was something guarded in his gaze, as if he absolutely knew what had caused them but didn't want to say.

Thea took a step closer to him, closing the distance just a little so she could lower her voice.

"It was the dragons, was it not?"

The twitch that raced through his frame was

answer enough for Thea. *She* knew, but was uncertain until now that he did.

She nodded even though he did not verbally agree, taking initiative. "I was in the woods and saw the first one attack. I—"

"Meyer! Meyer, you must come at once. Jeremy has fallen ill." Bethany called from a short distance away, her tone urgent.

Meyer set a fatherly hand upon Thea's thin shoulder, his gaze sweeping back from his wife to the young woman before him. He spoke low and conspiratorial. "Meet me at the Copper Kettle tomorrow at noon. We will speak then, aye?"

"Aye, tomorrow." Thea said. She watched as he turned and jogged toward the farmhouse where Bethany had already disappeared, sending up a silent prayer that the child would be all right.

Thea climbed into the wagon with the men. She stretched her legs out and rested her back against a hay bale.

She needed sleep and a meeting with Phae. Jasper should have returned by now with news. The wagon rumbled along the bumpy road, ferrying the exhausted men and one pale blonde woman back to town.

"He has tracked the dragon to its lair," Claudine said. She was a different kind of pale than Thea, with strawberry blonde hair caught back in twists and loops at the back of her head. Her fair skin had not a blemish on it and her green eyes, moss green compared to Thea's own pale version, were kind. Like the rest of the women in the hollow, Claudine little resembled the ugly witches of lore.

She led Thea through the forest as dusk gave way to the first shadows of evening. They were within easy walking distance of Faulkon's Cross.

Startled, Thea glanced aside and up at Claudine, who stood a head taller. "Where?"

"It is not close. Look, I have something to show you."

Tired and bruised and aching, Thea felt a surge of energy at the thought of surprising the dragon in its lair. Claudine gestured just ahead of them between the trunks of two huge trees. A shallow, dry creek bed covered with layers of dirt, pine needles and old maple leaves, ran through the middle of a small clearing.

At first Thea didn't understand what she was supposed to be seeing, and glanced around, then up at Claudine. She adjusted the bow and arrows, which she had retrieved before leaving Meyer's farm, on her back.

The witch smiled and continued to stare around them.

Thea left her side and wandered into the creek bed. Had there been water trickling through, it would have only come to just past her ankles. Above them, the limbs of the trees tangled to create a cool canopy. Vines slithered and twined around boughs and over the roots on the ground.

Suddenly, she smiled.

"This is like the hollow in Malmsbury!"

Claudine nodded, and stepped forward. She took the girls battered hand and led her toward a patch of ivy—and then right into a cottage. It opened up into a gentle living area with a chaise and chairs and a small round table tucked near the windows. The furniture was made of curling, twisting strands of thick and thin wood. The women manipulated nature, which always worked with them instead of against them, to suit their needs. As all the other cottages, the décor ranged from soft pastels to natural earth tones and gnarled beams from the trees along the domed ceiling. Miriette and Phae had fashioned all the cushions by hand. The floors were made of smooth stone.

"We thought we should have something closer to Faulkon's Cross now that Eugenia is living here permanently," Phae said from the doorway behind them.

"Soon, Thea, we know that you too will want to live amongst the citizens of town. We would rather be close to you and Eugenia than farther away, no matter that we can cut the travel time down with magic," Claudine added.

"It's lovely! I do not ever think I will move back into town, like Eugenia." Thea said, examining the rooms closely. She did so with a loss of the utter exuberance she'd had as a child and more with the keen curiosity of a blossoming woman. The door to her room had her name engraved upon it, surrounded by carvings of hawks, fuzzy rabbits and deer. It opened into a quaint space with plain but pretty dressers, a desk against the wall in front of the window, and a closet for clothes. A domed ceiling sported white beams instead of brown. Some of the childish things, such as the rocking horse, were replaced with new arrows, a new cloak and other hunting items.

Claudine and Phae traded a knowing look at Thea's remark.

"Perhaps you will remain with us, darling, and that suits us well. All of your things are still at the other cottage and you may bring whatever you wish here," Phae said from the bedroom doorway. Claudine hovered just behind her.

Thea faced them, pleased. "Thank you. I know Eugenia will be ecstatic.

"Yes, she will. She has expressed a desire to have

us closer," Phae said. "I believe she has met a young man she is smitten with."

"There is something else, Thea. We bid you not to seek out the dragons just now, dearling," Phae said, apparently aware that she had come into knowledge that Jasper had discovered the lair.

"But what if it leaves? What if I wait and it comes back and burns the whole town? So many people could die. Meyer Lyon knows about the dragons, too. I mean to speak with him tomorrow about it." Thea admitted.

"Then speak with Meyer Lyon, learn more now that you know where they are. We gave you this gift to use wisely, not to rush in and find yourself in deeper trouble. You have learned much, but you are not quite ready to confront two dragons at a time," Claudine added.

"You cannot deny that my archery skills are second to none," Thea said. She looked between the witches and followed them into the living area.

Darkness finished cloaking the land, making it impossible to see much past the windows. Even though the weather was mild, a small fire blazed in the hearth.

"Second to *none,*" Phae said, smiling. "Will you not wait just a little while, Thea? Let us find out all we can before you go."

Thea knew they were right. All she wanted to do was bathe, eat and fall into a deep sleep. She was no good without Jasper, without any energy.

"I will speak with Meyer tomorrow if they do not return tonight to finish what they started," she said.

Claudine smiled and rested a pale, calm hand on her shoulder. "Rest this evening, child, in case you need your strength tomorrow. You have been hard at work all day."

Thea gave both women very affectionate hugs and

kisses to their cheeks. They were her surrogate mothers and she loved them.

She retreated to her new room and closed the door to begin the process of unwinding. An hour later, washed and fed and tucked into her warm bed, she stared up at the ceiling, waiting for sleep. She was so tired that her eyelids burned.

The dragon—no the dragons—were almost in her grasp.

Soon, soon, they would feel the bite of her arrows.

And she would say, "Do you remember me, dragon? I am Thea..."

The forest, the forest, the forest.

Too dark to really see.

Branches cut at her face and leaves thrashed as the wind ripped through them.

She knew it was close.

The dragon.

Every fierce flap of its wings teased the treetops.

It was trying to flush her from cover and into the open. She could see the meadow beyond the thick trunks with bark so rough it shredded her skin off.

Running, running, zig-zagging her way anywhere but into the open. It felt like a maze, though after twenty feet there always seemed to be nowhere to go but out. Out –there-, where it would get her. She felt a gust of hot breath down her nape and swallowed a scream.

Left.

Right.

Left.

Suddenly she burst into the open.

No!

Spinning around, she stumbled and put an arm up to ward off an attack.

It swooped down for the kill, blue eyes glowing in the gloom. It looked even more sinister here with ambient moonlight turning the black scales blue. Its talons were wickedly sharp and extended.

For her.

It opened its mouth—look at those teeth!-- with the intent to snap right down over her body.

She felt the hot sting of its gaseous breath... and suddenly there were no dragons, no fire.

She stood before a much taller man, dark hair brushing against his masculine jaw, staring down at her intently. They were in the midst of an exchange, fingers brushing as he grasped her dandelion and straightened.

His eyes were blue, so blue.

It was the only color in the gray meadow, under the gray sky.

They narrowed, almost becoming slits. Reptilian.

She knew those eyes.

Around the dainty stem of the weed, his fingers grew claws.

He took a step closer; she took one in retreat.

Her spine became ice, drip-dripping numbness into her legs, which didn't want to run when she told them to.

He laughed, a growling, gravelly sound. His hand shot out to grab her--

"Thea! Thea, it is just another bad dream, child. Wake up," Phae said.

Thea snapped awake, sitting up with her breath in her throat. "It is here! It was going to—"

"Shh. It is not going to get you. It was just another dream child. You know I will not let it get you." Phae pulled her close with one arm and kissed her temple.

"I hate them," she whispered.

"I know, dearling. It is over now though. Go back to sleep. You will not be troubled by another nightmare tonight."

Thea knew the witch would make it so.

She hugged her and sank back down into the covers, shuddering.

"Sleep sweet," Phae said, rising to leave. She closed the door quietly behind her.

Thea knew there was something the dreams were trying to tell her. Every time she woke up, she could not recall exactly what it was. The most prominent images were those of red, of fire, of blue eyes and black scales. Sometimes it was the lone dandelion, a vivid spot of yellow in an ashen landscape.

She wondered if her dreams were prophetic, signaling her demise. Perhaps she would *not* win the duel between beast and human after all. Claudine had a gift to see into the future—maybe she should ask her to look.

The thought was scarier than she wanted to admit. She decided that she would let fate play out as it would without foreknowledge of the outcome, fearing it would affect her abilities should she discover the dragon, the hateful dragon, won in the end.

$$Chapter\ Nine$$

The Copper Kettle, a busy tavern at the far end of the main street, had a distinct sign hanging from the eaves: white and square with copper colored lettering set at a slant. Just over the door, someone had hammered a copper kettle into the wall, positioned with the spout down like it might pour tea over the heads of the patrons. The building had been spared in the attack, showing no signs of damage or fire.

Thea found it with ease, and after a curious glance at the awkward kettle, she stepped inside. She was a half hour early. Brushing a hand nervously down the front of her clothes—fawn breeches, a snowy linen shirt and a sage green tunic belted below her breasts-- she scanned the faces of the patrons and then to the available seating.

She took a seat at a table out of the way, the scrape of the rickety chair on the floor making her wince. Several men crowded against a long bar glanced her way.

She pretended not to notice.

This was her first foray into society besides her rush to aid yesterday, and her memories of interactions were thin and vague.

A rotund keeper, jovial with a gap toothed smile, arrived to take her order.

"Wha' it be, missy?"

"Warm cider, aye?" She smiled, looking up. The scent of raw meat, blood, crusty bread, ale and sweat assaulted her senses.

He grinned wider, exposing crooked teeth around the gap in the front. His apron wore streaks and smears of food and fluid, some of which she did not want to contemplate.

Thea fished out a few dented coins and dropped them into his meaty palm. He winked and waddled behind the counter, efficient, she noticed, even with his attention scattered about.

A moment later, he sent a young boy, perhaps his son, out with her drink. Large gray eyes peered past a thick fringe of dark bangs, the tray lifted with her mug sitting in the middle.

Thea plucked it up. "Thank yo—"

He fled, cheeks flushed, before she could finish.

Thea thought he was about the same age she was when the dragons attacked Malmsbury. At least he had been spared the horror of watching his mother, or father, be murdered by the dragon.

Turning her mind from those dark thoughts, she sipped the cider and returned to observing the other patrons. Most of them were men ranging from middle age to boys entering adolescence.

The attack left them rattled. Their mood volleyed between relief to be alive and outraged fury. She heard several mention a hunt and a few others making plans for a trap.

A group of angry farmers came in with their

cheeks flushed and curses on their tongues, their peasant shirts dirty from hours of dragging burnt debris from one place to another. The process of rebuilding and salvaging was in full swing.

Some weren't sure exactly what it was that had attacked them, and rumors grew wildly, taking on a life of their own.

Thea could have put them out of their misery but she didn't want to draw that kind of attention to herself. Phae had cautioned her to mind her tongue. If they ever caught wind that she knew where its lair was, they wouldn't ever let her rest until she told them where.

She understood their anxiety but she had spent too many years nurturing revenge and had plans of her own. Still, she considered sending Jasper to follow any hunting parties.

The door to the tavern opened, distracting her.

Meyer stepped in and was immediately accosted with cheers and back slaps. He received no less than three toasts from haggard looking men at the bar. Thea observed it all with a small smile. Meyer seemed to be quite a popular, respected man. Gone were the stained, grimy clothes he'd worn to save his farm. In their place were beige breeches, a linen shirt of white and a vest of brown with the buttons carelessly undone down the front. His knee-high boots were polished to a shine.

When he saw her he headed her way and took a seat opposite her at the table.

"Miss Thea, I hope I did not keep you waiting long," he said. He rested his elbows on the table and regarded her across it.

Thea shook her head and set her mug down. "No, Mister Lyon. I hope your son is well?"

"Meyer, please," he corrected.

"Meyer," Thea said.

"He is doing better this morning, thank you. I—" Meyer paused, leaning forward a little, as if he meant to begin delving into the topic that brought them both here. A rowdy outburst of fresh anger from the farmers at the bar seemed to change his mind.

Instead, he said, "I believe we should walk."

She met his eyes and read his expression perfectly. She nodded and finished her cider. The chair scraped against the floorboards when she stood up.

She winced again, feeling several pairs of eyes turn their way.

Unlike other women, she was unencumbered by wide skirts and feminine baubles but still managed to draw her share of attention. Automatically, she reached back to adjust her bow—when she realized she'd left it and her quiver of arrows hidden in the woods.

"Of course, Meyer," she said, eager to be gone.

Meyer pushed up from his seat and escorted her to the door. He held it open above her head and stepped out in her wake. She heard him exhale and wondered if he was relieved.

Overhead the sun shone bright and high. Spring was in the air, the vague scent of flowers and green grasses tickling the senses. She breathed deep and fell into step beside the tall, broad man, clasping her hands studiously behind her.

They were a striking pair; Meyer distinguished and graying at the temples but still imposing and strong, and Thea, thin with pale hair in soft waves down her back.

Several people glanced their way.

Meyer met them all with a nod or a small smile or a wave of his hand, quelling any rumors that might have started with his easygoing attitude. Certainly, if they were about an affair, he wouldn't be parading her right down the center of town.

Impressed with his handling of it, she glanced aside, studying his profile.

When they were well out of earshot of anyone, he began again.

"I was unaware that anyone else had seen them until you spoke of it," he said.

"It was by sheer chance that I happened to be near," she said. It was only a little white lie. Not quite chance, but the complicated workings of the witches and their animal spies. "I believe these are the creatures that took the town of Malmsbury."

Meyer met her eyes as she spoke. "After all the fire and the ravaging, I believe you may be right. I do not know where they come from, or why they chose these towns to attack. Have you any idea?" he asked.

"I do not know where they come from. One attacked my mother and I quite viciously. As you know, I survived and she did not. I have not seen any until now since that fateful night," she said.

"Do other people know of them? Are we the only ones who have seen?" he asked.

Meyer seemed like he was groping blindly in the dark. Like it felt surreal to be speaking so openly of dragons. Mythical beasts he always thought existed only in someone else's imagination.

Thea commiserated with his tone, his confusion, even if she had known about their existence longer than he.

"I have little contact with the people of this village, or any other," Thea admitted. "I am aware, as are a few ladies that I live with."

"So you come from another town? Which? It canno—"

"In the woods. We live –"

"The witches," he said. Meyer stared curiously at her, but did not break his stride.

"Aye," Thea said, finding no reason to lie. It would not help her cause later. "They saved me. Raised me." She looked away from his face. People bustled everywhere at once, their steps brisk, determined. A group of them, dressed all in black, somberly walked toward the graveyard.

"I fear that they, or the one, will be back to erase this town from the earth," he said.

"I know where the dragon's lair is, Meyer," she whispered. Thea stopped walking and faced him, her eyes serious.

Meyer looked utterly shocked and stopped as well. They were at the far end of the main street, the end that had not been scorched by dragon breath and fire.

"Where and how do you know where the lair is?"

"A hawk, Mister Lyon. I have a hawk that tracked the dragon and I know it will lead me back there."

"Lead *you?*" Meyer reared his head back a little, aghast. "You do not intend to seek it out, do you?"

She forced herself to go slow. It was tempting to rush through the whole explanation, all her plans. She resisted that folly and schooled her expression so that it didn't appear that she was anxious to do battle with the beasts. She was unaware how her pale eyes gleamed, how her delicate jaw tensed expectantly.

"Yes, actually, I do. I *am.* This is why I wished to speak with you when I realized you had seen it, too. Perhaps we may both go and finish the dragon before it finishes us," she said.

Thea couldn't decipher the complicated stare that Meyer leveled on her. She read shock well enough, but there was something else. Something deeper.

"You surprise me," he admitted. "I expected to be

approached by a flock of men—"

"Instead of a young girl? I am old enough and strong enough to fight."

"I do not doubt your heart or your desire," he said. "But the other men and I might become distracted over your safety—"

"Other men? No, Meyer, I mean for us to go alone."

Once more, he looked taken aback.

"Two people against *that?* I do not think for a moment they will be easy to kill. What if we follow it to its lair, and there are ten more waiting?" He shifted uneasily and crossed his arms over his chest.

Thoughtful, she frowned. "True, I only planned for one. My arrows will kill them if I hit the right target—they are vulnerable here." She used an index finger to thrust up under her own chin at the juncture where it connected to her throat.

"You have come somewhat prepared, my lady," Meyer said. He did not mock her, but sounded slightly impressed. He gestured for them to start walking.

Thea noticed several people were staring. She turned and walked with him, contemplating the dragons and their lair.

"I also have a little magic at my disposal," she confessed.

Meyer glanced at her, a thick brow arched. "Will it protect you—us—from their fire? We will have to get very close for your arrow to pierce its throat."

"Yes. I have spent years training for this," she said, meeting his gaze. "Maybe we will get lucky and find it asleep."

She had visions of sneaking upon one only to be incinerated after it tricked them and lured them in. She shuddered.

Meyer considered her plan of action seriously. She knew by his intent look and the muscle that kept flexing in his whiskered jaw.

"If we are going to do this," he said. "We must be quick about a plan. See what you can learn about their lair—entrances and exits and the like-- and meet me at the well tomorrow at sunrise."

Thea nodded; they had drawn water from the well on his land to fight the fire. It was well away from prying eyes. And ears.

"Aye, tomorrow then."

Meyer set a fatherly hand on her shoulder and squeezed before pivoting away in another direction.

Thea stood on the side of the road and watched him go. She trusted him to be discreet about the secrets she had shared and had faith in his strength.

If there was a man in Malmsbury capable of helping her, it was Meyer Lyon.

Thea retreated to the woods. She found her hidden bow and arrows and slung them onto her back, making haste for the hollow.

With any luck, she would have a sketchy map of the lair come meeting time.

On his way home, Meyer spoke to no one. The clop of hooves on the dirt road acted like a metronome, luring him into trance-like contemplation. His horse snorted and tossed its head.

When he passed the spot where Trimble had stepped from the forest however, he reined the steed to a stop. The animal turned a tight circle in place, as if there was some lingering, upsetting scent clinging to the leaves.

He wondered why the man hadn't aged, where he

had been all these years. He wondered what Nehemiah Trimble *wasn't* saying. Maybe the man knew the witch women, and they had gifted him with some special herb – he cut that ridiculous thought off before he could finish it.

Trimble, taking herbs to preserve his youth. Ludicrous.

He tried to calm his mount, but the horse wasn't having it. They made another pirouette, the hooves kicking up dust.

Meyer spurred the anxious animal on toward the farm, taking the last stretch of road at a gallop. He found Bethany and his two sons inside, and after stopping to kiss each on the forehead, he headed out to the fields with a shovel in hand. There were many hours left in the day and he meant to use every one wisely. He needed to think about Thea's plan, needed time to come up with a few of his own. It felt like suicide to go alone with a young girl to kill a dragon. Her heart was in the right place, he had no doubt, but he felt this specific task required strength in numbers.

Still, his need for revenge, and to keep his family safe, was strong. If he did not kill it first, he feared it would come back again and he was not willing to risk Bethany or his children. He was not without cunning of his own and he had always been a strong adversary in a fight.

She had magic and the witches on her side.

He glanced at the spot he'd seen the dragon standing over its kill, and suddenly his steps veered that direction. On the way, he jabbed his shovel into the ground. It stuck straight up, the handle smeared with dried blood.

The ground looked as if many men had chipped away at the surface with blades. He had the impression of scales grinding into the dirt during the battle. Blots of darkness were blood, he knew, and he avoided stepping on it. Maybe it would melt his boots, like the fire-melted bodies.

He grunted at his unusual thoughts.

A spade shape, black and as wide as his palm, thrust up out of the earth. He stopped and crouched down, eyeing it from every angle.

Not blood.

Not a root brought to the surface by claws.

He reached out to snag it and yank. The earth yielded its prize rather easy. Thick as his finger, the underside was smooth while the surface felt mildly rough. He tried to bend it, using two hands, and could not flex it at all.

Like a piece of armor, he thought.

Stronger.

And black as sin.

He grunted, watching the sunlight gleam off the surface. An iridescent blue glittered over the black and he recalled seeing the same thing during the fight. It was a weaker color here, he noted. It had been much more brilliant under the moon.

He stood and pushed the scale into the pocket of his breeches. It barely fit.

The rest of the afternoon he continued the laborious process of renewal and salvation. While he bent his back to manual labor, his thoughts strayed to dragons, lairs, and a pale haired girl determined to take them all on.

Chapter Ten

Fall
Dragons, my Brethren

An impossible event has occurred. Several impossible events, if I take the time to be honest. The most important being that not one but two of my brethren have attacked Faulkon's Cross on the same night. We do not work in tandem, or as teams. We also do not live communally or in packs, but alone in separate parts of the world. Yet these two were undoubtedly working together.

The odds of them attacking on the same eve accidentally is too much to be believed. I was forced to kill them both, which is not shocking in itself.

What is disturbing is that I chose to do so over men. Human men. They were not challenging me or threatening my existence, or perhaps would not have, until I did so first.

The second dragon was burning Meyer's lands, intending to take his home, and it enraged me. It prompted me to act in ways I normally would not.

Meyer, Meyer.

I saw him two days ago and I could see the shock on his face when he realized I had not aged a day. It is too blatant to be missed. I went so far to tell him that there were things he did not understand about me, and to confirm that what his eyes told him were true. I have not aged since he last saw me. At least I have not aged in appearance. The actual years are counted among the many I have been alive, but dragon years are much different than human years in terms of lifespan, and I will never look older than I do now.

I will never obtain the gray that Meyer has in his hair, nor will my face grow lined and creased with wrinkles. I allowed him to live and walked away leaving him wondering after my secrets.

To tell him what I am is cause for his demise. Humans have too much trouble keeping information like that to themselves no matter how hard they try. First he will tell his wife, and she will tell her mother, and so on until the entire town is caught up in the tale. Then they will gather and hunt me.

It is very possible they will hunt me anyway, or hunt the dragon, for Meyer saw us in the field. After all the care I have taken to spare him, he saw. He stared hard, gaze locked with mine, and I wonder. I wonder.

But no. He could not place me with the beast in the field. I gave him no cause to think I was not human, only that I had not aged and there are many other superstitious reasons for that. Humans thrive on tales and lore. I know he will come up with something that has nothing to do with my beast.

I admit that it makes me uncomfortable to think about the consequences if he has guessed what I truly am.

I close for now to heal and repair my wounds.

Dréoteth

Dréoteth healed at a rate that normal men did not. All of his kind did. He spent the entire next day curled in his cave, tail looped over his snout, expending energy to fix his wounds. It started on the inside, knitting and fusing, working outward through bone and flesh until he was utterly healed. The process was not a comfortable one, especially on the deepest cuts, and took many hours to complete.

His sleep was not the deep, endless sleep that might keep him under for eons, but a dozing that left his slanted eyes half slit. He was not afraid that someone might find him, for dragons chose their lairs well; he did not slip under because the niggling uncertainty about Meyer would not let him. It festered, the doubt, until he rose from his fitful rest with a grunt of acrid breath.

Several scales that had been pushed from his tough skin lay scattered over the ground.

The transformation from dragon to man took mere seconds. His nose retracted, like his talons, the tail disappearing while the scales seemed to melt into his skin. He stretched his arms and his spine, gauging the level of soreness from healing.

He felt renewed and complete.

After a brief dive into the pool, he changed into a pair of simple buckskin breeches and a loose shirt. Clothes were not necessary, not even his preference, but he had learned over time that it was better to be prepared when living anywhere in the vicinity of humans. He took the sloping tunnel up toward the surface, dragging a hand through the damp strands of his straight hair. The dull thud of his boots resonated off the jagged walls.

He surfaced into a mild spring night, the breeze buffeting in from the east. The scent of oak and pine and spruce mingled with tiny wildflowers that grew around the edges of the clearing.

His thoughts inadvertently swerved from Meyer and Beth to his brethren. For what had to be the hundredth time, he puzzled over why they had been hunting together. The answers were not any clearer today. They had been alpha males in their prime, younger and less experienced in battle. That detail had cost them their lives.

"I saw you speaking with a human."

Dréoteth only became aware he was not alone when a voice bled out of the night somewhere behind him. Whirling, he did not take a defensive posture so much as one that resembled a man about to take a large leap.

A woman, with hair so pale he could only call it white, stood twenty feet behind him.

He knew she was one of *them* immediately.

Two dragons attacking in tandem earlier and now a female alone.

Something was very wrong here.

He did not speak, staring hard and breathing deep to take in her scent. Diminutive, she was much shorter than he was with a deceptively fragile build. He knew her to be stronger than she looked; all females were. They were also cunning and clever and often times unpredictable.

They had to be to survive.

"Are you going to stand there and say nothing?" she asked.

"What would you have me say?" Dréoteth said.

He listened for sounds of others in the woods around them, drew in several more breaths for scents that did not match her own.

"I am alone," she said, as if she'd read his thoughts. "Alone now that you have killed both of my companions."

Dréoteth could not fathom her reply. He wore his surprise openly, just for a moment.

"Your companions?" he repeated. The question was rhetorical. "Do you mean to say the three of you traveled here together?"

She inclined her head a fraction, no more. Draped in loose material of deep burgundy and dark green, it only enhanced her paleness and the striking clarity of her skin.

"I know what you are thinking," she said. "But things in the world beyond us have changed. Out there," she swept a hand toward the west. "Humans have built towns bigger than you can imagine. In some places, they have built right to the edges of the forest and their numbers have grown too great to safely accommodate us. To survive, we have been forced to leave for less and less populated areas."

Dréoteth eased a little as he listened, the forest quiet around them.

"There are still vast amounts of earth where no humans tread at all," he argued. "And why here? Why this town?"

"One of the others remembered it from years ago. We all returned together, not realizing you were here."

"Yes. I recall the attack years before." He regarded the pale woman with an astute, critical gaze. "I would never have believed that our kind agreed to travel together and hunt together had I not seen it with my own eyes."

"It becomes necessity if you want to survive," she said. "I am Feline." It was a sign of respect and the burgeoning edge of trust to give him her name.

Fel-een. Dréoteth rolled her name through his

mind, trying to decide if it fit.

He looked openly skeptical over her announcement and almost sneered in derision at the thought of being dependent on another, even one of his own, for survival. Wisdom held his antagonism in check.

"Feline. I am Dréoteth."

They stood there, faced off against one another, tension thick on the air while they went through these preliminary and necessary introductions.

"Dréoteth," she said, as if affixing his name in her memory. "What were you and the human speaking about?" Her blunt question lacked direct accusation, but there was something in her pale eyes that set him on edge.

"That is none of your business, Feline. My suggestion to you is that you keep heading east. Go several hundred miles away from here lest you find yourself in the same condition as your companions." He all but spat the last word. The more he spoke, the more he thought about the entire thing, the more hostile he became.

Feline arched a blonde brow at the increasing vehemence in his demeanor, but she did not back down. "It is my business to know if he is aware you are a dragon."

"No, I believe that is *my* business," he said. He took one small, aggressive step toward her.

Feline held her ground. Her eyes narrowed, body strung tight with alertness.

"Dréoteth, I am not your enemy. If you do not believe what I say, that we, you and I, *must* work together then come with me and I will show you. With your own eyes you will understand that things are not as they used to be."

"Go with you where? Back to the bigger cities that you say you fled out of fear?" His upper lip curled in disdain, but he did not advance another step. "If you are so weak, Feline, then you deserve your own death. I am perfectly capable, as you can see, of surviving without you."

Her lips tightened into a thin, disapproving line. "You should not be so quick to dismiss what you do not understand. After all, *two* other males were hunting and traveling with me. It is a small matter of verification," she said. "There is nothing holding you here."

He saw her question as a challenge, to prove that this town, this land, these humans meant nothing to him. He took another threatening step forward, fingers flexing in and out of loose fists. At the same time, he found himself curious over her insistence that the world was all but coming to an end simply because men were building and expanding.

A sneer rippled across his lip. "Very well, Feline. Let us go see this *threat* that has you in such a snit." Quicker to anger with one of his own kind for the danger they posed, he nevertheless proceeded with caution around her. Females were known for their vicious skill, especially when they thought they had something to gain. She did not intimidate him, but he respected her possible power. That she thought she needed him to survive knocked her down the danger scale quite a bit, however.

There was none of the protectiveness for her that he had seen Meyer and other male humans display over their women. He felt no sympathy for her, *their,* supposed plight. Belatedly, he also realized she was right about the land. There *was* nothing for him here any longer.

Dragons did not covet material things—although he had his collection of paintings and books-- in the same way humans did, nor did they own homes or tie themselves down to one piece of property for life.

In their eyes, the entire earth was their playground.

Their hunting ground.

Dragons often traveled far and wide, rarely settling for extended periods unless they fell into their deep sleep. He had been in one place far, far too long.

He wasn't sure what to make of the knowing gleam in her eyes when he agreed. She seemed satisfied, but didn't gloat.

"When shall we go?" He posed the question expansively, sardonically.

"Tonight, if you are – tonight, yes," she said. She clasped her hands demurely before her, apparently unbothered by his aggression other than to keep watch and make sure he didn't suddenly attack her.

"Let us go then. Show me how civilization has changed." He gestured mockingly toward the open pasture behind him.

Feline stood there for a second at his gesture, staring at his eyes, before turning to make her way past him.

It was a brazen move to give him her back.

She moved like all the rest of them did, graceful and sleek, unhindered by the confines of her clothing. Feline did not seem as wary of him as he was of her, which was suspect and cause for consideration. He had little time to wonder over it.

He followed, stalking in her wake, a grim grin on his mouth.

She took a few running steps and launched off the ground with a powerful leap, her body erupting into her dragon.

He was shocked to discover that she was not black, like the rest of them. But *white*. The moon glimmered off the pearly scales, tinting them blue. Smaller than him by a few feet, thinner through the body, she had a slender snout and wicked, curved spikes along her spine.

There could be no question that she was of his bloodline.

He leapt into the air right on her heels. His wings snapped out sharply, winging him away from the earth. Ahead, she seemed to glow against the dark sky, and he wondered at her ability to have stayed alive this long. He counted on his coloring to blend in, to keep his true form hidden from humans.

Her coloring, the whole situation, distracted him as they climbed above the treetops, heading west.

When they passed over the edge of town, he cut a look down toward Meyer's farm. The fire was out, his scorched fields counting for less than half of what he owned. The homestead stood intact.

Blowing hot hair out his nostrils, he said a silent good bye to the only human he'd ever befriended. Even if he came back to Faulkon's Cross, which did not seem likely, he did not intend to ever see Meyer again.

Chapter Eleven

They flew for five nights, seeking shelter during the daytime. Dréoteth had never hunted with another dragon and when Feline suggested it early on their first morning, before the sun came up, he almost denied her. The gnawing hunger drove him into the skies with her and he took to the hunt with a vengeance.

He was wary that first hour, suspicious and cautious. She flushed the game from the bush with impressive skill, maneuvering sleek and sharp through the mist.

They herded their prey into dead ends and ate their kill with a respectful distance between them. She never encroached upon his, and he never infringed on her own.

By the third evening, he looked forward to their hunting hour. He learned new strategies with a companion, and quickly anticipated her habits.

He knew when she meant to corner the prey, and when she wanted to pluck it straight off the flat plain of a meadow. She was a very amiable partner, which both intrigued and annoyed him.

He didn't want her to make it so comfortable to co-exist.

It wasn't supposed to be this way.

Not only was she a competitive hunter, he found that she was intelligent and well read with interesting views on humans.

"So after you killed the Lords of the land, you invaded their homes and their libraries to learn about them?" He asked.

It was just before dawn on their fifth day. In their human guises, they had taken shelter in a cliff with a large cavern that stretched far back into the rock, giving them both the room they needed. Their bellies were sated with food.

Feline nodded. "Yes. It is better than going among them in daylight, although I have done so when I was forced to."

"What about their servants and family?" He asked, curious.

"If they had any, and I could not get around them, then I hunted them until they were gone," she said.

Sitting near the wall, she had her arms looped loosely around her updrawn knees. She watched him with an avid but veiled expression. The pale strands of her hair had been twisted and looped away from her face.

"What was the longest you stayed in their homes? Or castles?" Dréoteth asked.

"Oh, I never lived there. I only took what books or maps or papers I wanted and left."

"Why not?"

Feline arched a slim brow. "Do I need to explain? Surely you know the answer to that."

"You could have read ten times the books, gained ten times the knowledge if you had stayed under their roof for a few weeks instead of taking what you could carry and leave," he said. Dréoteth sat against the other wall but with his long legs stretched out before him.

"You sound like you know from experience."

"I have never targeted certain men for their homes and libraries, no," he admitted. But he had for paintings. And then, "But I did live amidst them for a time."

He watched surprise and the beginnings of loathing start to cross her face.

"You lived *among* them? As one of them?" Feline seemed incredulous.

Dréoteth appeared impervious to it, as if he was above any chiding. "Yes. I spent years studying them, learning their posture and language and habits. It tested my control more times than not," he said, wry at the admission.

Mild amusement replaced her incredulousness.

"That is the first time I have heard one of our kind willingly living among humans. What was it like? How did you not go on killing sprees?"

"Sometimes it was difficult, I confess. But I discovered that there were a few humans worth knowing, if only so I could learn things one can never learn in books, no matter how well written."

Feline considered that for long minutes, teeth scraping light over her lower lip. "And you became closer to a few of them than you ever thought possible, am I right? Such as that man I saw you speaking with that you refused to tell me about."

He lacked the open hostility that he'd shown the first day, replacing it with arrogant languor. As if he didn't really care what she thought of his interactions with men. He did, and he didn't.

"Yes," he finally said. "If there was ever a human I could term as a 'friend', that man would be it. We have known each other a long time in human terms." Dréoteth watched her face very closely for reaction, or revulsion, or any other emotion that might suggest she thought him insane.

The silence stretched out again while they regarded one another, and he swore he could almost hear her mind spinning through the implications. On the one hand it amused him and entertained him; dragons loved risk and chance and he'd certainly opened himself up for it here.

Feline showed no derision, but she was very obviously dubious of his decisions. The smooth plane of her brow wrinkled with consternation. Instead of mocking him, she asked a pertinent, intuitive question.

"What if he would have accidentally discovered you?"

"Then I would have ended his life and went on with my own." Dréoteth put conviction and nonchalance behind every word; whether or not he really would have was an issue he refused to contemplate at the moment.

"They are only a means to an end, Feline." He thought that was a lie, but his face never gave him away.

"Perhaps. What was it like then? Living as one of them?" She sat forward, bending her spine comfortably.

"They make life much harder than they need to. Over the smallest, trivial details they fight and bicker. What means nothing to us means everything to them. While I loathe it," he admitted. "I also find it morbidly fascinating. At times, I have wondered how far humans will allow these inconsequential things to divert them from what is important."

"Sleep for five hundred years or so," she said. "And you will find out." Feline smiled, the first real smile since she'd met him. It was a subdued but genuine expression, one that reflected in her eyes as well as on her lips. "Or maybe you will get a better idea when you see what I have brought you to see."

Dréoteth inclined his head in agreement, and very likely, that exact thing would come to pass. It was how they'd spent the last several centuries, after all. "Let us rest then, and tonight we will take a look at the city."

She seemed like she might ask him another question, but unraveled her arms from around her knees and curled down on the stone. At her back, the uneven wall curved up and over them, just high enough for them to stand upright without slouching. It was not big enough to accommodate their size as dragons.

Although they slept in the same cave, they stayed as far away from each other as physically possible. He stretched out on his back, one arm behind his head, boots crossed at the ankle. There was enough space between them that he would hear her moving should she risk the unthinkable and attack him. His slumber was light, his body still and slack.

He woke only once and knew without looking that she stared at him through the gloom.

He didn't ask what was on her mind.

They emerged into a tepid evening just as the sun sank below the horizon. He felt no effects from his battles when he stretched, the muscles flexing powerfully. Anxious to get airborne, he glanced over to see her staring at him, apparently trying to read his thoughts.

He gave her nothing but a nod and they took to the air.

Flanking her in the sky, they flew over an orange

and red landscape. Shadows chased the color over the terrain like hungry dogs, replacing it first with the gray of twilight and then the black of night.

Less than fifteen minutes later, the first glittering lights of a city came into view. Sparse at the edges where farmland made large squares against the earth, he picked out random homes nestled near trees and thin, snaking rivers. The clusters of light grew thicker and closer together, until it seemed to explode in every direction as far as he could see.

They did not fly directly over the middle of the sprawling city for fear of being seen. Even on the fringes, he was shocked at the growth. The sharp spires of white churches were like beacons, drawing his gaze.

The darkness did not hinder their sight. From this height, he could easily see people bustling along the roads.

So many.

They were *everywhere.*

He thought four or five thousand people must live here.

Four or five *thousand!*

He was used to villages and shires that housed several hundred to a thousand, at the most.

A thousand people had seemed crowded and suffocating.

Faulkon's Cross, a town he'd once thought immense, looked positively tiny next to this.

Feline winged by the city, instead of circling it. He wanted to examine this monstrosity below more closely, but he kept pace with her, cutting through the night swift and sinuous.

Orchards replaced the roads and buildings. He could smell the different scents of the blooming fruit trees. Newly sown crop made square scars of farmland that eventually replaced the hectic array of lights and roads.

On the outskirts again, he tore his gaze off the last flicker of candlelight in a house window and looked ahead.

There must be something else she wanted him to see.

They hadn't gone more than a mile before he saw pinpricks of light amidst the trees.

More homes.

Another town.

Not a large as the last one but much larger than Faulkon's Cross. In dragon terms, these towns were right on top of each other. The amount of land they took up was staggering, and he was aware that hunting here would be a challenge.

They were so close that he wondered if it was an extension of the last one. He split off from Feline, curving through the sky to the left, and gained altitude. The colder air didn't affect him at all; his scales and his tough skin deflected it. From this vantage, he could see that there was enough of a break between the two towns, a swath of unrelenting black that separated them.

It was not even a half-day ride away.

He circled around again, back to the right. Down below and ahead, he saw more lights. The entire earth seemed dotted with humans living in clusters with only small spaces between cities.

For the first time ever, he felt disoriented, as if he'd flown into a massive spider web of which there was no easy escape.

Every direction he turned, lights.

More lights.

Homes, churches, buildings.

People.

An *incredible* amount of people.

Feline cruised in and flanked him on his right,

pale against the inky sky.

Blowing out a disturbed breath through his nose, he caught a darting look from her glowing eyes and they shared an understanding that transcended words.

She was right.

Humans had advanced much more steadily and more prolifically than he could have imagined.

They made enormous circles around the perimeter of the towns. They seemed never ending.

Before they could get too embroiled in the thick of it, they cut away, back toward the cavern. He had been prepared to mock Feline for what he was sure had been extreme exaggeration, but as they coasted onto the broad ledge and bled back into their human guise, he realized he *was* disturbed over the situation, and while he was not of the exact mindset as she, he better understood her.

He drug a hand through his black hair and followed her into the mouth of the cave.

"So many," he said. "So *many* of them."

"Yes," she said.

He felt her assessing gaze on him. Her point had been roundly made.

Reaching the far wall, she put her back to it and slid down to the ground, leaving her knees bent. She watched him, calm and collected.

Dréoteth paced, agitated.

"This is just the beginning," she said. "There are more. Many more. Of course there are vast expanses yet without a human in sight for miles, but the game is limited there, the land sometimes inhospitable. Small shires and villages are in shorter supply than we realize."

"I see that," he said. Dréoteth glanced between her and the ground as he made a circuit of the cave. "What of the other dragons? I know there must be more. Where have they gone?"

"Some of them have been hunted. One of my companions, Excelion, heard that a band of humans killed three of our kind. Dragon hunters, out to annihilate us."

"Mmm." Dréoteth began to speak but the words ended in a growl. He might not live in communities with his brethren, but he would band together with them to avoid becoming extinct altogether.

"We have been forced deeper and deeper into the wilderness and mountains and valleys. In another thousand years, Dréoteth, we will be living in arid deserts and the arctic because there will be little place left to hide," she said. Feline sounded annoyed that humans might drive them to that point, but also vaguely worried.

"A thousand years? No, half that, I think." Pivoting on the sole of a boot, he stalked his side of the cave, gaze cast down in thought. "Fear not, Feline. There will always be places on this earth that man will not dare to tread. They may not be precisely *perfect* hunting grounds for us, but we will adapt. As we always have."

Their process of adaptation had been agonizingly slow however over the centuries with so much open land.

"I will not live in the arctic," she said. "As ironic as it is, seeing that I would blend in better with my coloring, I loathe that climate on a constant basis."

"Your coloring, yes," he said, changing the subject even though his mind was still on what he had witnessed. "You are the first white I have ever seen. My mother told me stories before she left me, but that is all."

"As far as I know, I am the only white alive. If there is another, it has not come to my attention."

"It makes things more difficult in crowded areas,"

he noted.

Feline inclined her head. *Yes.*

"If we gathered all the dragons together, we could find and attack the smallest villages, working our way toward the bigger ones. But then they will only hunt us harder and smarter," he said, thinking aloud. "I know many areas near Malmsbury and Faulkon's Cross that have miles upon miles of untouched land. Closer to the mountains where you found me and beyond them. I know of only one small village nestled within the pass. Otherwise, humans have traveled through there but few have made their homes. It is too isolated. We might take a stand in a place like that, but eventually they will come."

For a dragon, hundreds of years went by in a snap. They had learned to think ahead in decades and centuries instead of months and years.

"It leaves us little choice but to do the latter, and deal with them when they finally do encroach upon our territory," Feline said, frowning. That choice did not seem to sit well with her.

They had few others.

Dréoteth paused and glanced down at her. A shank of raven black hair threatened to cover one eye. "Does it? What if we integrate into their societies? What if we do what I have been doing for years?"

Immediately, Feline scowled and curled her upper lip in distaste. "You cannot be serious."

"Can I not?" He arched a brow. "It will take less than a thousand years for humans to encroach to the point that it makes it dangerous for us to survive. We need hundreds of miles of untouched land and deep caverns to sleep where they cannot find us. Perhaps it is better to live on their fringes, learning their ways even better and more efficiently than I have, so that we may be overlooked."

"I loathe the idea," she said. It was clear in her tone that she meant every word.

"Do you enjoy living?" Dréoteth mocked her.

"Of course I do. We are *dragons*. We bow to no one. We shall not be forced to integrate to live. This is our world as much as it is theirs." Feline, agitated, rose to her feet and paced on the other side of the cavern.

"You are right, except I do not see it as bowing to a greater power. I view it as ensuring our survival. In my eyes, it is the smart choice. It also allows us to know what they are thinking and planning. If there is to be a hunt, we will know about it and be able to take steps to prevent our own death. Sometimes," he said. "It is best to hide in plain sight."

"I have never attempted to move amongst their society other than on the fringes. What if one angered me and I snapped?"

"It is a thing I have had to deal with for decades." Dréoteth might have laughed at the irony of the conversation he was having if the situation wasn't so dire. "You must take one step at a time, and lucky for you, you have me here to guide you. That is, if you wish it."

Feline snapped a look across the gloomy cavern, illuminated only by a thin thread of moonlight spilling in from the mouth of the cave. Neither of them had any trouble seeing the other and would not have even if there were no light at all.

"It is much for me to think on," she said at length.

"Yes, for me as well. We will have to choose another town anyway because Meyer knows there is something different about me. A pity. I had made great inroads, such as they were, in Faulkon's Cross," Dréoteth said.

"Kill him. He is only one man," she suggested.

Dréoteth shot Feline a hard, quelling look that would have made most women and many men shrink in fear. "He deserves better than death."

"Then make him one of us," she said. It was not a suggestion she put forth lightly.

Dréoteth hissed his surprise at her audacity. Some dragons would have killed her outright for the suggestion. His gaze narrowed upon her and they both paced through the cavern, keeping on opposite sides of some invisible divide.

"Impossible. I cannot believe you suggested such a thing," he said.

"It is not impossible." She started to correct him, like he didn't know the ways of their kind.

"I *know* it can physically be done," he hissed again, his tongue lashing against his teeth. "I will not subject him to that kind of change. When in recent history has anyone even attempted it? Not in the past several centuries that I am aware."

"Not for ages," Feline admitted. She paused to put her back to the wall, but did not sink down to sit. "It is better than his death," she pointed out.

"Meyer does not have to die. He does not know what I am. Whatever he has seen will end up like all the other dragon stories of lore, either set aside as imagination or an overtired mind."

"Starting over in another town will not be difficult if you have gained experience doing so these past years. We will chose another, then," she said, changing the subject.

He had the distinct impression that she was trying hard not to anger him. So far as he knew, he was the only remaining dragon she had come into contact with other than the two he'd killed in Faulkon's Cross.

"Yes. Perhaps we should take a hard look at that

small village nestled in the mountains. I do not recall the name at the moment," he said. He eyed her speculatively. "There is an immense cavern in the range you found me near. It will serve as a good shelter until we scout out that village." Dréoteth decided to accept this new turn of events in the manner of one used to change that sometimes came quickly. He tried to adjust to the thought that Feline would be part of his existence for the foreseeable future. Immediately a suffocating feeling swept through him and he tried to dismiss it.

Perhaps he would grow accustomed to her over the years.

"Tomorrow evening we will head back." Feline accepted his authority without argument. If she had any other thoughts about Meyer, she did not say.

Deep in contemplation, they settled down to sleep.

Dréoteth lay awake, staring at the ceiling. Unwittingly, he thought about the ancient ritual that he'd heard about once upon a time. It was so far back in his life that he could barely recall the process. It wasn't especially *difficult,* but the chant had to be precise and the words were hazy in his memory.

Why was he even thinking about it? The concept would never come to pass. Feline had planted a seed and he was annoyed that he spent any time at all contemplating it.

Converting a human was rarely ever done, and others did not condone it. The risks were extraordinary, if they even survived. He knew of two cases, stories passed down from the ancients, and both had died.

Meyer had a family and children. He had another on the way. There was no reason to contemplate it further.

The words were better forgotten, left to rot with the corpses of their ancestors in the far reaches of the earth.

On the trip back to his mountain, he became pensive and quiet. Feline did not encourage conversation, and sometimes he wondered what she was thinking. Was he as decent a companion as the other two dragons? Did she secretly resent him for killing them? He never caught her looking at him with anything other than curiosity.

But he wondered.

During the day, they slept. At night, they hunted together and ate apart. Several times he knew she wanted to dip into conversation, but he discouraged it by keeping his eyes averted.

The constant companionship started to wear on his patience. She did nothing to incite him; he was simply unused to someone spending so much time in his personal space.

He didn't know how humans did it night after night, day after day. Just when he thought he'd grown used to her presence and to accept the changes they needed to make, he felt stifled and suffocated by them.

Such a contradictory creature.

Relief swept through him when the terrain became familiar. At the very edges of Faulkon's Cross, they flew over several farms on their way toward the mountain. Night cloaked the land, providing them cover. They landed in the same meadow, touching down with a final flap of their wings. Talons clutched the earth once, and in the next step they were human feet, trotting forward through the momentum.

Dréoteth spent a moment in the field to breathe

deeply, seeking scents that did not belong.

Deer.

Rabbits.

Fox.

No humans or dragons had passed through since they'd been gone. He led Feline in through the hidden mouth at the base of the mountain, stalking through the winding tunnel with the bare thud of his boots on rock.

He felt her behind him, following at a cautious distance. Her steps were quieter than his, as if she was wary to make too much noise in his domain. Dragons never shared their lairs and he knew she must be as uncomfortable as he was. This was different than sleeping on opposite sides of random caves; this was his sanctuary. Without being told, he knew that her other two companions, now dead, had slept in their own caverns and caves.

He didn't intend on sharing his, either.

The tunnel opened into the great interior, and he glanced back to see what she thought. A strange luminescence gave the large space an ethereal glow. The soothing burble of water that bled from a vein in the rock smelled fresh and inviting. He saw her brow arch and knew she was impressed with all this particular cavern had to offer. Most had no freshwater pools.

"You have found yourself a jewel of a lair," she said.

She went over to the pool, crouching down to scoop a palm full of water. Tasting it, she made a small sound of approval and rose to finish her examination of his space.

"It suits," he said, understating it.

The look she gave him said it more than suited.

When she passed by the flat ground of his resting place, she gave it a wide berth. His scent was strongest there.

While she explored, he walked over to the stone pedestal where his journal sat. With a deft motion of his hand, the tome disappeared into a crevice in the rock. There it would stay, unharmed and safe, until he chose to retrieve it. He owned nothing else that he worried about her seeing, or taking, beyond the large number of oil paintings against the walls. He could do nothing about them now.

A few clothes sat folded on another outcropping; shirts, breeches, boots. The serviceable collection lacked any fancy jackets, vests or other adornment. She left those alone, barely glancing at them.

The stacks of paintings against the wall earned a disturbed frown from her. Standing before them all, hands clasped demurely behind the small of her back, she stared at the depictions like they were an affront, unworthy to be in her presence.

Before she could ask—and he knew she eventually would—he said, "There is a separate cavern through that tunnel." He did not need to point it out; the opening yawned wide and broad at the other end.

Feline turned from the paintings, clearly disapproving of their presence within his domain, and glanced at him like she had gleaned all his dirtiest secrets on her way to the mouth of the tunnel. Her hair glinted silver in the strange light of the cave.

He felt the weight of all the words she did not say when their eyes met and in his typical, arrogant way, refused to explain his collection. He bristled under her blunt stare, ready to growl a warning when she disappeared into the shadow of the snaking corridor.

Listening to her fading footsteps, he stripped off his tunic and undershirt. He took the time to fold them instead of throw them haphazardly on the floor. His boots came next, landing with dull thumps on the uneven rock. He left the breeches on out of deference.

He knew the terrain she explored intimately: the tunnel with three turns, smooth walls, and veins of minerals deposited into a modest cavern with a soaring ceiling and space enough to accommodate their dragon. A slithering stream of water, an offshoot from his pool, circled around a flat bit of stone for resting. Fresh air breezed through from hidden crevices and small, wispy green plants with waxy white flowers clustered around the stream from a crack in the ground.

Bits of marcasite glittered in the walls, winking in and out like distant stars.

Two more tunnels led off from there, one crawling deeper into the mountain, the other meandering its way outside. He knew she would learn every crack, every niche, every corridor, like he'd done.

If she used the other entrance, she wouldn't have to constantly traipse through his cave, a thought that appealed. It kept her close enough to keep track of, and far enough away not to smother him.

Making his way to the pool, he knelt there and cupped water in his palms to splash over his face and shoulders. He drug his fingers through his hair, dampening the dark strands, and shook it out like a dog shook its fur. Hunched forward, the teeth of his spine were prominent under his dusky skin from nape to waist.

He glanced over and saw her standing there near the corridor, staring at him. It wasn't in their nature to make smarmy 'see anything you like?' comments and he cared little that he was half naked in her presence.

"Do you think it will suit?" he asked, rising from

the edge of the pool.

"It suits me fine. I—"

"Good. Then use the other entrance and exit from now on."

Her eyes narrowed at his cool words. "I can find another lair far from here, if I am that much of an inconvenience."

"Did I say you were?"

"You did not have to," she bit back.

He was aware that his impatient, dismissive demeanor contradicted the relative ease of their travels. Moving from one extreme emotion to another were not unusual traits for dragons. She was on the verge of doing so herself. He baited her temper while he walked to a stack of books tucked between two boulders.

"You came to me for safety and protection, remember. If I find you an inconvenience, do you think it wise to complain?" He scanned the spines and plucked one from the row.

"You have a certain way of twisting things to your liking. Tomorrow evening we will fly over this village you spoke of." Her crisp retort preceded her retreat into the tunnel.

He took grim satisfaction in her withdrawal.

The evening next, Dréoteth stalked out of the mountain and into the open. Pregnant clouds hung low in the sky, bellies ready to burst, and he filled his lungs with the undeniable scent of ozone and rain. Wind gusted through the limbs in the trees, thrashing the leaves noisily together. Energized by the oncoming storm, he turned his face into the downdrafts, seeking the scents of his prey. He was anxious to hunt. Outlined against the darkness by a pale shirt and dark breeches, he made his way to the middle of the field.

He wondered if Feline expected them to hunt together from now on. He scowled and decided right then that he would not be bound by expectations.

Hers or anyone's.

Movement at the other end alerted him to Feline's presence. She must have traveled to her other lair, wherever that was, and retrieved her things. The dress, a blue so pale it was almost white, made a sharp contrast against the deep green of the forest around her. He could see, even from that distance, the darker embroidery around the scooped neckline and fitted cuffs.

He wondered whether she'd chased off the noble lady it once belonged to, or whether she'd eaten her. Either way, it fit her petite shape well.

"Will you hunt in the rain, Dréoteth?" She asked, drawing closer.

"Alone, yes," he replied. He searched her eyes for offense at his forthright declaration and found none.

"The terrain around here is rich with game," she said, letting him know that she had already gone hunting without him.

He snorted.

Perhaps they were more alike than he realized.

Meyer froze behind the thick trunk of an evergreen. It towered tall above him, the branches fanning wide and elegant. The sound of voices paused him and he strained to make out what they were saying.

A man and a woman, that much he knew. A prickle of something uneasy made the fine hairs on the back of his neck stand on end.

Maybe it was the oppressive weight in the air from the storm. In the distance, thunder rumbled ominously.

He touched the rolled map tucked into the leather belt at his hips but thought better of taking it out and opening it. He was sure he hadn't taken a wrong turn. Thea's witch friend had drawn it up and he had faith she hadn't made a mistake.

No farms or homes were located this far out from Faulkon's Cross. What were the man and woman doing out here, so close to the dragon's lair?

Branches blocked his view and another peal of thunder made it difficult to decipher their words.

He needed to get closer.

He needed to do so quietly, without alerting them, until he could get some kind of feel for what was going on here.

Stepping from behind the tree, he picked his way from one trunk to another until he had a clear shot of the field and the couple. A seasoned warrior, he knew better than to stand in plain sight. He secluded himself in a shadow and behind a thin veil of leaves.

One palm held the hilt of his sword to kept it from banging against things and making noise.

Mute shock gripped him when he realized the man was none other than Nehemiah Trimble.

He started to step from behind the tree and call out when something, perhaps bone deep self-preservation, stopped him.

He didn't recognize the woman. She was delicate and petite and quite beautiful and he was sure he wouldn't have forgotten her had they crossed paths before this.

The color of her hair alone was memorable.

Standing together, they looked like any other couple except, he noticed, they did not touch affectionately or look at each other like lovers.

Was this woman the source of Trimble's... lack of

aging? Could she be a witch, a sorceress of some power that granted him long life?

Did he really believe in those things?

A thousand different questions rioted around his mind.

The topmost being what the devil they were both doing here, so close to the dragon's lair.

Maybe they were hunting it. Maybe Trimble sought justice and hadn't wanted to involve him.

Thunder growled in the heavens, closer now. Streaks of lightning illuminated the sky, ripping through the belly of the clouds.

The first *pat-pat-pat* of rain hit the leaves above his head.

And then Trimble snapped a look *right* at him, eerily pinpointing his spot in the tree line.

Meyer knew he hadn't moved, hadn't made a sound. He'd done nothing to draw attention.

The blue—why was that so familiar?—of Nehemiah's gaze sliced across the field and locked onto his own. Struck by a severe case of déjà vu, he glanced at the woman. She stared, forthright and unafraid.

Suspicious.

He had the impression she was displeased.

"Meyer Lyon," Dréoteth called, casually stalking closer. "You needn't hide in the trees."

It sounded so blasted normal, like they were greeting each other in town on the eve of the festival instead of under a deluge at the front of a storm in a desolate clearing.

He felt foolish and stepped out from the branches, brushing them aside with a broad hand. He hadn't shaved in several days and a dark layer of whiskers lined his jaw, the mustache thick and lightly peppered with gray.

Rain sluiced over his weathered skin, dampening

his hair and the dark tunic he wore over equally dark breeches. His boots, a well-worn and favored pair, laced snug up the front to the knee.

He smiled at Trimble and the woman, one hand casually resting on the hilt of his sword.

Nothing unusual in that.

"It is always best to scout out unknown locations. I am surprised to find you here," Meyer said, careful to keep accusation from his voice.

Trimble held his gaze in a way that might have made other men uneasy. He was used to the man's unusual demeanor and didn't think more of it than that.

This was Nehemiah, not some heathen with an axe.

"Yes it is. Are you hunting deer, quail?" Dréoteth asked.

The rain came harder, a sheet of silver needles from a black sky.

It sucked Dréoteth's shirt against his skin, outlining his broad shoulders and collarbones.

Meyer glanced past him a moment to the woman. He fancied she seemed tense and either ready to run —or ready to fight.

"Miss," he said, inclining his head.

A strange, awkward pall settled around them. Meyer felt it straight to his core. He looked back at Trimble when the woman didn't so much as nod his way.

"Yes," he replied, hesitating over his answer a second too long. He glanced between them and could tell by the looks on their faces that they knew he was lying. "Looking for new quail and turkey grounds. What brings you and your companion—I am sorry Miss, I did not get your name—so far from town?" He thought he heard her hiss when he reached up to scratch his wet whiskers. Frowning, he glanced past Nehemiah who cut her off from his view with an innocuous side step.

Meyer met Trimble's eyes.

Again, he had a strong sense of déjà vu.

"Meyer Lyon, this is Feline," Dréoteth said. He did not provide a last name or any title.

Meyer grew a little annoyed. How was he supposed to meet anyone with another body in the way?

"Miss Feline," he said, going through the motions anyway.

No answer.

The night was filled with silent hostility.

"Feline has family in Summerville. We are thinking of moving there," Dréoteth said, recalling the name of the village in the mountains at the last second.

With each word, awareness built between them. The kind of awareness where people know something is wrong, that someone is lying, and that things were probably going to go badly.

Despite the deluge, Meyer's palms started to sweat. Beads of rain dripped from his hair and onto his cheeks, ran slalom through his whiskers, and fell like glittering diamonds from his jaw.

He inhaled. He exhaled.

He let the moment stretch like taffy between the fingers, unsure what kind of danger lurked here. His rational mind tried to assert that it was only Trimble, just Nehemiah the scribe, that there was nothing to fear.

His gut demanded he take out his sword and start lopping off heads.

The tension was thick enough to cut.

As if the Gods were at war, lightning blitzed the sky and thunder cracked like cannon shot, shaking the very ground they stood on.

Meyer swallowed hard and realized his grip on the hilt of his sword had tightened uncomfortably. If he glanced down, he knew the skin over his knuckles would be white.

He dared not look away from Trimble's face.

"I think you should go," Dréoteth said.

It was a warning, clear and simple.

No inexperienced youth, Meyer searched Trimble's eyes and read the warning accurately. With a curt nod, he turned on his heel and marched toward the trees. A patch of saturated ground sucked at the soles of his boots.

He had no answers, only more questions. Survival instinct kicked in sharp and hard; he held his tongue. A tingle bloomed across his skull where he felt sure Nehemiah and the lady Feline bored holes with their stares.

A hundred more feet to the forest.

Like black, wet snakes, Dréoteth's hair stuck to the sides of his neck. From the ends, rivulets of water twisted over his skin, sliding down into the soaked material of his shirt.

Tension made him aggressive, made his shoulders bunch and tighten, made his jaw flex and pulse. Inwardly dismayed at finding Meyer here, he wondered over the inevitable question: *how had he found them?*

Every scenario he came up with didn't seem plausible.

What he *did* know was that Meyer hadn't come searching for new quail and turkey hunting grounds. Without a doubt, that was a lie.

He knew it. He knew *Meyer* knew he knew it.

The downpour and whipping wind made it difficult to detect anyone else in the immediate vicinity. Were there groups of men in the woods with pitchforks and swords, ready to do battle? Had Meyer guessed who and what he was?

Why then, hadn't he pulled his weapon to attack?

Why weren't there cries of rage and shouted promises of death?

Relieved that Meyer heeded the warning, he stared at the back of the scholar's head. The swirling questions of whether he had been discovered fell away to a much more intense debate over whether to end Meyer Lyon's life.

The seconds balanced on a razor's edge, teetering uncertainly.

His beast writhed with anticipation, eons of bone deep survival instinct whispering insistently to end him while a sliver of humanity—was it really that?—stayed his hand. Like the crack of a whiplash, he processed all the dangers and the answers and the consequences against the absolute knowledge that he didn't want to.

He didn't want to end Meyer's life.

Images of Beth, round with child and two clinging to her skirts flickered across his mind. He owed her something for all the hours and days she'd spent trying to befriend him. Always gentle, kind.

She had disregarded any strangeness and accepted him for who he was, better or worse, which was more than he could say for the bastard Sean.

No, no.

He was still in control of this situation.

There were other lairs, other mountains.

When Meyer was a safe distance away, he would melt into the storm, into the darkness, and leave the entire area behind.

A leathery flap of wings and a *whoosh* of air immediately above his head ended his grim satisfaction before it could start.

Momentarily, a solid body blocked out the rain.

"Fe*line!*" His tongue carved her name like a sharp curse, cutting the syllables in two.

In her dragon, she was far too quick and powerful for him to knock off course. Gliding in, she ducked her sleek head for Meyer, who didn't realize the danger until he heard the shouting. Recoiling, he raised his arm in self-defense. Like that feeble limb might do any good against the needle teeth and the vise like jaws bearing down on him. There was no time to draw a sword.

The pale dragon snapped and missed when Meyer ducked, but her talons, wickedly sharp and deadly, dug into his sides, ripping wide gouges along his ribs. Clutching him like he was a lost toy, she drug him several feet, snapping her jaws down again; she caught his shoulder and he screamed.

From a standstill, Dréoteth crouched and launched off the ground, a roar of fury overlapping a loud *boom* of thunder. His outstretched arms turned into legs and claws, wings emerging and snapping against the weather and rain.

Feline swerved away from the trees at the last possible second, the tip of one wing scraping against branches and leaves. Too close to the ground, she struggled to maintain her death grip on the male and gain height.

Dréoteth slammed into her broadside but didn't have time to clutch and drag her as she'd done to Meyer; he pulled up at an incredible angle to avoid a collision with the trees.

Feline dropped Meyer and impacted the ground, lithely twisting and tucking one wing to prevent it from breaking. Scales, white and glossy like piano keys, became covered with mud and debris.

Meyer rolled and came to a stop on his back, momentarily stunned. A geyser of blood, red against the silver rain, spurted from a vein turned into a spigot.

Ripped off during the attack and still in its sheath, his sword lay several yards away. Useless.

Dréoteth carved a circle against the night, coming around at a tight angle, aligning his landing with Meyer's prone body. His feet touched down –dragon to human-- and he ran forward, wet hair slapping against his scalp.

He felt the earth tremble as Feline's tail smacked down. She regained her feet and heard her struggle to lift off. Her wings beat at the air, raindrops ricocheting off her muddy scales.

Landing on a knee, he put his hands directly over the gaping, raw wound in Meyer's side. Feline's talons had ripped through the layers of clothing as easily as they'd ripped through skin. Dréoteth knew the injuries were grievous, unrecoverable. He lied anyway.

"It is not that bad, Meyer Lyon. Just lay still."

The scholar, fear in his eyes, skin pale with encroaching death, feebly tried to push his hands away.

Dréoteth read the truth on Meyer's face. There were no secrets any longer.

The rain lashed down with armageddonish strength, lightning freakishly streaking in every direction. It illuminated the dark puddles collecting beneath Meyer's body, the water stained red across the rippling surface.

Meyer's life tried to pour out between the creases of his long fingers. Dréoteth pressed more firmly against the wound. He bought time only; there was no way to save Meyer Lyon now.

"Trimble, for G... god's sake man, I have a family," Meyer said, teeth chattering. "T... tell Bethany and my children that I fell in battle. Do not let them think I wandered away and left them alone."

"Dréoteth," he corrected. "I will not leave her wondering over your fate."

"D... dréoteth."

"I did not ever mean for you to find out." Dréoteth knew guilt and remorse for the first time. These foreign emotions fueled his rage and the glance he shot across the field, through the rain toward Feline, promised retribution.

She sat like a pale stone gargoyle on an outcropping over looking the clearing, wings tucked against her sides.

Waiting patiently, it seemed, for death to claim her victim.

"I would not have told anyone. We were f... friends," Meyer said.

Dréoteth glanced down at the scholar. He understood that in his feverish, dying mind, Meyer believed that to be true.

He also knew better.

He'd been there in the aftermath of the dragon attack on Malmsbury, watched Meyer grieve and suffer. Doubt and suspicion would have eroded their friendship until Meyer felt compelled, for revenge and out of fear, to kill him.

He felt a peculiar need to abolish any sins Meyer might think he committed.

"I was not the one who burned Malmsbury, but it *was* me that day in your field," he confessed. The day he'd taken two other dragons down, chosen humans over his own kind.

Meyer gasped and shuddered; his body was shutting down, beginning the final descent into death. Like a melting tallow candle, his skin appeared waxy, cold.

"... saved the.. farm," Meyer said, stuttering. He

stared at Dréoteth with glossy eyes. "T... tell B.. beth. ... the baby..."

The children. The baby. They would never know Meyer, never really understand his intelligence and fierce love of family.

All of it made sudden, irrevocable sense. Pieces of a mystery puzzle snicked into place with startling clarity. He would never truly *feel* these things the same as a human, but in this singular moment, he understood what loss really meant.

His hands left the wound and gripped Meyer's tunic up by the throat, lifting his head off the ground. Forcing the man into a startled second of lucidity.

"If you could live, Meyer, to see your children grow, with exceptional circumstances, would you decide to?" Dréoteth asked. "Would you do *anything* to return to your life, no matter what the personal cost?"

Meyer looked between Dréoteth's eyes. He wheezed, "Yes, *yes.*"

"*Anything?*"

"Yes!"

Turn him into one of us. Feline's words whispered through Dréoteth's mind.

An impossible, implausible, consideration.

Dangerous.

What was he thinking?

A man turned dragon. Unpredictable. Torn between the violent beast and the instinct to protect his family. It was almost cruel.

Dréoteth knew that Meyer would suffer confliction far greater than he himself did. Would it eventually drive him to madness?

Tick, tick, tick. The time on Meyer's life clock grew increasingly short.

Overhead, the storm raged, reaching a furious

peak. The atmosphere felt electric, the wind driving the rain sideways.

"Do it," Meyer pleaded. He could not know what he asked.

Dréoteth eased Meyer back to the ground and examined the wound. Meyer sputtered through a groan of pain while he prodded at the shredded edges of flesh. Feline's talons had ripped deep into the cavity, tearing tendons and muscle like knives through melted butter. He reached up, smearing the tips of his fingers under his own tongue; they came away slick with saliva. Before the rain could wash it away, he stuck them into the gash, swiping his spit against the sides.

From the deepest recesses of memories more ancient than his own, he pulled arcane words to the surface and wove them into a chant from a long dead language recalled in a most desperate hour.

Although his whispers could not have been heard above the rain, Feline roared in fury. The sound rattled the already rattled night.

Dréoteth watched Meyer's shocked face, read the struggle to stay conscious in the fathomless dark of his eyes. He didn't know what was happening to him —but soon there would be no escaping it.

Meyer arched on the ground, suddenly, and Dréoteth let the repeating chant fade. He took his hands, covered in blood, away from the wound. A wet, gurgling noise inched up Meyer's throat, until he was shouting and twisting through the mud and red-tinted puddles.

He looked to be in the midst of a massive seizure.

His immediate work done, Dréoteth pushed to a stand. He was soaked completely through, his clothes hanging lank and limp on his wiry body. He gave his head a quick yank, removing the clinging hair from his face. One wrist smudged sideways across his upper lip.

On the ground, Meyer howled and thrashed.

The rain tapered from a deluge to a patter, and then into silence, as if Mother Nature was wary of the strange magic taking place in the clearing.

Dréoteth slanted a stark look at Feline. She glared at the scene, tense and disbelieving.

They met and locked gazes, his posture dominant and arrogant, his mouth a grim line. The situation was quite dire, but Dréoteth refused to be baited into another hasty decision, even if he badly wanted to take to his dragon and kill her. There were more pressing issues to be concerned with.

He looked back at Meyer. The man arched and writhed in agony, his blood on fire, his muscles cramping and seizing. Cells broke down and were reconstructed, remade, reborn. Meyer's body fought the process, seeking to purge the intruders, setting the temperature of his skin to unthinkable levels.

Dréoteth remembered what his first change felt like, though being born as a dragon meant they didn't suffer like Meyer suffered now.

It went on for long, agonizing hours. He paced a slow circle around the scholar, saying nothing. Meyer wouldn't recognize anything or anyone until the master of his pain laid down the puppet strings and let the marionette sleep.

The storm abated, but thick clouds remained, roiling like a witch's brew, blotting out the moon.

Finally, not long before the sun breached the horizon, Meyer's screams abated and unconsciousness claimed him.

Chapter Twelve

Burning, burning, burning.
Deep in his lungs, couldn't breathe.
Searing pain.
Pain that radiated out through every limb, every pore.
He felt like nothing but an instrument of someone else's torture.
In his head, visions.
Dreams.
Nightmares.
Fire and heat and scorched flesh.
Chasing and hunting and running.
Babies. Sweet baby smiles.
Distorted faces, beloved faces.
Talons and death and blood and wicked teeth.

It lasted for five days.

Meyer swam in and out of consciousness, never fully surfacing. He writhed and twisted and sweated and rolled around the floor of Dréoteth's cavern, filling the space with screams.

One whole day, he slept. Curled on his side, feverish, he barely moved. Barely breathed.

Lost in delirium, he didn't know where he was, who he was, or what was happening. Incoherent mumbles meant nothing, had no shape, no discernible syllables. He smelled things that confused him, heard footsteps echoing in his mind.

Every time water touched his tongue, he realized he was parched. So thirsty he could have drunk barrels of it.

On the morning of the sixth day, his name roused him from a dead sleep. His mouth felt like a cotton ball, tongue swollen, joints aching. He must have been in an accident.

"Meyer, it is time to wake up," a voice said.

He recognized it.

Trimble.

He slit his lashes open and saw a pair of legs standing close to his head. A pair of shins, to be exact, covered in the bindings of boots. His eyesight was so acute, so sharp, that it hurt to leave them open too long.

"Meyer." Sharper, slicing through the fog.

"Mmh," Meyer said. It was half grunt, half acknowledgment.

He felt... so very strange.

"It is time to rise. Tell me how you feel."

Meyer rolled onto his back—he hurt everywhere—and discovered he was *ravenous*. His stomach growled insistently.

"I feel," he said, licking fuzziness off his teeth. "Hot. Hungry. I—what is that *smell?*"

His head felt like it was going to pop open and expel all his brains. He keened in pain, holding his palms against the sides. Memories surfaced: *rain, blood, dragons, dragons, dragons, talons and mud and agony and death.*

He became acutely aware of new hurts, new changes.

His back felt like someone had hit it repeatedly with a hammer.

"What have you done?" he whimpered, trying to hold his head together. "*What have you done?*"

"What you asked me to," Dréoteth said.

"I never asked for *this!*" His voice bellowed into the cavern.

Turning onto his other side, he retched all over the floor. Bile, bits of blood, meaty looking tissue that he could not put a name to.

He howled, writhing away from the vomit back toward the boots. Onto his knees and elbows, still holding his head.

Would you do anything to return to your life, no matter what the personal cost?

Yes.

The words came rushing in with more memories: the pale woman, a white dragon, relentless rain, roars and teeth.

Decisions.

His decision to live.

He could never have dreamed Trimb—Dréoteth would do this. –but what exactly had he done? Beaten him?

Something niggled at the back of his mind, something he refused to name. To acknowledge.

No.

No.

"It will take you a while to adjust to the changes," Dréoteth said. "The process of becoming a dragon is not an easy one."

No!

"*What have you done?*" Meyer's mind whispered

the truth of it. His senses, so startling and clear, confirmed it. He was something other than what he'd been born.

No longer a man.

No longer *just* a man.

"Focus on your children, on Bethany. On all the reasons you decided to become what you are," Dréoteth said. "I have given you a gift."

"You have given me *nothing!*"

"I have spared you death. Now, with work and effort, you will be able to see your children grow." Dréoteth sounded annoyed. "Is that not what you wanted?"

"I did not ask to become a beast! You have turned me into that thing I loathe!" Meyer choked on the irony, resting his forehead against the cool stone. Already he regretted agreeing to anything. He'd foolishly hoped for some magical intervention that would have left him the same. Meyer.

Not, not *this.*

Rage stirred in his blood, hot and demanding. It rose so quickly, so intensely, that it obliterated these few moments of lucidity and he slumped to the ground, unconscious once more.

Dréoteth strode out into the early morning sun. The field had dried out some from the deluge, leaving only small puddles in the places where the grass was spare. A family of raccoons hustled into the trees and a bird veered away from the clearing, deciding to do his hunting elsewhere.

He stretched his back, his arms, his senses extending as they always did. On the alert for the unusual or the unwanted.

For prey.

For Feline.

He had not seen her since that night and knew that she hadn't slept in the adjoining cave. A wise move, for his mood was unpredictable regarding her interference. Spending so many days watching over Meyer had cooled his fury and had allowed him to do some deep thinking on his situation.

He was still torn over what to do. Feline would be a valuable asset, at least on the field of battle, in the coming decades and centuries should man continue expanding his empire. Unless a natural disaster or a plague hit, he saw no reason why they would not.

He thought she would have severe difficulty integrating in any way into their society, as he'd done. Her actions would raise suspicions and then they would have to defend themselves, becoming outsiders and ostracized, or leave for another new town to begin again.

She emerged from the trees on the other side of the field, approaching him with wary, angry eyes. The pale dress had been exchanged for what appeared to be stable boy breeches in dark brown and a loose fitting shirt of cream that scooped along her collarbones. Her hair had been whimsically tied back in wisps and twisting strands.

He waited until she was closer to speak, his voice carrying easily even though he didn't raise it or shout.

"You had *no* right to take control of the situation like that," he said.

"Perhaps not, but you were going to allow him to retreat after seeing both our faces, and while you might feel some security in the fact that you are 'friends'," she stressed the word. "I do not. I will not pay with my life for your weakness with humans."

Her bold words infuriated him. Dréoteth closed the distance before she could flee, wrapping a strong hand around her delicate, slender throat. He stared down into her eyes, his fury barely contained.

"It is not *weakness* but curiosity," he said. "*I* very obviously have a handle on it because I still live, do I not?"

"Yes, but—"

"No," he said, cutting her off. "There are no buts and what ifs and maybes. I had plenty of time to discern the danger and act. *You* acted first and thought later."

Beneath his tight grip, her throat worked small swallows down. Her eyes were wide and sharp on his face. He dwarfed her in size and while he could have easily crushed her windpipe, he left her just enough room to breathe.

"It matters no longer. He is one of us now. Leave off, Dréoteth," she said. They were brave words, considering his anger. A small hand lifted to wrap his wrist in an effort to get him to release her.

He did so with a snap of his hand away from her skin and her fingers. But he loomed there over her, glaring, impressing upon her that she should not challenge him again. This was the way of the dragon, and especially so since he was male and she was female.

"You stretch my patience," he said, just before he turned away from her to stalk back into the cavern. His plan to spend time outside came to a grinding halt. There was too much tension. He couldn't trust her not to make an attempt on Meyer with the man weak and unconscious.

Two evenings later, after assuring himself Feline had gone off on a hunt, he went out on one of his own. He returned in short order after filling his belly, too wary of Feline's motives to leave Meyer alone for long.

Stepping into the gloomy cavern, he found Meyer gasping and rolling around on the floor, clutching at his throat.

"Take a drink from the pool, it will ease the pain," he said.

"I feel half dead," Meyer said. His voice sounded sandpaper rough. Raw.

"Shortly, you will feel more alive than you ever have."

Meyer growled, a sound not quite human.

Dréoteth watched him crawl to the pool and drink deep after gagging on the first few mouthfuls. Meyer looked better today than he had so far. His clothes were ripped and ragged and dirty, but his skin had a healthier cast and his eyes didn't look so glassy.

Standing near the rock pedestal, he met Meyer's gaze. Instinctively, he knew the man battled rage, that uncontrollable fury that gripped their kind.

"You... deceived... me!"

Dréoteth stripped out of the loose shirt he'd worn, laying it across the table, such as it was, in anticipation. He knew what was coming. Stepping away, languid and unhurried, he crossed to the wide, open area where he slept in his dragon.

"You may not appreciate what you are now, but you will. When your new child is born, you will thank me." Dréoteth, utterly confident, stood with his hands hanging at his sides.

It enraged Meyer and he rose, not without great effort, to his feet. He stood as if his spine was permanently crooked, one shoulder dipped lower than the other. His balance was precarious. A roar built in his throat and spewed into the cave, growing louder and stronger. The noise seemed to startle and galvanize him; he charged across the floor, staggering to stay upright. Red faced, with veins standing out against his skin, he looked bent on destruction.

Dréoteth expended little energy when he grasped the man by the shoulders and threw him to the ground. His balance, honed and sharp, made him especially lethal in a face-to-face fight. He growled a guttural, low warning.

Meyer landed with a crash and a grunt and then a howl of fresh pain. He rolled twice and clumsily crawled into a crouch. His dark eyes glittered. He smelled like bile, blood and urine.

"Stay down, Meyer. Stop this nonsense," Dréoteth said. "Get control of your anger. Funnel it into healing your wounds." He counseled the man like they were scholars at the School instead of beasts.

"I do not want this! End it, end *me!*"

"I will not," he said, neutral and calm.

Meyer lurched forward, reaching out for Dréoteth's throat.

Dréoteth caught him, arms wrapped around, and slammed him hard against the stone floor. He straddled Meyer's back immediately and leaned down to growl behind his head.

"Stay. Down."

Meyer started to struggle and Dréoteth cupped the back of his head with his hand. A touch of magic whispered from the elder dragon to the young one. Slowly, Meyer slumped to the floor.

Dréoteth stepped away toward the tunnel leading into the other, smaller cavern. He stopped at the entrance and listened. He heard the faint trickle of water and nothing else. No soft rustles, no gentle scrapes, no breathing. Satisfied, he stalked the long, winding tunnel back outside, into the night.

He caught air on the run, transforming from human flesh and muscle into hard scales, deadly claws and snapping teeth. His wings stirred the trees around the edges of the clearing as he climbed higher, his sharp gaze slanted down through the leaves and branches on the search for game. He flew for a while simply to enjoy the flight, the feel of his powerful dragon body, before he really applied himself to the hunt.

It only took him ten minutes to scare several deer from the underbrush and he was especially vicious when he brought two of them down; one with a cruel snap of his teeth and the other with a gouge of his talons.

He devoured one himself right there at the edge of the clearing, viciously rending it apart limb from limb, and drug the other one back across the ground. It left a bloody trail through the low grass. Just before the opening of the tunnel, he whittled down to his human form and manhandled the deer into the cavern.

It was a messy task. Usually, he did not bring his game inside, but he decided that Meyer needed to eat.

Perhaps it would improve his disposition.

He dumped the deer next to Meyer and waited for the scent of blood to rouse him.

Dréoteth stalked over to a meandering trickle of water that fed the pool and leaned in, cupping a mouthful to drink. He heard Meyer start to stir and glanced over, smearing his wet hand up along his temple and into his black hair. He shook it out, and perched upon a rock outcropping to watch.

Meyer slowly wobbled to his knees. Dirty and haggard, with dark whiskers lining his jaw, he looked a wreck. The dead deer sat right in front of him. Meyer stared first at him, then at the deer. An inhuman sound of indecision and need tore from his throat.

He knew Meyer experienced, for the first time, what *true* hunger was. At the same time, he could see the revulsion on his face. Nevertheless, Meyer fell upon the deer, ripping at the hide with his fingers and teeth. This was not the way they usually fed, but Meyer was not ready to change from a man into a dragon. At a cellular level, his body knew the difference. The physical shift took time to get used to.

Meyer found gouges that Dréoteth's claws had made and ripped them wider, gorging himself to the point he choked and gagged. Twice he vomited up what he ate but that did not stop the frenzy.

Covered in blood, Meyer fed with the hunger of a thousand men. Dréoteth said nothing, didn't attempt to slow him or give advice. This was all part of the learning experience and every dragon did it differently.

A half hour later, Meyer slouched back. He'd consumed far more meat than any man should have. Most of it turned into energy inside, fueling his recovery and allowing his mind to process things with more clarity. He looked disgusted and repulsed; he also looked sated.

"Do you feel better?" Dréoteth asked.

Meyer paused to think about the question. "Yes, a little."

"It will be better in an hour, and even better an hour after that."

Meyer seemed to consider it, breathing heavy. He no longer groaned in pain, though he winced every now and then. Sometimes he stared at his hands as if they were numb or different, flexing them in and out of loose fists.

"Is it like this for everyone?" he asked.

"No," Dréoteth replied. "Nearly all of us are born this way. Very few humans have ever been turned. You will not have every single capability that we have, not all of the magic, but most of it."

"Magic," Meyer said. He swabbed his tongue through his mouth, collecting the residue of blood. "How is this possible?"

"It is possible because I made it so," he said with a degree of arrogance.

"I have the urge to kill things," Meyer announced.

Dréoteth laughed. It had been a long time since he'd done so. "Yes. That is a part of your nature now. It is not so different than when you hunt deer and turkey, hm? It is just more... uncivilized. In time, you will learn to control your urges and not *be* controlled by them."

"Will I ever feel normal again?"

"What is normal, Meyer Lyon? You will feel empowered, strong, and invincible. You will *be* those things, although it is possible to be killed. You would be wise to avoid humans for the very near future until you learn yourself. I believe you will come to appreciate the changes."

Meyer looked doubtful. He stood up off the ground and stretched out his body. Not altogether steady on his feet, he stayed in a partial crouch and extended one arm, then the other, getting a feel for the changes.

Dréoteth observed these initial explorations curiously. "The more you use your body, the more you exercise it, the faster you will become accustomed to it," he said. "Already your mind is adjusting, accepting, realizing your new potential."

"I wish to see Bethany," Meyer said at length.

"You need time," Dréoteth said. "You are not in control of yourself or your body. It is possible that if you push yourself before you are ready, you will descend into fury and do damage to those you care for."

"I would never—"

"You *might*," Dréoteth said, cutting him off. He

did not need to speak above a murmur. "Is it worth the risk?"

Meyer flexed his thick fingers in and out and rotated his wrists. His extremities moved like they used to. There was nothing different about that. "No," he finally said.

"You must also face the fact that you will not get along with all humans any longer. We do not necessarily like them, no matter that you and I built a friendship over the years. It was the first time for me, and the last," Dréoteth confessed.

Meyer's lips thinned. "You hid it well, your dislike of me."

"You were one of the very few I did not mind being around. Tuttle, Upham. They were others."

Meyer's gaze sharpened at the memory of the fire and the devastation. "It could not have been you who set Malmsbury ablaze, for you were with me. Was it the white dragon?"

"No. Not the white. Others, like me," Dréoteth explained. "I have killed two of my brethren. One of them attempted to attack your farm."

Meyer did not need to be told why Dréoteth did so. He was quiet for long, telling minutes. "I am indebted to you for that at least. For saving the farm. Even if I cannot... cannot get back to my family, she will have the house for the children."

Meyer rubbed a hand down his face, smudging blood up into his disheveled, dirty hair. "I should clean up. The smell of the blood is enticing me, and I stink," he said.

Dréoteth never would have guessed that he might find humor in this situation. It flared briefly, and vanished. "Yes, you do. I will discard the carcass. From now, we eat *outside*. There are clothes that will probably fit you there," he said, pointing to a stack. "Until we can get you more."

Dréoteth stalked across the cave and grabbed the remains of the deer up effortlessly. In a show of dominance and complete confidence, he turned his back to Meyer—a risky thing at the moment—and started to haul it to the tunnel. He paused at the entrance, turning his head enough so that Meyer could see one of his eyes.

Just one.

"If you ever attack me again, I will kill you."

Dréoteth did not wait for an answer. He disappeared into the darkness with the deer.

Chapter Thirteen

Fall
After the Change

An unexpected thing has happened. Meyer has become one of us. I cannot recall any time I have ever had to watch a human be changed, so this is a learning experience for us both. Oh, I have heard stories, yes. I know the lore, the tales. We all do. But it is different hearing it and seeing it with your own eyes.

Meyer is handling it well so far. It has been four days since he awoke and with each one, he masters the skills of the dragon with impressive speed. I am not so surprised at that part, simply because I have seen him excel in other things in his life that are similar. Meyer is a strong man and a fast learner.

One of his issues, as with all of us, is his sudden unease for his former kind. Humans. He discussed it with me yesterday and confessed that he has had urges to seek them out and kill them.

This is not unusual. I have explained to him how it is with us, though I realize it will take him some time to understand. It is possible that he will never fully be able to control it or himself. Some humans do poorly and end up victims of stronger dragons who cannot abide them. I am teaching Meyer as we go, trying to get him to learn about his new abilities instead of focusing on the anger. It surfaces here and there and one time, he went through an entire rage that took hours to work him out of. He wanted to raid and pillage and slaughter.

He did nothing more than abuse his fists against the stone in my cavern for I would not let him leave and I did not allow him to change. Once or twice I have seen the ripple through his body, that beginning want to shift into his dragon, but I have brought him down every time. He is not ready. Not yet. His desire to see his family tears at him but I cannot and will not leave him yet to go tell Beth lies in his stead.

Feline keeps her distance while he is in this bare beginning of a new life, but soon, very soon, they will have to face off and overcome whatever ill feelings they have. Or, I should say, learn to control their desire to rip each other to shreds. She attacked Meyer, made the decision for him, and I am not sure that he would be able to control at least one attempt to kill her. Time will tell.

Tomorrow I plan to take him out in the evening and begin the lessons on hunting. I have not decided whether I will allow him to follow through with a change.

Dréoteth

"I wish to try the change." Meyer greeted Dréoteth with that news several evenings later.

Meyer had applied himself to healing, learning and accepting with more zeal and determination than Dréoteth could believe. Each and every day there had been great improvement and he saw no reason to delay with the next, inevitable step. Meyer had to learn to become what his insides and mind were already demanding he was.

Dréoteth finished lacing a boot, briskly tugging the ties. Straightening, he negligently tucked his muslin shirt into a pair of plain, brown breeches. Casual and comfortable, the way he preferred when he had to wear clothes at all. He eyed Meyer from across the cavern.

Gone were any signs of injury. Meyer looked healthy, robust. He had fed with a passion and hunger every time prey had been brought, which filled him out quite nicely after the weight he had lost during his week of unconsciousness. Black breeches, from Dréoteth's own collection, fit a bit more snug than they probably should but then Meyer had always been bigger, bulging with muscle. A simple shirt of white fit a little better.

"All right, Meyer. Let us see what you can do."

Dréoteth finished a goblet of water and set it down on the flat stone he used for writing or reading and other things of that nature. He started for the mouth of the tunnel, expecting Meyer to follow.

Meyer stalked after him, projecting a distinct aggressiveness. His steps were long and brisk, shoulders hunched slightly forward, fingers curled tight into his palms.

Dréoteth, subtle and sinister opposed to all that outward bristle, let him walk at his back. His years of experience lent him not just an air of arrogant confidence, but a supreme capability to handle whatever, and whoever, crossed his path.

They entered into the evening to find it balmy. Stars glittered bright like sparkling diamond chips all across the velvet sky, each one much more brilliant than Meyer could ever remember. He took an enormous, deep breath, pulling in fresh scents of new leaves and fresh grass and many others that were so strong and so numerous that it assaulted his senses.

Every time he came outside it was this way, and each time he enjoyed it more than the last. A low rumble rippled through his chest. Walking to the center of the clearing, he flexed his arms and back, preparing the muscles.

Dréoteth faced him and began to explain.

"The way to changing, which we all have to learn, will be more difficult for you," he said. "You will feel the heat first, a searing, burning sensation all through your body that will most likely surprise you. If you pull back, you will not change. You must allow it to continue, which will be uncomfortable the first fifty or so times until you get used to it. After the burning you will feel as if someone has grabbed your arms and legs and body and are all pulling in separate directions, like you might come apart. You will not."

Meyer detected subtle humor in the last three words. He paced around Dréoteth, listening, feeling a heat inside begin to rise. He let it, reminding himself not to panic.

"How painful will it be?" he asked.

"Very painful your first three or four times," Dréoteth said. "That will ease into something as common as breathing in the future. Think of that. Realize that these are the initial steps. Allow your body to go through the transformation no matter how awkward or how much you might want to stop it."

Meyer nodded curtly. "Is it that I concentrate? I already feel the heat, the beginnings of a burn inside."

"Yes. Concentrate. *Invite* your body to change," Dréoteth encouraged. "This also makes it easier. Or it will in subsequent transformations. Do *not* attempt to fly this first time. If you crash wrong, you may break a wing or your leg or something more permanent, like your neck."

Dragons had weaknesses just like any other animal.

Meyer continued to pace, his boots crunching over the ground, flattening the new shoots of grass in his wake. He rolled his head and sweat broke over his brow.

Dréoteth stood impassively by, in the same spot with his hands at his sides, keeping close watch as the changes started to manifest into something real.

Meyer grunted, and then growled. His pacing picked up until he was stalking in erratic circles and random patterns around the clearing, not seeming to really notice Dréoteth was there. He was totally preoccupied while the sweeping changes took hold.

He threw back his head and howled, the veins standing out on his neck. His arms and legs looked strange, the sockets bulging and stretching, the fingers growing long and sharp at the tips.

Several times the process seemed to stall with

Meyer right in the middle, his growls of agony rending the night into silence. Not one bird chirped for miles.

The pain the pain the *burning* pain. Meyer never knew such agony. It was white hot, like he'd fallen into a vat of something boiling. Somewhere in the back of his shocked mind he remembered not to fight it. His arms felt like someone had yanked them out of their sockets, and his body, his head, all grew long and deformed.

He was made of too many sleek, strange angles. The tail, the tail, my god he had a tail. It whipped at the ground, causing it to shake, and he roared hard enough that he felt a strange hissing gas shoot out his throat. Not fire, not that hot, but hot enough. It tasted odd on his tongue as well, almost sweet and smoky.

Flipping over, he gained his back feet unsteadily, tipping over again and again because he couldn't get his balance. His slanted gaze raked over a figure in the clearing – Dréoteth. Yes.

Dréoteth.

He was one of them now. Changed. A *dragon.*

He roared again, both victorious and enraged, flapping his leathery wings out into the air. The things he could smell, the things he could hear. Everything around him was a hunting ground.

A killing field.

Yes. He *owned* it all.

Wobbly steps brought him around the spacious meadow while he got used to this body, this *thing* that was both him and not him. His connection to anything human was so very minimal right now.

He snapped his jaws again at the air, at nothing. Testing.

He had never felt such power. He never wanted it to end.

"Meyer," Dréoteth said. The name sounded like the strike of a hammer on an anvil.

The dragon, his scales black as midnight with that surreal blue sheen, looked around at its name.

Its former name.

It was not Meyer any longer.

"Change back," Dréoteth said.

Meyer roared, ill content with the command.

"You must take it slow. Do not over extend yourself. Tomorrow we will come back and do it again."

The dragon, still wobbly and shaky, growled in protest. He realized, belatedly, that he didn't know *how* to change back. That was a lesson he had not learned.

Almost before the thought could complete itself, he concentrated in the same way he'd become a dragon, to become a man again. It did not happen immediately, and it was less painful than before, but finally, after long minutes of writhing and thrashing and howling, he found himself on the ground in his clothes.

Human again. Breathing hard with the sting of fire racing through his veins. For several minutes he adjusted to what he'd done, trying to put it into perspective. The dragon inside him already had, but the human part of his mind had to catch up.

He stood up slowly, trying to find his precarious balance. He faltered, staggering a few steps one way and another, tentative as a newborn foal. His legs held true and did not buckle.

"Amazing," he whispered. "*Amazing.*"

Dréoteth, resolute and unwavering, regarded the entire event without pleasure or disappointment on his face. Whatever he really thought about that initial attempt remained his secret. "Very good," he said. "How do you feel?"

"Like... I... " Meyer had trouble finding words to describe it. His clothes looked in fine shape and he smoothed his palms over the lay of it, surprised that he came back in them and not naked. "Like I can live like this. I *can* live like this."

Meyer had spent many days doubting, unsure.

"Yes, you can live like this. Can I trust you to stay in the cavern while I hunt?" Dréoteth asked.

"Why can I not stay here, in the clearing? I desire to be outside," Meyer said. It was useless to argue going on a hunt when he couldn't fly.

"Because you are still too vulnerable, and I do not know where Feline is," Dréoteth answered. "I doubt she would do something so foolish as to attack you, bu—"

"Why?" Meyer said. He almost spat the word. "She has before."

Dréoteth merely gestured. "That is why you cannot stay in the clearing. Now go inside." His authority was not to be questioned.

Meyer didn't like it. He snarled faintly, turning toward the mountain, regaining his balance and equilibrium in a few short strides. He had half a mind to seek the white dragon out for a confrontation while Dréoteth was gone. Disappearing into the hidden entrance, he followed the tunnel back to the cavern. Agitated, fueled with aggression from his triumphant first change, he crossed the cave toward the opposite corridor. The one that led to Feline's temporary lair.

The glint of gilded frames and oil painted faces paused him.

He had seen the paintings before, of course, and was curious why Dréoteth collected them. He'd been too preoccupied to bother asking. Changing direction, he approached and crouched in front of the one with slashes through the canvas. It reminded him of someone damaging something they cherished because they could never have it—or *do* it.

Dréoteth could have anything he wanted.

Almost.

Maybe it was the endlessly staring faces of strangers that had angered him, made him strike out. Doing a quick search, he found none of the other portraits were damaged.

He grunted and rose to his feet, sufficiently distracted from doing something foolish like finding Feline.

For seven days, Dréoteth counseled Meyer in the art of change. Every evening after the sun went down, they entered the clearing to practice. Meyer thrashed and growled and roared his way into his dragon, living with the pain.

By the seventh evening, he was able to switch almost immediately and more quickly than at any other time. He could sense that someday, the change would be effortless. It empowered him, driving his determination to new heights.

On the eighth day, Meyer approached Dréoteth well before they were due for their practice session. His control over his anger and rage had greatly improved, and he posed his question with confidence. "I wish to visit Bethany this evening. Soon, Dréoteth, I must return to my life."

Meyer's inner confliction between his beast and his family kept him awake for long hours. His growing urgency to return, for now, overpowered his desire to stay in the wilderness.

Dréoteth glanced up from his journal, letting the quill settle flat onto the stone. He considered Meyer in his forthright way.

"Are you sure you can control yourself? Have you considered that you might have issues with anger? What if you are surprised by your desire to kill your own wife and child? These questions must be given serious contemplation," Dréoteth said.

At first, Meyer wanted to denounce at once that he would never hurt Beth or his sons. She was pregnant with a third child Meyer had longed to meet and be a father to. He could not fathom injuring any of them.

And yet... and *yet* there was something uncertain deep down where his honesty lived. Something he could not name and did not want to give voice to.

"You have doubt," Dréoteth said, like he'd read

his mind.

Meyer put his hands on his hips and inclined his head. He had never made it a habit to lie in general, much less to Dréoteth, either in this guise or as Trimble.

"A little," he admitted, meeting and holding Dréoteth's eyes.

Quiet for a long, considering moment, Dréoteth finally said, "I suppose no matter how long you wait, there will always be doubt. Let us go then."

Meyer double-checked his clothing; black breeches that fit his muscular physique well, a shirt of white under a dark, plain tunic and a wide belt of hand-worked leather that had belonged to some other man he'd never met and never knew, but could smell in the material.

He thought it more than passable to see Bethany and his children.

The two men left the cavern on foot. Once they entered the woods, they broke into a languid lope. Part of Meyer's training involved learning to use the enhanced speed in running and the long distance endurance that allowed them to go for miles without stopping. Their heightened senses alerted them to dangers or prey as they went.

Meyer schooled himself along the way. This was what he had wanted, what he had gone through such agony for. He lived, thanks to Dréoteth, and now it was time to pick up the threads of his life. He was still a husband and father.

The deeply ingrained honor he carried throughout his whole life had not changed—even if other things had. He wondered if he would be able to control himself enough to fool Bethany.

It took them several hours to reach the outskirts of Meyer's property even after they spent a full hour running at top speed. He blustered through the forest on Dréoteth's heels, lacking the other man's skill and grace. They didn't press out into the open but stayed there under the gloom of the trees, lost in the darkness.

Dréoteth glanced aside at Meyer with a question in his eyes: *Are you ready?*

Meyer argued with himself over the answer. He nodded and stared hard at the familiar, distant farmhouse. It felt like he'd been gone for five years instead of a few weeks.

Holding Dréoteth's gaze, he argued with himself over the answer, nostrils flared wide to draw in the scents around them. He needed to get his breath back. When he was less winded, he stepped out into the field. He'd been cautioned to stay away from all the livestock and he did so, skirting the stables and horses and the cows standing close together under the broad branches of an oak tree. He could smell them all, though, and his fingers made fists as he fought off the urge to change into his dragon and hunt them down.

No, no. Not now.

Not yet.

When he got closer to the back of the homestead, two of his dogs started barking stridently. The fur stood up on the backs of their necks. His scent confused them and he tried to soothe their fear and uncertainty with quiet words that only served to make them more wary. One whined, one growled.

The back door opened slowly and Bethany stood there with a candleholder in her hand, the flicker of the flame illuminating half of her face. Almond shaped eyes, full lips, high cheekbones rosy with the glow of pregnancy.

Meyer stood there in the yard, easily able to see her despite the darkness, and something inside him hurt.

"Is someone there?" She sounded tentative.

Meyer paused, and then spoke up. "It is I, Bethany." To his own ears, his voice sounded gruff and different. He heard her gasp and the back door flew all the way open.

A gentle breeze blew her white nightgown against her body, outlining the swell of her stomach. She looked ready to deliver any day. She also looked both relieved and surprised as she carefully navigated the stairs to the ground. With an ungainly waddle, she made haste across the yard. When she reached him, she got on her tiptoes and hugged him with one arm, the other keeping the flame from his skin.

He stood still as a statue, all but frozen in place.

Finally, he wrapped his arms around her. She was so much shorter that he had to bend his shoulders down to make it easier.

"Meyer! Where have you been? I was worried," she said.

"I did not mean to leave without warning," he said. "I ran into trouble deep in the woods and was detained." It was not all a lie. He leaned back to look down into her face, a fierce desire to both protect her and... no. He had no desire to hurt her.

Certainly not.

That strange urge was something other. Something else. It was him getting used to these oddities, the dragon.

"Come inside. Shh! Buster, Brownie, be quiet." Bethany tried to hush the dogs that had their ears back and their teeth bared. She seemed too excited and relieved to see Meyer to understand their reactions.

Meyer glanced aside, struck by the wild urge to snarl and snap at the dogs. With effort, he resisted.

Taking the steps by twos, he crowded her on the

landing and let her lead him inside. Coming in from the back, they stood in a nook adjacent to the dining area. Wood floors creaked faintly, the smell of cedar mingling with the poignant scents of his sons and Bethany's sweetness. A sharp stab of nostalgia distracted him from the dogs.

Everything looked just as he'd left it.

He also felt suffocated and cloistered and had the desire to turn right back around and leave the house.

He couldn't breathe.

He thrust a hand through his hair, still dark with gray peppered at the temples, and followed her deeper into the hallway. The kitchen, illuminated only by the glow of the moon through the windows, smelled of chicken and bread and cheese. She led him through the living room, past Jeremy and Jonathan's toys, and up the long staircase toward their bedroom. He paused to run his fingers over a wooden rocking chair that he had crafted with his own hands.

"Tell me where you have been and what happened," Bethany said, seeking his eyes. "I feared I would have the babe and you would not be here."

She struggled up the steps with the candle held in front to light their way. Meyer could see just fine without it, but he said nothing. The close confines of the stairwell served to unnerve him and he felt his skin tingle.

There wasn't enough air. Not enough space.

The cavern was wide and high and large. It smelled of the earth and stone and water. He'd felt much closer to the wilderness there than he did here, amongst his own things. Oil lamps and hand painted portraits and desks with carved chairs. All his.

A part of him wanted to shun this life, these

trappings. At the same time, he couldn't totally shake the comfort they brought. It was disorienting to feel so torn in two.

And then, unexpectedly, he heard himself say, "It is a very long story, love. I only came to tell you that I am not finished with the business and I will need to leave shortly. But let me tuck you in and in a few days, when I return, I will explain."

"What do you mean you are leaving again? The babe could come any time!" Bethany made a sound of consternation and looked away from his face.

She struggled the last few steps and he cupped her elbow to help, an automatic gesture. A thing he would have not thought twice to do before. She set the candleholder on the nightstand and awkwardly slipped beneath the blankets.

Through the window, pale shards of moonlight filtered in, illuminating the space. Meyer drew the covers up to her chest, suddenly disgusted with such mundane tasks; he wanted to be hunting and flushing game into the open. He wanted to rip and tear and shred and snarl.

He realized that a low growl had built in his chest when he met Beth's eyes and she was looking at him not with fear, but wary confusion. Tamping down the rumble, he cleared his throat as if that's what he'd been about all along and leaned down to kiss her mouth briefly. It left him feeling strange inside.

He smoothed back a few strands of her dark hair and smiled.

"I will return soon and things will be back to normal," he promised. "Let—"

"*Soon?* How soon? Meyer, this is not like you."

"I should have my business taken care of by tomorrow. Sleep now."

He stared down into her face when she clutched his arm and squeezed plaintively. Any other time, he could not have been pried from her side when she was so close to delivery. He just needed one more day to... adjust. Guilt threatened to weigh him down at the accusation in her eyes.

Turning from her, he stalked out into the hallway without looking back.

He wanted to go.

He wanted to stay.

His footsteps led him into another room on the second floor just down from his and Bethany's. Pushing the door open, he found his sons sleeping soundly on their little beds, buried under the covers. Dark haired, flush cheeked, they looked like angels.

Proud and protective, he was pleased to note that he didn't have one violent thought when it came to the children. Encouraged, he strode to each of their beds and brushed kisses across their foreheads. Their scents, beloved and distinct, brought a fatherly pang to his gut.

But he had to leave the house.

Adjusting their covers, he palmed their small heads and left the bedroom. Descending the staircase, he found his way through the dark to the back door and stepped out into the evening. Immediately he drew a deep, cleansing breath. The smell of green leaves, dry twigs and raw earth soothed some of his discomfort.

The dogs started barking, bodies rigid and alert. He glanced slowly aside, hand on the banister, and snarled. They were not tethered to anything, yet neither animal wanted to come closer. Foam flew from their mouths, fur bristling along their backs.

It took all his willpower not to maul them.

He stalked across the open yard for the distant line of trees where the forest began, desperate to put distance between them before he did something he knew he would regret.

From the woods, Dréoteth watched Meyer cross the yard and enter the house. He heard the dogs barking hard and loud but Meyer seemed able to resist shouting or getting aggressive.

That was the first good sign.

Rather than wait to see what else happened, he turned away, sinking deeper into the shadows. He wanted to see if Meyer had trouble following his scent through the underbrush when he returned. He knew the man would not be able to stay the entire night, at least not on this first visit.

Out in the forest he heard the usual sounds of life: the hoot of an owl, the shuffle of raccoons through the brush, the grunt of a bear making tracks *away* from his scent. A master of stealth, he avoided brittle twigs and crackling leaves.

He was not surprised when he heard the faint sounds of footsteps enter the forest at the tree line. Meyer needed lessons in the art of stalking. Dréoteth strolled, hands casually tucked into the pockets of his breeches, letting Meyer catch up at his own pace.

He didn't slow down or speed up or make it harder for Meyer to find him.

"I could not stay," Meyer said beside him a few minutes later. He sounded riddled with guilt.

"I knew you would not," Dréoteth said. "You felt too confined, that the walls were close and suffocating."

"Yes. You know this because you feel it too whenever you are inside?"

"When I first began drifting into the villages as a human instead of a dragon, I found it very hard to stay inside the taverns and Inns. For the same reasons as you found it hard to stay in your own home. That too will ease as time passes," Dréoteth said. He tried to assess whether or not he thought Meyer could return to the life that he'd left.

Meyer looked disturbed in ways he hadn't when they left the cavern. One big hand rubbed at the back of his neck, like he was indecisive. Confused.

"Will it?" Meyer asked. He glanced aside at Dréoteth. "Everything feels very strange and foreign right now."

"Do you think you will be able to resume your life with Bethany, live as the man you were before?" Dréoteth asked. He could not entirely read Meyer's thoughts on that aspect. "It will probably take some getting used to."

"I... do not know. It was all I wanted before, when I was dying. But then I was not the creature I am now," Meyer said. "I cannot fathom not knowing my children. Not being there as their father. Yet suddenly I find myself too restless to even consider life on the farm. It is almost as if I feel transcended, *above* such mundane things as that."

Dréoteth knew they were not easy confessions for Meyer to make.

"That will be your most difficult task to overcome. Living amongst humans is trying even on the best of days. It might be easier for you than us born to it, because you were born to *them,* and have a deep relationship with children to help you focus."

Meyer's mouth curved into a wry smile. "It is a wonder you put up with me all these years and never gave yourself away."

Dréoteth laughed, a rare, raspy sound.

"Such were the tests I put myself through. It was a challenge to mingle with humans, especially so in the beginning. Many times I had to leave villages after only a few days because I was too tempted to go into a rage," he said.

"I did not have any violent thoughts about Beth or the children. That pleased me," Meyer admitted. "I *did* want to kill the dogs there for a few seconds when I left. If they continue, it wil—" He paused.

Dréoteth glanced aside. "If they continue, it will be difficult for you to function normally on the farm," he said, finishing Meyer's thought. "Not only will the dogs be aggressive and bark constantly, but the horses will shy and run."

"I did not think of that. I only thought to avoid them for my visit, not the extended consequences of my situation. I could get rid of the dogs and the horses, but Bethany will have questions. And how would we get into town? I cannot make them walk that far."

"Sell the farm and move closer into town," Dréoteth suggested. "Tell Beth you wish to lean toward teaching. You already have a position at the School anyway. There is another option, which Feline and I had discussed. Moving away to a much smaller village, where we might be less inclined to violence and where we might keep our true nature hidden longer."

Meyer grunted. "It is going to be challenging to hide what I am from her for a long period of time."

"Yes, because as you noticed with me, you will not age any more from now on. Not outwardly. This is as old as you will ever look," he said, removing a hand from his pocket to gesture at Meyer.

"When I can no longer hide it, I will have to tell her."

"You can *never* tell her," Dréoteth warned. "Or your children. Enjoy the years you have been given with them, Meyer, and prepare yourself to say good-bye when the time comes. Be thankful they will have a handful of years to know you and remember you."

Without warning, Dréoteth picked up the pace of their trek through the forest. Easing into a ground-eating run, he guided them back toward the mountain, hoping that Meyer took his words to heart. The consequences otherwise would be catastrophic.

Dréoteth led Meyer into the clearing at twilight the next morning. He repeated the instructions for flight one last time.

"You must not hesitate. When you push off the ground, imagine yourself going straight up into the sky. Imagine it, and make it real," Dréoteth said, pausing in the middle of the clearing. He made a gesture with his hand. "It will be disorienting when you get up there so try to stay around tree top level. That way if you crash the damage will be minimal."

Meyer glanced at the sky, hands casually resting on his hips. Anxious to master this next task, sharp eyed and intent, he absorbed the instructions and advice like a sponge.

Both men were dressed in casual breeches and loose shirts for comfort, their boots older and well broken in.

"How quickly does one master this skill?" he asked.

"Very quickly, or you will find yourself injured often. The smaller details will refine as you go. Learning to land and take off safely are the most important. Watch me," Dréoteth said.

He turned away from Meyer, jogging a few steps to gain momentum. He pushed off from the ground with a great lunge, thigh muscles bulging, his arms extended above his head. The transformation, seamless and smooth, happened between one blink and the next.

Amazed, Meyer watched from his spot on the ground, buffeted by the backwash of wind from the first strong flap of Dréoteth's wings. The black dragon looked enormous against the pink and orange sky of a new day. Meyer understood why they preferred to fly under the cover of night; they were impossible to miss for their size. No human could mistake them for a condor or other species of bird, even from a considerable distance. The long tail and wicked snout were distinctive.

Dréoteth cruised the length of the small clearing, staying below the treetops. He but skimmed the rim of the pasture, making a tight circle at the end, and glided back toward the center.

Awed, Meyer watched with rapt fascination.

Is that what he looked like when he changed? So deadly, so sinuous?

Dréoteth cut his wings in sharp flaps to land, coming down quickly. The last few steps he took were jogging ones; he transformed from beast to human in a few precious seconds.

"You make it look too easy," Meyer said.

"It will become second nature soon," Dréoteth promised. "Now you try, before the sun gets too high." He stood some small distance away to watch.

Meyer grunted and rubbed his calloused palms over his thighs. Concentrating, he stared up at the sky and let the heat and energy build inside. This he had practiced during their nighttime hunts, when they were running with more speed than he'd ever have as a human. Suddenly he took a few great leaping steps and launched himself into the air-- only to shout as he stumbled forward and crashed into the ground.

Dréoteth hardly seemed bothered. "Try again."

Meyer rolled to his feet. "I barely got off the

ground."

"Because you are a little fearful," Dréoteth said.

As brave as Meyer appeared, he *was* afraid of flying. Squaring his shoulders, he stood there for long minutes that stretched silently between them. He stared upwards, trying to imagine it, until he ran forward and jumped. This time he started to change, felt his body ripping into a new shape, felt the wings burst out from his back. He wobbled through the air, panicking, veering sharply one side to the other before he flapped his wings and climbed.

He climbed too high, of course.

Out of control and roaring in fear, he went higher simply because it was easier and he was afraid to look down, much less fly toward the earth. It appeared he might crash several times, lurching into a roll before rocking the other way. He caught glimpses of Dréoteth observing his sloppy technique from the middle of the field. Even when he thought he was going down, Dréoteth didn't panic or run forward or shout other instructions.

Meyer wasn't sure whether to be thankful or annoyed.

Finally, after so many minutes of wobbly flight, Meyer found a better stroke to his wings and figured out how to use the wind to his advantage. Disinclined to stay up too long, he glided toward the earth and extended his talons to land, concentrating so hard that he forgot to change back into a human. He lurched forward with his wings extended until his nose shuffled into the grass, tail in the air.

He came to a halt with a grunt.

Blowing out dirt and a hot puff of breath, Meyer gazed triumphantly across the field at Dréoteth.

"Not a bad landing. It would have been easier in your human guise," Dréoteth said. "I do not think you should go up again until nightfall, when there is less risk of someone seeing you."

Meyer growled, malcontent with the order. He slid back into his human form and brushed a few blades of grass from his breeches. "It is very strange to be so high above the earth. But what a view!"

"You will spend much time in the air I think. *After* dark."

"Dréoteth, I do not understand why dragons take human shape if they loathe them so," Meyer said, sticking a blade of grass between his teeth. He had wondered over this for weeks.

Dréoteth walked over to a collection of boulders at the base of the mountain and sat on one, looping his arms around the bend of his knees. "We were not always able to take the shape of a man. Ages ago, a Fae woman with great pow—"

"A Fae woman?" Meyer's brow furrowed.

Dréoteth smiled. "Yes. You have heard of the Fae? They possess incredible magic."

Meyer snorted. "They are not re—"

"Are they not?"

Meyer switched the blade of grass from one side of his mouth to the other and sat on an adjacent rock. Dréoteth had a point. *Dragons* were real, and he would have never guessed before seeing one. "Aye, go on."

"She came upon one of us in a field, gravely injured from battle. Young and impetuous, she decided to save him, temporarily changing him into a man because he was easier to care for. That was her first grievous mistake. Nurturing him in a cave, she saved his life and became enamored with him. When he awoke and realized what she'd done, the dragon-man tried to kill her. He failed, because Fae are clever, tricky beings, and she refused to remove the spell that allowed him to change. She used his pure hatred of humans as his torture and made it so that he passed the curse along to his offspring and any females he mated with. Worse, she made it so the females had to be in their *human* guise to give birth, so that every dragon thereforth was born a human. The Fae's wrath knew no bounds."

Meyer listened, frowning as the tale unfolded. "Even though the first dragon did not *have* to change into a human again after she cast her spell on him, the following generations were born that way and they probably felt tainted."

"Yes," Dréoteth said. "You understand this because you have a small ability to reach back through generations of dragon memories and retrieve their thoughts and feelings. It is not, and will never be as developed as mine, but you can sense basic emotions. Even the knowledge that he had been a man, and *could* change drove the dragon mad. But he had spread his seed far and wide before he died, ensuring the curse would go on. Eventually the unaffected male dragons perished, leaving only the females and cursed generations to carry on."

"Bloody hell, what a triangle," Meyer said. He spit out the chewed blade of grass. "Now I am a human, changed into a human-hating dragon. The irony defies imagination."

Dréoteth laughed. "I had a great many reservations about doing it."

"Then why did you?"

"Because I thought you might be strong enough to overcome our natural instinct enough to allow your children to know you."

"That suggests some kind of compassion for humans," Meyer said, arching a brow.

"If I had developed none at all, Meyer, you would have been dead long before now."

Meyer discovered he could not argue with that.

At dusk, Meyer began practicing his flying again. Transforming came much easier now, with less pain, and he looked forward to discarding his limited human guise for black scales, sharp teeth and sharper claws. Several of his landings were rough; pitched forward, snout in the ground, back end hiked in the air. He had grass in the hard ridges above the slits of his eyes and dirt up his nose.

He managed to land every time without damaging his wings. Flying became less scary, until all he wanted to do was soar on the currents, swoop over the trees, and dive at extreme angles. He saw Dréoteth watching him from the meadow, standing casually near the stump of a tree.

One dragon became two as night fell, and Meyer tried hard to keep up with his mentor. Dréoteth made him feel incompetent and sloppy with his sleek maneuvers and skill.

It only made him try harder, practice longer, fly smarter.

Dréoteth suddenly swooped down toward the trees in pursuit of game, and Meyer joined the hunt. It was a bear they were after, he could smell it even from here, and he roared with the thrill of the chase. Hunting with a bow and arrow in the brush looked like child's play compared to this.

He was not as big of a help to Dréoteth as he wished he could be. His technique needed work. He frightened off more game than not, excitedly roaring and thrashing his tail in the wind.

Dréoteth flushed the bear into a meadow and caught it with his talons; he left the wounded animal for Meyer and carved a turn with his wings, off to find his own meal.

Meyer understood why Dréoteth insisted they eat in separate meadows when he ripped into the bear on the ground. He felt fierce and possessive over the kill, snarling and growling even though there wasn't another predator around. He wasn't sure how he would have felt to have another dragon in the field with him. Perhaps in time he wouldn't feel so threatened. Those were distant, muddled thoughts; he was consumed with feasting and filling his rumbling belly.

He flew back to the clearing when he sated his hunger. In a sudden fit of confidence, he came in to land and tried to transform into his human just as he touched down, thinking to spare himself a mouthful of dirt. He wound up tumbling ass over ear, nearly breaking an arm, until he flopped spine down and stared up at the stars.

It hadn't gone quite as he'd expected.

He was still lying just like that when Dréoteth landed some minutes later, switching effortlessly, though Meyer knew it wasn't meant to mock him.

Still, he chortled.

"What is so funny?" Dréoteth asked. "And why are you laying like that? Did you hurt yourself?"

"Not really. I was laughing because your landings are so smooth and mine are mini-catastrophes."

Dréoteth wandered over to stare down at Meyer from on high. He looked amused. "You have been at this a very short time, in the scheme of things. I have been doing it for centuries."

Meyer grunted. "Aye, so you have said. What will happen with Feline?"

Dréoteth glanced away and across the landscape, staring at a distant spot. Thoughtful.

"I do not know. I have not decided if she will die for trying to kill you."

The cold calculation, the sheer *confidence* Dréoteth radiated made Meyer appreciate not being his target. He would not stand a chance in a battle with his mentor.

Meyer stood up, finally, and brushed off his clothes.

"Do you think she should?" Dréoteth asked.

"That is a difficult question. What is done is done, and she has not tried again, knowing you will kill her. Perhaps it is best to live and let live." The situation was complex for him, not easily decided one way or another. Had Dréoteth asked him that last week, he would have said unequivocally that yes, Feline should die for the attack.

Today, after the thrill of the flight and the hunt, doubt surfaced.

"It seems, for now, that she lives," Dréoteth said, putting an end to the speculation.

"I could have had that bear on my own, you know," Meyer grumped, changing the subject.

"That bear made you look awkward and slow. I suspect you would still be doggedly chasing it a week from now, miles from here, unless I intervened."

Meyer laughed and clapped Dréoteth on the shoulder. "My friend, while you give me lessons in hunting, I will give you lessons on a thing called subtlety. You need some."

Fat lot of good he thought it would do.

Chapter Fourteen

"But I know something is wrong. He would not have stayed gone this long, not with Bethany so close to her time," Thea said. "I *know.*"

The conversation had been going on for five days. Thea paced around the quaint living room of Phae's house, agitated and frowning. She suspected the women knew exactly what fate befell Meyer, but they sidestepped her questions or successfully and skillfully distracted her.

Not today.

Today, she wanted answers. She glanced at each one, gauging their mood.

Miriette, Claudine and Phae seemed unfazed by her restlessness. The pastel colors of their loose fitting, casual dresses complimented their flowing hair, their delicate features. Each of them wore their concern for her and for Meyer openly.

"You cannot go traipsing after him alone," Miriette said, for at least the fifth time. She stood next to a birdbath with a long, carved base and a shallow bowl with whimsically scalloped edges. The water was clear enough to expose the odd symbols and runes painted onto the bottom. Ivy that had found its way inside via a window twined around the base and over the edges.

"Then come with me. One of you or all of you. Nothing bad will happen if you are with me," Thea said. She knew her reasoning was sound. "At least tell me if he is injured."

Miriette glanced down at the water and smoothed her palm across the top.

Thea stepped over and tried to peer over her shoulder. She knew how the scrying pool worked, but every time she tried to use it to detect Meyer's whereabouts, she only produced a blackout, the water clouded like someone had dumped the contents of an inkpot into it. She suspected one of them had cast a spell upon the stand to prevent her from discovering what happened.

Something bad, her gut said. Meyer was still gone with no word, no contact, and every day she grew increasingly antsy.

There was nothing in the water beyond the unrelenting black she was too used to seeing. She half suspected the witches could see whatever images were there just fine and that she was the only one who couldn't.

Perhaps if she snuck off to a pond in the forest, she would get a clear reading.

"I see nothing, dearling. No images, no sounds, no smells. Perhaps being too close to the lair prohibits us seeing anything substantial. Dragons have always possessed a startling bit of magic," Miriette said.

"Yes, that is quite logical, and probably accurate," Phae said from her spot on the arm of a divan. She sat there, hands resting on her thigh.

Thea stepped back, glancing between the women. "What if he is dead? I—"

"He is not dead, sweetling," Phae said. She sounded very certain.

"But how can you know?"

"Death is an inescapable understanding. If he was dead, we would know."

Thea bit her lip in consternation. She glanced down at the toes of her shoes, missing the glance the women passed between them.

By the time she looked up, they were watching her again. She adjusted the bow across the shoulder of a sand colored tunic. Attached to her back by strips of leather, were specially designed arrows. On her feet, boots made of soft leather covered dark brown pants to the knee.

She glanced at the door.

"Give him another week, Thea. If he is on some other personal mission then perhaps he will complete it in that time and come home," Phae said. "He could very easily have come across other game hunters and been invited along with their group."

"Another week," Thea said, dismayed. "I will not seek the dragon without Meyer's aid but I fear time grows short. And really, Meyer does not seem the type to leave his pregnant wife alone when she is due," she pointed out.

"The dragon will not go far from the lair, child. It might be gone for a day or so, hunting, but it will not vacate completely unless something drives it out. Meyer could be hunting extra meat because he knows he will not have much time to leave *after* the babe comes," Miriette reasoned.

There was little else she could do besides grumble her agreement and go outside to practice on a still target with her arrows. She needed to burn off the brunt of her impatience with physical activity.

Eugenia was there, practicing with her own bow. She smiled at Thea and they engaged in a rousing contest of archery.

When Thea was gone, Miriette glanced at Phae. "She grows restless. Perhaps it is time to lure the dragons far from here. Or kill them. I had hoped they would battle and do the deed for us."

Phae, long hair streaming down her back, looked thoughtful. "We have ever been careful not to do anything they can retaliate for. Their magic is strong, as you said. If they can find us, they will hunt us as humans hunt them. Ellery and I have been working on a spell that will probably drive them across the continent and out of her reach."

"Then it is a simple matter of illusion," Claudine said. She stood by the door, listening. "I will fake their death and call her to look in the water so that she will believe they are truly gone. Then, finally, she will be free of her need for vengeance. As soon as the white dragon returns, we will put our plan into action."

He could see Feline resting upon a jagged bit of outcropping that overlooked the clearing. Her wicked shape made a frightening outline in the shadows of night, wings pulled close to her sinuous body, talons clinging tight to keep her immobile against gusts of wind.

Dréoteth had kept them separated while Meyer adjusted to his new status as dragon, but tonight he meant to try and close some of those gaps. Feline had returned from seclusion and there was no time like the present to start.

He still had his doubts about them all trying to live communally, a thought that went against his natural instinct. Being forced to work and train Meyer in such close quarters had helped him overcome some of it, but he had his moments where he wanted to shoo Meyer and Feline away from *his* mountain, *his* clearing, and tell them to get on with life.

It was an adjustment for everyone.

If he was honest with himself, the newness of being around other dragons and engaging a human who had just gone through the change provided a challenging diversion and distraction. His forays into society to begin with had been for the same reason.

Of course Meyer had thought the idea of working together and living around each other a great idea. When he had explained the press of humanity to the scholar, and that their hunting grounds were dramatically shrinking, Meyer's mindset had closely mirrored his own. Instead of waging utter war, he thought it better to live on the fringe, even if he struggled with the desire to be hunting and doing dragon things rather than lounge around smoking parlors, discussing the fate of the world.

Meyer was as torn as Feline and himself, but for different reasons.

Dréoteth had been integrating for years and would have the easiest time of them all. The utter irony had not escaped him.

Feline simply found humans too repulsive to easily embrace it, or at least she had the last time they spoke.

He glanced once more down the field to where she lurked, silent and still, then back to Meyer.

"Ready?" he asked Meyer.

Meyer nodded. "Yes."

Dréoteth made a gesture with his hand toward Feline.

Her wings unfurled from their tight clutch against her body, and she launched off the rock, swooping down toward their end of the clearing.

He felt Meyer tense beside him.

"She would not dare," Dréoteth said, confident the white dragon did not have killing on her mind tonight.

"She dared once before," Meyer said, grunting.

Dréoteth stepped smoothly in front of Meyer in a way that didn't insult him, like he couldn't protect himself.

With as much ease as Dréoteth, Feline glided to the ground and touched down as a human. One moment she was a ghostly, ethereal shape in the night and the next she was a pale haired woman in a deep blue dress. The style, square necked with tight sleeves giving way to wide mouthed cuffs, suited her.

She seemed hesitant to approach them, warily eyeing Meyer.

The tension ratcheted up another notch.

"Meyer, this is Feline. Feline, Meyer," Dréoteth said, making easy introductions. By his tone, one would never think he was on alert and ready to intervene at a moment's notice.

But his eyes were sharp, assessing, reading their expressions and body posture for signs of aggression. He stepped aside so that they could make their stilted greetings.

Meyer cleared his throat, fingers flexing in and out of his palms. "Feline," he said. His voice was gruff.

Feline came to a stop a few yards away.

"Meyer." She inclined her head a small fraction.

"Now that we have that out of the way," Dréoeth said, getting down to business. "We need to discuss our future plans. This will not work if you two think either one is going to attack the other, so let us dispense with all the hostility and get on with it."

Meyer grunted.

Feline narrowed her eyes.

Dréoteth glanced between them and was satisfied enough with their responses. No talons were out, no one was changing, and no one had charged.

That was a decent beginning.

"Living here in this part of the mountain would be convenient, I think we all agree, because of the extensive caverns. It gives us all privacy and the hunting grounds here are heavily populated with game. *However,* it does not allow us to become a part of any society, or begin the process of integration. Deeper in the mountains, there is the small shire of Summerville with perhaps one hundred citizens. I think that is a much more fitting setting than Faulkon's Cross with its vast and growing population," Dréoteth said.

"One hundred people are more manageable than a thousand or two," Feline said.

"Staying in Faulkon's Cross is out of the question, I agree," Meyer said. "If I noticed the changes so easily in you," he glanced at Dréoteth. "So will everyone else. It will raise suspicion. I can sell my farm and move Bethany and the children with us. She will not take kindly to it, for all her family is here. But I believe she will follow where ever I lead." He frowned, rubbing a rough finger against his lower lip.

"It is a fresh start," Dréoteth said. "You will have to deceive Bethany as long as you can, for she is not slow and will soon guess something is amiss."

He grunted again. "I... will worry about that after we make the transition. She is due any day with the babe. We can scout out places to stay in Summerville and when the time comes, I will move my family there."

Feline, quiet until then, said, "What if she realizes that you are not now what you were when you met?"

"Let us worry about that when the time comes,"

Dréoteth said, intercepting the question. "He has ten years or so before his lack of aging becomes a serious issue. We need to find new lairs closer to Summerville, which should not be too hard considering it sits in the valley of the range itself."

Feline parted her lips like she meant to argue it now, but closed them again without a sound. She inclined her head in agreement.

"So it is settled then. We can begin the process of relocation in the meantime." Dréoteth needed an evening to look for flaws in the plan, although just now, he did not see any. The only obstacle was Beth. She presented more of a problem than he wanted to admit to anyone.

"Aye," Meyer said. "I should return home. She is due any day and I need to learn to ... become a husband and father again." He seemed hesitant to speak about his reservations any deeper than that in front of Feline.

"When you return, if you do not find us here, then seek us out in Summerville," Dréoteth said. He did not think Meyer would have trouble locating them. The town was small, and there were only so many ways to get in and out of the mountains.

Meyer nodded curtly and turned away from them both. He took a few running steps before leaping into the air. His transformation was not as effortless as the other two, but he gained his dragon and wheeled away into the night.

Dréoteth observed until Meyer was out of sight. He glanced pointedly at Feline before striding away toward his tunnel and the cavern beyond.

"Really, Bethany, nothing is amiss. I am simply exhausted from so much travel," Meyer said.

He paced around the living room that had once

seemed so spacious. The ceiling seemed too low, barely above his head, and several times he accidentally knocked into a piece of furniture or a misplaced toy. He felt too large for this place. His presence alone overflowed every room.

For the last four hours he had walked the halls of his own home and felt like a stranger doing it. He'd visited the children, kissing their foreheads—they were asleep at this late hour—but found peace nowhere inside. Reading in his favorite chair held no appeal.

Beth had been delighted to see him. She looked fit to pop any minute, her belly enormously distended, and seemed more than ready to have him settle in for the duration. She'd told him she was having mild cramps every so many hours, signs of imminent labor. She hazarded a guess of a day or two before the arrival of their newest child.

Such a short amount of time to re-adjust.

"Come, tell me what is on your mind," she invited. She sat in a chair near the fireplace, patting the arm of his wingback. "We should decide on a name, too, aye? We left it until the end this time and …well. The end is almost here."

He glanced at the chair, then at Bethany, so swollen and uncomfortable. She had that glow though, the one she always got when she was carrying a child. A few strands of curly, dark hair escaped the knot atop her head and tickled her rosy cheeks.

He raked his fingers through his own hair and approached his chair, sinking down into the cushioned confines. Once upon a time, reading stories to them from his collection of books had been his favorite thing to do. He sprawled out, legs stretched long, his spine pressed flush against the seat. He was achingly aware of his inner power, of the energy coursing through his system.

"I have been thinking we should move," he said, broaching the subject tentatively. He glanced away from the lapping flames in the hearth to Bethany's face.

She looked as shocked as he suspected she would be.

"... move? But Meyer, we have just settled into the farm here. Why would you even think of moving? You love it here," she said.

Meyer cleared his throat. "Yes, but—"

"And mother, father, my sisters. I cannot leave them, Meyer," she said, interrupting him. Her eyes were wide in her face, expression aghast.

"Perhaps they will consider moving as well. Later," he said. Planting his elbow into the arm of the chair, he lifted his fingers to his jaw, fidgeting with his whiskers.

"You have not said *why*. Mother will never leave here. Ever. And father will not go without her," she said. "I prefer to stay here. Jeremy and Jonathan love it here, and the crops—"

"Will grow some place else," he said, cutting her off. "There are other homes, Bethany. Better ones, bigger ones, to raise our family in."

"Bigger ones? Meyer Lyon, you raved and ranted and praised this house because it was large enough for us and at least four children to live comfortably."

"Comfortably? Putting two children to a room hardly seems comfortable," he argued, but remembered how excited he had been when they'd moved in. Now it seemed tiny, suffocating.

"What has made you change your mind about Faulkon's Cross?" Beth asked, close to tears. "All you could talk about for months was how much you loved this land and planned to live out your whole life here."

He could hear the thickness in her throat.

"Does there need to be a reason?" The sharp snap of his voice made the dogs outside start barking. They had done so again when he'd arrived, baring their teeth, hackles raised. He fought off a growl of annoyance when they didn't immediately quiet down again.

"Yes," Bethany said, snapping back. "There does. Because this is not like you, Meyer. You almost do not seem yourself."

Meyer couldn't help but smile thinly; one of the things he'd loved about Beth from the start was her feisty nature. She wouldn't go down without a fight. Or at least a decent argument. Bethany might be pregnant and slow to move around, but her mind was still sharp.

The dogs brayed and barked harder. He hissed under his breath and lunged up out of the chair. He'd had enough.

"After you have the babe, we should at least go have a look. Will you do that for me, Bethany? Just take a look at the village and see. I desire change," Meyer said. He leaned over to brush a kiss to her brow.

"Perhaps. For now, all I can concentrate on is delivering us a healthy child," she said.

Appeased that the seed was planted, he grasped her gently under the elbows. "Come, let me help you to bed."

"Are you not coming?" She rose from the chair with a small, feminine grunt, gripping his forearms with her hands.

Once she was upright, Meyer scooped an arm behind her back to steady her. He led her toward the stairs and suddenly swept her up into his arms like a bridegroom on a wedding night. This would go much faster if he just carried her. He had no trouble at all holding her while taking the stairs in pairs.

"I am going to see what those bloody dogs are going on about. Something must be prowling the yard," he said. The lies left a bad taste on his tongue but he was desperate to get outside. Just for a few moments. Stretch his arms, his legs, catch the scents on the breeze.

He carried her straight to their room and laid her carefully on the bed.

"Hurry back," Beth whispered.

"I will." He stroked a hand over her hair and turned away, stalking into the hall.

Meyer strode from the room and down the stairs with an impatience that almost choked him. His boots thudded over the floor and he knocked the back door out of the way, gulping in huge draughts of night air. The dogs, already agitated, barked harder when he startled them. They barked so hard their feet twitched off the ground, ferocious protectors that were not quite ferocious enough to charge him.

He stalked away, snarling, and headed for the tree line. He just needed one more flight before he turned in. One more change, one hour as his dragon.

He thought if he burned away some of his inner tension, getting through the rest of the evening in the house would be easier. In short order, he came upon a smaller, unplanted field. Due to his recent circumstances, the crops had been neglected.

Concerned about changing too close to the farmhouse, he glanced back toward the homestead to gauge the distance between here and there. If Beth bothered to look out the second story windows, she had a good chance of seeing his black silhouette against the dark sky. He doubted she would get out of bed in her condition and counted on her falling asleep so that she wouldn't be tempted. At least the dogs had shut their yapping traps.

Running, he leapt into the air, transforming with unbelievable ease. His preoccupation must have distracted him from fretting about the change, for once, and he reveled in how effortless it felt. He sought the current, leathery wings flapping against the air. Rising just above the treetops, he skimmed them, staying low. The sensation grew more pleasing every time he sought his beast and took to the skies.

This was where he wanted to be.

This was what he wanted to be doing.

He opened his elongated maw and snapped his teeth on the breeze.

Testing.

Meyer discovered that flying was addictive and that he could cover an enormous amount of ground in a minimal amount of time. His keen eyesight allowed him to see much more than he ever would as a human. The forest stretched for miles around Faulkon's Cross in several directions, breaking for meadows and fields with crops already starting to bud. He stayed within a few miles of the farmhouse, careful to avoid any other properties where he knew people might see him.

Something darting through the dappled shadows of the trees below snagged his attention. Quick motion always did. He honed in on it, instinctively following its jagged pattern. Every time he flapped his wings, the treetops thrashed, making the – was that a human?—change direction. It seemed to be heading for a small clearing north and east and he encouraged it to, growling just loud enough to penetrate down past the boughs and the leaves.

His predatory instinct kicked in just as it burst from the edge of the trees into the clearing. He swooped down closer to the ground, following its erratic, zigzagging dash with his eyes.

The human ran faster, the dark cloak snapping at its heels like rabid dogs.

Meyer wanted to kill it.

He wanted to close in and snap his jaws over the intruder, although he had no claim over this particular bit of land.

Or did he?

Meyer felt like he owned it *all.*

He tried to follow its hectic pattern and was forced to pull up when it darted into the safety of the trees, denying him a chance to attack. Soaring high, he tilted his streamlined body into a circle and came around again, attempting to pinpoint the human. He spotted it through the shadows, a flicker of motion and heat. The desire to flush it back into the open was heady and electrifying.

Improving his technique by the second, his maneuvers became tighter, more controlled, the disorientation righting itself quicker after each sharp turn.

The human swerved and dashed into the open unexpectedly; he felt a thrill sweep through him when he cut through the air, right on its proverbial tail. The rush of adrenaline obliterated rational thought. He wanted to roar his triumph, damn the farmhouse and witnesses, and declare premature victory over his victim. He felt the beast trying to take total control, where he became nothing but a killing machine, hunting and ravaging and sating his unholy lust for violence.

He picked up speed when he swooshed down past the very edge of the trees into the clearing, snapping his jaws. The human ran with impressive speed but it was no match for him; the distance closed quickly and the roar he tried to contain spilled free of his throat when he opened his mouth, eyes gleaming,

sharp teeth shining.
Thirty feet.
Twenty.
Fifteen feet from his first kill.

Thea crouched before a small puddle of water trapped between the rocks of a narrow, trickling creek. Her fingers left ripples on the surface as broken images flickered and died before she could really make any sense of them. She caught glimpses of black scales, long snouts, gushes of flame and not much more. Like a broken mosaic, none of the scenes seemed to make any kind of sense. She couldn't tell if this was the past, present or future. Her spellcasting in this area needed work.

At least it wasn't the back nothingness she'd conjured before. She wondered if it had to do with the fact she was so far from the hollow. Her wandering had taken her further than she meant it to.

Dressed as dark as the shadows around her, she peered at the water intently, adjusting the collection of arrows over her shoulder. Her bow was hooked on her back, a sword strapped to a belt at her waist. She never left the hollow, even on short excursions, without them.

Around her feet, a layer of dead pine needles and fat pine cones littered the ground. The edge of her cloak caught on one and she flicked it twice to get it unstuck, muttering under her breath when the pine cone refused to come loose. Picking it up, she tugged at the material and it gave with a small tear. She lobbed the cone into the water, creating a mini tsunami that swamped the stones around it. Grinning, forgetting about scrying pools and magic for a moment, she breathed the scent of mountain laurel, holly berry and damp ferns, an earthy cocktail she'd grown to love.

She considered picking some of the blooms and leaves to take home with her when a shadow flickered at the edge of her vision. Gasping, she glanced up. Almost as if her scrying had conjured the real thing, the dark silhouette of a dragon passed just above the trees.

Déjà vu struck her hard and she lurched to her feet, darting away from the creek, her cloak flapping sharply at her heels. It seemed to stalk her from the air, veering and turning whenever she did. She risked a glance up; it was right there, blotting out part of the moon.

Even though she was some distance from the hollow, she still knew all the nooks and crannies of this part of the forest like the back of her hand. She knew where the hidey-holes were, where the gnarled roots stuck up the highest, sure to trip her, and where the forest gave way to a clearing.

At first she ran out of fright, startled by the proximity of it. Slowly, though, a plan began to take shape.

This was what she'd been waiting her whole life for.

It was what she'd trained for, hoped for. Confrontation with the dragon was the only thing she could think of for years.

Now was her chance for revenge.

She dashed left and broke from the safety of the trees, running out into the open, daring it to chase her.

Luring it.

Testing its abilities, its turning speed.

The hair was up on her nape, heart pounding a frenetic rhythm in her chest.

She thought she could feel the heat of its breath

on her back and that was enough to send her fleeing into the tree line, panting, silently reciting spells of protection. Flying past rough trunks, bark snagging her cloak like demon fingers, threatening to rip away the hood that hid her pale hair, she made a haphazard U-turn. It hissed somewhere behind her and she expected the forest to erupt into flames.

Galvanized, she fortified her determination and burst from under the protective canopy onto flat ground, her bow bouncing against her spine.

She heard the *snap-crack* of tree branches when it dipped sharply downward and didn't need to look back to know it was coming in for the kill.

She sensed it, felt its lethal intent.

Bravely she stayed upright, breathing hard and fast, arms and legs pumping madly, knowing that any second it was going to grab her up in its jaws.

This was it.

This was her chance.

Maybe her *only* chance.

When she felt the heat of its breath close all around her like a warm blanket, she ripped the sword out of its sheath and pitched forward, hitting the ground already rolling. She angled the gleaming, rune-carved blade so that the tip was upward and she thrust it just as the dragon's head passed not a foot above her body.

It thought it had her and instead she pierced its throat, finding that impossible soft spot between scales that was not as hard here as the rest of the body. It took strength and skill to penetrate the hide, and more than a little luck. Phae had cast a spell upon the blade as she had the arrows in her quiver, helping to assure that it pierced the dragon either through the scales or the skin.

The dragon, roaring in pain and surprise, ripped the sword right out of her hands. It clanked against the ground some feet away, the whole upper half coated in black dragon blood.

Thea rolled onto her stomach just as the beast impacted the earth, shaking the ground beneath her. Wheezing, she watched it twist and flip, one wing caught under its body until it broke with a sickening *pop.*

All of it happened in a matter of seconds that felt like years, as if the whole world had slowed down to a strange, surreal crawl. She pushed up, trying to get her shaky legs beneath her. The hood on her cloak fell back, exposing her braided, pale hair. Several wayward wisps framed her face, dirt marring one cheek.

The dragon thumped into the trees, wounded but not dead, roaring and thrashing wildly. Leaves rained down and bark flew in every direction.

Thea ran forward unsteadily, reaching a hand down to gather her fallen sword. She needed to finish it off before it realized she was coming and blasted her with dragonfire. Fear felt like a writhing, live thing in her chest.

Between one violent twist and the next, the dragon suddenly disappeared. There was no way it could have taken off or ran into the forest. She would have seen it.

Shocked, she slowed to a walk, gripping the hilt of her weapon so tight her fingers ached. Where the devil had it gone?

From the ground, the prone shape of a man stirred amidst the dust and tried to gain his feet. His clothes were disheveled and askew and he staggered, one hand at his throat, his back to his attacker.

Of all the things Thea had expected when confrontation came, it hadn't been *this.* She sheathed the sword and took the bow from its holder, snagging an arrow to notch between. Her fingers shook; it took her three tries to align it correctly.

This was for Mother.

Father.

Her older brother Thad.

She exhaled, concentrating.

Standing in the clearing, she resembled a warrior, posture perfect and still. The battered cloak settled around her like a dark curtain. The arrow flew and her aim was as good as the years of practice she'd put behind it. She struck the stricken dragon-man in the side and he howled, twisting around to face the threat. Blood streamed from the wound on his neck and glistened between his clutching fingers.

And suddenly, Thea had a much bigger shock; she found herself facing off with Meyer Lyon. Another arrow was already notched and ready but she faltered, stared.

Meyer.

Meyer was the dragon.

... The dragon was Meyer.

Thea simply couldn't make sense of it in her mind.

The familiar man garbled words that sounded wet and tangled, hand at the gash in his throat, an arrow sticking out his side. Whatever he was trying to say she could not understand, but what she *did* know was that he had deceived her.

Tricked her.

Lied to her.

Maybe Meyer had intended to lead her to her eventual death.

The next arrow flew and it struck him high through his left shoulder. She'd been aiming for his heart, but her nerves were taking a beating, forcing her shot off the mark. Surprise had her tight in its grip.

Meyer went to a knee, eyes wide with shock, balancing precariously like he was about to propose to a bride.

Unsure that his wounds were fatal, too close to her goal to stop now, she dropped the bow and arrows and reclaimed her sword. It slithered free of the sheath with a tinny hiss. She stalked forward until she stood over the fallen, kneeling, wheezing man.

His face was a mask of tortured horror, disbelief.

Thea was devastated by his duplicity, his lies.

"Deceiver," she whispered.

Meyer shook his head. *No.*

She arched the blade back and swung it hard, feet braced.

Meyer's head toppled to the ground and his body fell the other way, landing with a thump on the grass.

His blood was *everywhere.*

Thea barely had time to feel vindicated in her revenge. Something stirred on the air behind her and she reacted before she thought; throwing herself to the side, careful not to land on her own blade, she barely got out of the way of vicious, snapping teeth that shredded the air an inch from her body.

Another dragon, as black as the one she'd just killed, nearly had her. Gasping, she lurched to her feet as the dragon's tail whipped to the left, missing her by inches. She ducked, stumbling over something and glanced down straight into Meyer's dead, staring eyes. No amount of counseling and preparing and planning could have prepared her for *this.*

She screamed, a short, sharp sound, and ran into the clearing instead of the trees. Her bow and arrows were right there where she'd dropped them. Did she

have time to get to them before *it* got to her? She
risked a quick glance back. The dragon zoomed
down from the sky like an angry god, wings
stretched wide, its ethereal blue eyes all but glowing
with hatred. Somehow, she knew this one would be
much harder to kill than the last one.

She wasn't going to make it.

The bow and arrows were too far.

Panting, she veered away for the trees, refusing to
drop her sword so she could go faster. She needed
something.

Barely making it into the trees before it caught
her, she didn't go deeper into the shadows but
stopped, turned, and rushed right back out into the
clearing. She counted the seconds lead she gained
while the dragon wheeled in the air.

This time she was going to make it. She had to.
She'd committed herself and now she was in the
open like a sitting duck.

She didn't let go of the sword until she was right
on the bow and arrows, which she plucked hastily
off the ground. Nerves jangling, she notched one and
turned --- only to find the dragon gone.

Startled, she glanced the other way.

Straight ahead, a dark shape loomed. Rather
than chase her down from behind, this dragon chose
to counter her and come at her dead on, its eyes
narrowed into menacing slits.

Thea took a stand right there, breath thick in her
throat, adrenaline pumping through her system like
a hive of busy, buzzing bees.

In her ears, her own blood roared so loud that it
almost drowned out the one the dragon made as it
cracked open its jaws. She aimed the arrow and let
fly; it disappeared into the dragon's open mouth.
Thea crouched into a small ball a second later when
the dragon thrashed its head and snapped the arrow

lodged far back in its throat.

It wasn't enough to kill it. Not nearly enough, though she hoped the runes and symbols in carved in the shaft would take effect quickly.

They were not quick enough to prevent it from opening its mouth as it careened toward her, strafing a line of fire that she could not escape.

Panicked, she clutched the bow and arrows in her arms and pressed her palms together like she was about to administer her own last rites. Interlocking her thumbs, she shouted stridently, reciting a chant Miriette had taught her.

The fire came right up to her and she turned her head.

Sure that she was about to burn, she held her breath.

It raced around her, flames on all sides, scorching the meadow and part of Meyer's headless body.

But it did not touch her.

The heat seared her skin, unbearably hot.

Unable to hold her breath any longer, she gasped. Her throat burned and it felt like there was not enough oxygen to sustain her. She wheezed, tears streaming from the corners of her eyes.

The flames doused almost as quickly as they'd come, leaving only tiny tongues of fire that flickered on the verge of going out. A rush of fresh air came in its wake and she staggered forward through the charred grass, turning to see that the dragon, in her distraction with its fire, had gone down.

It hadn't crashed as hard as the other—as Meyer —had, and it showed all the signs of severe disorientation that the spell on the arrow had promised.

Shaking uncontrollably, struggling to function in the aftermath of battle, a battle that still wasn't over, she faced the dragon and set down her bow and arrows. Her sword was somewhere to her right in the middle of the field.

Turning her palms toward the ground, another chant broke free. She called upon nature, bringing forth from the earth roots and vines that slithered over and around the dragon at her command. Rough and smooth, thick and thin, they hooked and wrapped and coiled. They trapped its legs, circled its snout, and smothered its wings. Too late, it roared in fury when it struggled against the bonds.

She was too shaken, too untrusting of the dragon to waste any time. Running, avoiding any bits of flame, she picked up her bloody sword, steeling her resolve.

Would this dragon turn into a man? Who would he be? Someone she knew, had once trusted and laughed with as a child in Malmsbury?

Betrayal ran deep.

Stalking across the field, she approached the writhing, furious beast. "Do you remember me, dragon? I am Thea. Now it is *my* turn."

The magic from the arrow made it dizzy, confused. It growled dangerously, a warning, or was it acknowledgment?

He would not be easy to kill, for she had no other tricks up her sleeve. The business would have to be done by hand, hacking at the throat until she severed its head all while dancing clear of its razor sharp teeth.

It turned a look full of hate upon her, trying to fight against its bindings.

Sweat made the grip on her sword slick and slippery.

"Thea, no!"

Startled, she stopped and snapped a look toward the sound of her name, the sword held at a defensive angle toward the dragon, as if she feared it might break free and charge her.

Eugenia Bailey ran toward her, red hair flying like a banner. Dressed in black breeches and two layers of shirts, gray and white, she held a bow in her hand, the quiver tied to her back.

The dragon swung a menacing look that way, too, its eyes narrowing.

"What do you mean, no? I will finish this and we will be done with them for good," Thea said. She swallowed and panted for breath.

Eugenia slowed as she neared Thea, caught upon the dragon's eyes. She stared—and stared.

Something uncanny seemed to have gripped her.

"Eugenia, what is it?" Thea asked, more than a little unnerved at the stares the dragon and the woman were trading.

"I... I... no, do not kill it," Eugenia said, without breaking eye contact.

"Have you lost your mind, Eugenia? The other dragon was Meyer Lyon!" She pointed with her sword toward the headless, half burned body.

Eugenia tore her gaze from the dragon, looking first at Thea in disbelief, then to the vacant, staring eyes of Meyer. Even in death, at this distance, she recognized his face. Eugenia caught a sob against her palm.

"So you see, Eugenia, this one must die, too. It could be a man we know, who walks among the people of Faulkon's Cross. It cannot be allowed to live," Thea said, chilled by her own words as much as Eugenia's hesitation to eradicate them from the earth.

What was wrong with her? Perhaps because Eugenia had not watched her own mother and father and brother perish, she did not have the same determination to see them dead.

It mattered not; she had enough determination for them all.

Thea stalked forward with intent.

She would end this here and now and never be worried about dragons again.

Eugenia Bailey, torn with indecision and unease, glanced away from the blue-eyed dragon, to Thea, to Meyer.

Or what had once been Meyer. Shocked to her core, sickened and disheartened, she struggled to make sense of it.

So much death.

She had been following Thea in secret at the behest of Miriette, coming late to the scene of all this destruction after she'd lost the girl's trail in the woods.

Now Thea meant to kill this last dragon—was it really the last one?—and fulfill her wish for revenge.

Eugenia could understand Thea's desire, knowing she'd lost her whole family to early, needless graves. Thea had almost been taken to her own grave right along with them, had witnessed her mother's death personally.

Watching Thea grow from child to a young woman in the hollow, Eugenia loved her like the little sister she'd never had. She'd provided a shoulder and an ear when Thea needed both, listening to her plans for retaliation since the beginning.

Thea had waited a long time for this.

She glanced at the dragon again. It was looking at her rather than the pale haired girl with the sword who meant to end its life.

Eugenia swallowed, staring. She dropped her bow into the grass.

A chill raced down her spine.

She stepped forward, bathed in the glow of a fat, silver moon, and wrapped her hand around Thea's head. Her palm pressed snug against her brow and she whispered a sleeping spell into her ear.

Thea had not been the only one learning from the witches.

It was an easy spell to remember and perform, and Thea went limp, the blade thumping harmlessly onto the grass. She caught the girl under her arms and pulled her along the ground away from the dragon.

They were far too close.

She hadn't thought what to do *after* this, of course. Thea, although slender and light, was still rather heavy for her to pick up and carry. Easing her to the ground, she took her gaze from the steady stare of the dragon and crouched, sliding her arms under Thea's back and knees.

She had to try.

Grunting, she lifted, only picking Thea up a foot off the ground before she gently set her down again.

That would never work.

"Did no one ever tell you not to turn your back on the enemy?" A ragged voice said.

A yelp of surprise flew from her throat and she staggered backward, losing her balance. She landed on her backside, staring up at –

"Nehemiah Trimble!"

He looked drunk, clothes dirty and torn along the seam of a shoulder. He swayed while he walked, barely putting one boot in front of the other.

"What are you doing here, Eugenia? Why did you —"

"*You* are the dragon? Were you the same dragon that almost attacked me the ni—"

"Yes. My name is not Nehemiah, it is Dréoteth."

The illumination of the moon backlit his body, making his features difficult to read.

Eugenia crawled backward, hands gripping the dirt. Had she made a gross mistake, letting him live?

"D... Dré—what are your intentions?"

He staggered closer, looming, and reached forward to snatch her right off the ground.

She smelled as sweet and feminine as she ever had. Dréoteth, past the disorienting fog in his mind, remembered that much. He felt sick inside, injured and broken and strange.

It was all he could do to pretend like everything was normal.

He snorted.

Nothing was normal. Meyer was dead, beyond saving this time, and Thea, the little girl from so long ago whose weed still rested in his journal, had killed him.

He set Eugenia on her feet, strong enough to do that, but it cost him in pain. Maybe his ribs were cracked. It hurt every time he breathed.

"I *should* kill you," he said. And he absolutely should. He should end her, end Thea, and after finding the witch hollow, blast them all into ash. Even now their poison and magic ate away his insides, doing unimaginable things.

He surprised himself by saying, "But I am not going to. Thea has you to thank for her life. If you had not come when you did, I would have killed her."

"She was about to use her swor—"

"I was luring her in. She thought I was trapped—and it was a good trick, calling up the bonds—but all I had to do was change back. It loosened the roots long enough for me to escape. You tell her when she awakens, so she does not make the same mistake on other prey."

"But—wha... I do not understand all this," Eugenia whispered.

"It is simple, is it not? I am a dragon. Meyer was attacked by another and I made him one, too." He wondered if he slurred his words as badly as he thought he did.

Was he even making sense?

Her face became slightly distorted, and he felt her hands suddenly clutch his arms. She must have been terrified, yet here she was, the brave and bold Eugenia Bailey, lending him aid. He steadied his balance and smiled grimly.

"Let me take you –"

"To the witch hollow? No, I think they would not like that," he said with a hazy, raspy laugh. "You have done more than enough, Eugenia Bailey."

"That sounds like good-bye, Nehemiah Trimble."

He wondered, too, if he imagined her voice shaking.

She touched his face, a fleeting wisp of fingertips across his cheek. He twitched at the gentleness—and found it was not as distasteful as he thought it would be.

"It is. Look after Thea and tell Bethany, tell her... that Meyer perished in a hunting accident," he said.

When he should be doing everything in his power to get to his lair, he was standing here making arrangements for humans. In this last hour, a startling epiphany occurred to him.

He realized that it was possible to be a dragon and still care about humans. Not *all* of them were the enemy. Some of them had irresistible artistic talent, some could play fascinating, moving music, and others were genuinely charming or witty, prepared to befriend even the most abrasive personality.

Like Meyer, Eugenia, Beth.

Part of his reptilian mind rebelled against the idea of caring--it always would-- but Dréoteth knew.

He knew because he found it hard to say good-bye to the firebrand Eugenia Bailey. He knew because he felt sorrow for Bethany who would never see her husband again, for the children stripped of their father.

He knew because he ached over the loss of his only friend, Meyer Lyon.

It took death and dying to realize what they had been trying to show him all along. He reached across to cup his long fingers under Eugenia's chin, his first and only act of tenderness, and stared at her eyes.

He saw her struggle for words that he hushed when he moved his hand and pressed a single finger over her lips.

Then he staggered away, sinking into the blessed shadows of the trees.

Today was as good as any to die.

Epilogue

The cool stone beneath his body smelled familiar. His limbs felt heavy, like they were made of lead. He tried to slit his eyes open and couldn't. Every time he moved, he couldn't tell if he did, or if it was a figment of his clouded mind.

Where was he? What had happened?

Something sat over his snout, and he realized it was his tail.

Water burbled distantly, just a trickle, and he smelled it on the air. Clean, fresh.

Breathing brought him pain somewhere deep, and it reminded him that he was injured.

Injured and sick.

He couldn't remember how, or why.

Darkness surfaced and tried to drag him down. Down into a welcoming abyss where nothing, not even the pain, could touch him.

It took too much energy to fight it.

Sinking, sinking, sinking.

He breathed in. He breathed out.

And the eons wore on.

Born and raised in Corona, California, Danielle started her first novel at age 11 on an airplane flight from California to Texas. The unfinished 'book' was tucked away as a memento. Her love of books and writing led her to start several other novels over the last decade, none of which ever got to the publication stage.

Dréoteth was written during an exhaustive but exciting National Novel Writing Month exercise, which she completed, and has now become a full-fledged book. It is her first published novel.

Danielle lives in Texas with her husband, two sons, and their black cat Sheba.

Visit my blog for updates and new novel release information:

www.daniellebourdon.com

Follow me on twitter:

www.twitter.com/wildbloom

www.ingramcontent.com/pod-product-compliance
Lightning Source LLC
Chambersburg PA
CBHW060534180626
46817CB00002B/570